GW00888883

Best Wishes,

[signature]

About the Author

Alan Brown was born and educated in Tunbridge Wells. He and his mother escaped when a German rocket wiped out their street during World War II. He has worked for local newspapers in Kent then moved up to management, covering the country and setting up promotions for two London companies. He and his wife Barbara have also run three successful businesses of their own.

He has now retired to a village in North Devon which has three pubs, reasoning he can afford to get thrown out of two. With his wife's support he finally finished this book, the idea for which was conceived forty years ago whilst on holiday in Guernsey.

THE HOUMITS OF
SEYNORGUE

Dedication

For my lovely wife Barbara – without her support, encouragement and typing skills, this book would never have been written.
For my family and friends who have provided the inspiration for the good characters in the story.
Special thanks to Frankie for his knowledge of computery things. And last but not least, our friend Maggie who gave up the last day of her holiday to complete the last proofreading.

ALAN BROWN

THE HOUMITS OF SEYNORGUE

AUSTIN MACAULEY

A CIP catalogue record for this title is
available from the British Library.

ISBN 978 1 84963 152 5

www.austinmacauley.com

First Published (2012)
Austin & Macauley Publishers Ltd.
25 Canada Square
Canary Wharf
London
E14 5LB

Printed & Bound in Great Britain

The Family Ethel

Ethelfoot Baron of Dorsetshire – Father of those below and many more unaccounted for.

Etheltread – First legitimate son who inherits title when his father dies.

Ethelethel – Returns to run the household with her daughter Ethelegs when she is ditched by her lover.

Etheltar – Thrown out by his father – becomes a slave trader.

Ethelbert – Earns a fortune robbing coaches which pass through Dorsetshire.

Ethelete – Butch sister.

Ethelgay – Runs a boutique in Lyme Regis then joins Britain's first boy band.

Ethelred I and Ethelred II – The two gingers.

Ethelegs – Daughter of Ethelethel finally runs away to join the Houmits.

PREFACE

Long long ago before some clever chap had discovered how to make electricity, but a long time after some even cleverer chap had invented the wheel, the term Merry England was first used although nobody knew exactly why. Our story starts on this particular day at 11.26a.m. precisely with a high tide in Dorset.

At that time further out to sea than the projectory of land called Portland on which stood Portland Bill, there was a much larger piece of land, Bill's big brother, Portland Willey – but because of the unkind names used against the residents they had renamed it Seynorgue.

Using single carved letters which were still attached to a broken plank washed up in the harbour from an old viking ship, they concocted the name Seynorgue. When the letters were displayed on the craft they had spelt GAYE NORSE in honour of its very strange, and now very drowned, captain and crew.

The letter A had lost its middle bit and was now turned upside down and used as a U thus the name SEYNORGUE was now nailed to the rockface to the side of the causeway where it joined Willey, giving various travellers a clue as to where they might be.

This causeway was even narrower than the one joining Portland Bill to the mainland, at Weymouth, being only wide enough for a horse and cart, but with a couple of wider points along its mile length providing passing places.

Over the years the sea had eroded the white rock, which made up the road, at one spot breaking completely through underneath the highway, creating a tunnel for the swirling water.

During the winter months the causeway between Bill and Seynorgue nee Willey was often impassable at high tide, but it was now May and the roadway was a good ten feet above the sea.

Living on the piece of land beyond Portland Bill were the Houmits of Seynorgue. They had once been hermits, following solitary lonely existences, each living in one of the many caves amongst the rocks. But because of the taxes imposed by the Baron of Dorsetshire on each dwelling, they had integrated into larger caves, and "family" groups were formed.

Swiftly adapting to this form of living and indeed finding a liking for it, the families grew even larger.

Soon it was apparent that even larger accommodation was needed, so the first hovels were built of mud, stones, cow dung and straw.

Most of the hovels were grouped together and now formed the main village on Seynorgue, with dwellings varying in size and grandeur. Shops and taverns were added and now encompassed the market square.

No longer being hermits and not wishing to be classed as lowly serfs or peasants, the same as the rest of Ethelfoot's subjects, they had settled on the collective name of Houmit to maintain their identity.

On the mainland the closest town was Weymouth, and a few miles to the north east of this was the Grand Manor, now residence of Etheltread, Baron of Dorsetshire, eldest son of the recently deceased Baron Ethelfoot who lived in a grand manner with some of the family Ethel who had not left home.

The Baron's lifestyle was far removed from that of his serfs, never wanting for money food or warmth, waited on by his servant Burghers.

CHAPTER ONE

The Family Ethel and their Houmits

Etheltread Baron of Dorsetshire came from a long line of Ethels, he had taken the title after the sudden death of his father Baron Ethelfoot.

Ethelfoot was buried where he lay after an unfortunate hunting accident on the family estate, having been "mistaken" for a wild pig whilst frolicking in the bushes with the wife of a house guest, who had "mistakenly" put three arrows into him.

Being an exceedingly large man and a bit of a mess, it was decided to dig a hole next to him and roll him in.

Any mention of Ethelfoot being under foot or six foot under was now frowned upon by members of the family.

Author's note: The house guest and his wife continued to be "happily" married and were last heard of when they bought a pig farm in Denmark.

Etheltread being the eldest son had informed the family's solicitors of the old mans' demise. He had gathered together all those bearing the name Ethel to hear the reading of the will.

However, it was with some feeling of insecurity that the family gathered in the Great Hall at the Grand Manor wondering who else might show up and lay claim to the baron's riches, as it was well known that Ethelfoot had never been faithful to any of his many wives, all of which had long since departed.

Mr. Grumblegut of Grumblegut Grumblegut and Grumblegut, solicitors to the family Ethel, was in fact the second G, and suffered the same as his partners with raging gout.

Today was no exception, and the stagecart journey from his offices in Dorchester had not made him any merrier. The track was littered with potholes, the cart driver seemed intent on finding every one. He had been guaranteed safe passage by Baron Etheltread, also Ethelbert who ran the stagecart service trading under the banner of "Bert's Buses".

15

In his briefcase he carried the will which he was about to read to the family of his gruesome client. The contents of the will made him very nervous, he and his partners had drawn straws as to who was going to be the unlucky one to deliver the news, he knew that item number five would cause an uproar.

However, another swig at the bottle he kept secreted in his inside pocket, and the thought of the huge fee he would be charging, made him start to mellow as the cart bounced through the grand, now open, double wooden gates set in a high stone wall which encompassed a thousand acres of land tended by Burghers, the Ethel's servants, for their exclusive use.

Ethelfoot had been given the land and the title of Baron by a previous king, for whom he had led missions to foreign lands, spreading christianity and killing unfortunate locals who didn't agree with his point of view.

The unsavoury Ethel's, and their even more unsavoury Burghers, relishing a new found freedom since the demise of Baron Ethelfoot who had ruled his family with a rod of iron, were now making frequent visits to Seynorgue, getting very drunk and extremely rowdy in the village square, which was one of the centres for nightlife in the district.

The Houmits of Seynorgue were aware changes were afoot, since the news of Ethelfoot's death had been spread hotfoot through his lands.

The Houmits grew vegetables, tended fields of corn, and kept sheep, goats, cows and pigs.

Their animals and their produce were sold every Tuesday in the village market square, quite often seriously interrupted by rowdy Burghers, delighting in shouting out bids at the auction, less than the bid before.

Every day fisher Houmits put to sea in their boats and landed their catch at the quayside around six in the evening. Ethels and Burghers had been claiming the best of the catch for themselves, then refusing to pay, although the Ethels already collected taxes from all the Houmits.

One of the many sources of income on Seynorgue, was the sprawling trufflemouzer farm where trufflemouzers, a unique breed of dog, were bred for hunting wild boar, vermin and truffles.

The pups were sold to ever increasing admirers throughout Dorsetshire, and they were fast becoming a must have item in many of the better establishments.

Their fur was used to make hats which nearly all the Houmits wore.

Recently, two drunken Ethels and several Burghers had been to the farm making faces, and calling out rude names to the trufflemouzers seriously upsetting their breeding and their general well-being.

It was, therefore, a very pleasant sunny Tuesday morning in the market place, business was flourishing at all the various stalls, also at the auction of cattle, devoid of the presence of any Ethels or Burghers. In fact none had been seen on Seynorgue since the previous weekend.

Amid the throng of merry market goers was an incredibly smelly Houmit, who made his living collecting dung from the small farms with livestock, and transporting it on his cart to the Houmits growing crops. He was the only one in the market place who wasn't jostled and pushed; a rancid odour gave him an invisible cordon from the rest. His one good friend, was a tatty individual by the name of Sidney, whom he spied making his way towards him.

"Whatcher Sid," he called gleefully, having had a good morning in the market place with orders from two new fruit growers. Usually his day at the market was spoilt by Ethels and Burghers, commenting loudly on his bodily odours.

Sidney proceeded towards his friend; there was a slight breeze, so he ensured that he was upwind when he stopped four paces away. This arrangement suited the dung seller. Sidney had terribly bad breath as well as a dreadful stutter.

"No sign of 'em this morning," the smelly Houmit greeted his friend cheerfully, "praps it wasn't just Ethelfoot who died," he added even more cheerfully.

"Fffat ppigin chance," replied Sidney.

At that precise moment who should slide off a nearby haycart but Ethelegs, the grand-daughter of Ethelfoot.

"What day is it," she screamed at nobody in particular.

"TTT," started the stuttering Houmit.

"Tuesday," chimed in his smelly acquaintance.

Jumping up and down shaking bits of hay out of her hair, Ethelegs proceeded to accuse anybody within earshot, which was quite a long way around her, unless they were very deaf, "why didn't you wake me up? The last thing I can remember was playing darts in Burgher's Bar on Sunday night."

With that she took a flying leap on to a nearby horse and headed out of the village towards the mainland and her home in a cloud of dust.

Mid afternoon sun was sliding over mossy buttresses, then squeezing between grills set in the outside stone wall of the Grand Manor completing its journey illuminating the drab place.

Opposite one of the grills, a large fire of various timbers was sparking and crackling on a hearth under a grimy canopy, the wood bringing different smells and warmth to an otherwise dank and unwelcoming room.

"Is everyone here?" enquired Mr Grumblegut to the gathering of Ethels in the Great Hall.

"All except Ethelegs," sneered Ethelete who spent her time weight lifting and exercising with other hairy females, but had always been jealous of her niece's looks and way with the boys.

"I'm happy to wait," said Grumblegut, who decided he would charge his huge fee plus so much an hour.

"Well I'm not," piped Ethelgay, stamping his foot.

"I've got fresh summer stock coming in all the time now, and if I'm not there to supervise I just know nothing will be right."

Ethelgay a slightly built fair haired clean shaven individual ran a boutique in Lyme Regis and lived over the shop.

Gaygear as it was known, specialised at this time of year in summer smocks which were in pretty colours, appealing to gentry and serfs alike, fed up with the usual grey/brown sackcloth.

"There there," soothed Ethelethel the eldest daughter of Ethelfoot. "I'm sure your young helpers do very nicely without you."

The young helpers were a wannabe boy band working at Gaygear to earn cash between very infrequent gigs.

"That's what I'm worried about, how nicely they will do for themselves without me watching."

"Let's all have a drink," said Ethelethel, whose brief marriage to a travelling tinker had ended sixteen years earlier, when he ran

18

off with a group of passing gypsies, leaving Ethelethel with a year old girl. She named the girl Ethelegs. Even as a child the little girl had sported a fine pair of legs, which had become even more shapely as she grew older. Moving back to the Manor with her baby she had taken over the roll of Mother to the rest of the family, and only referred to her ex husband as that little tinker.

"Oh, I see you've started already Mr. Grumblegut would you like a piece of bread to dip in your flagon of gin? And you two gingers stick some more wood on the fire," she said without pausing for breath, to the two youngest members of the family, Ethelred I and Ethelred II who were known affectionately as gingers. The pair had just managed to drag the biggest piece of timber from a pile next to the hearth and heave it on to the already huge fire, when the front door flew open causing smoke to billow out and fill the room.

"Sorry I'm late," panted Ethelegs.

"You should be ashamed," screeched Ethelgay, "look at my best pink blouse covered in soot, and look at the state of you, you look like you've just got out of a haycart."

"It's always you we have to wait for, Mr. Grumblegut said he can't hang around here all day," lied Ethelete, always ready to get a dig into her niece.

"Stop them picking on me Ma," yelled Ethelegs.

The three wolfhounds who had been lying in front of the fire, upset by all the noise and smoke, started to fight, unluckily for the two Gingers who were drawn into the fray.

"Hell's bells, shut up all of you," bellowed Etheltread striding into the fracas, pulling dogs and gingers apart.

"You are showing the very worst side of us Ethels to Grumblegut."

The smoke slowly cleared disappearing up the chimney.

"I didn't think I had a worst side, did you Ma?" simpered Ethelgay, "but look at my blouse, it's ruined."

"Can we get on with this?" demanded Baron Etheltread, "Grumblegut get rid of your drink and start reading."

The solicitor deciding the best way to get rid of his gin, tipped his head back and emptied the rest of the flagon down his neck, some inside and quite a lot outside.

He rose unsteadily to his feet, took a pace forwards and fell over a wolfhound.

"Will you help Mr. Grumblegut up dears?" asked Ethelethel, of the two gingers, "you are very pretty and I will get your blouse washed Gay - you are not as pretty as you should be. Legs get yourself tidied up are you alright now Mr. Grumblegut?" she continued without pausing for breath.

The last two male Ethels, who had been sat in the corner of the huge timbered room swilling beer as quickly as possible, then trying to out belch each other, finally got up and came to join the rest of their siblings who had gathered round the table. Neither of them could stand the smell in the corner any longer, as the belches were often accompanied by explosions from lower parts of their bodies, producing huge guffaws from the pair.

These two were the third and second eldest on the male side of the family after Etheltread.

Ethelbert controlled the transport through their domain and as far afield as Portsmouth and Exeter.

Etheltar, who as a boy had been deemed by some the nastiest as well as the strongest of a rough family, now enjoyed being a man of the sea, and it was a lucky coincidence that his ship was moored at the harbour in Seynorgue when the old Baron died, and a message was sent to him to attend at the Grand Manor. Etheltars relationship with his father in the early years had been strained, to say the least.

The two gingers had helped Mr. Grumblegut to a chair at one end of the table, on to which his head had dropped and he was now fast asleep.

"Wake up Grumblegut and read the piggin will," shouted Etheltread in his ear.

Grumblegut stirred and started to snore.

"I'll read it," volunteered Gay who had always been a clever little chap and liked to pretend he could read.

"He might as well," said Etheltar who could only read a bit.

"Go on then," chimed in the gingers looking nervously at Etheltread.

Baron Etheltread opened Mr. Grumblegut's bag and handed a sheaf of papers to Gay. Looking very intelligent, Gay thumbed through the documents pausing occasionally to comment.

"How kind, very nice, thank you," to himself but for all the rest to hear.

"Rather than read out all the boring bits it says that everything is left to me. So I might as well chuck these on the fire," he said, moving to do so.

"Hold hard sailor," shouted Tar moving quickly for a big man and grabbing the papers from his younger brother's hand.

"I might not be able to read but I ain't piggin stupid."

Etheltread jumped from his chair. "Go and sit in the corner Gay before we all set about you." Ethelgay started to cry.

Mr. Grumblegut meanwhile had regained consciousness, he took the sheaf of papers from Tar and started to read.

CHAPTER TWO

Pig in a Pub

The market was closing down on Seynorgue, the sellers counting their money and the buyers wondering if they had paid too much for their purchases.

Many were mooching off to their hovels, some made their way to the quayside, to buy some fish for their tea.

One small wizened Houmit was loading a pig he had swapped for a barrel of apples (the bottom ones being quite rotten), and feeling decidedly chuffed with his day's transaction. Suddenly the animal leapt off his cart and ran higgledy piggledy back through the market place.

Some trufflemouzers who had been scrummaging through the general rubbish left on the cobbles, broke away from their snuffling and gave chase. Several other Houmits joined in the fun and took after the pig, yelling and whooping as they went.

Seeing an open doorway at the top of some steps the frightened creature rushed in with the trufflemouzers hard on her heels. In the darkened room she barged into a table, upsetting food and several pints of beer and cider over the customers of The Hungry Houmit, the favoured pub in the market used by the locals.

The Burghers Bar on the other side of the square tended to cater for visitors.

Squealing loudly she rushed through another door and disappeared from sight. The Houmits came to a halt in front of the doorway. Finally catching up with the chase her wizened owner gasped, "Where's my sow."

"In there," came the general reply.

"Well go and get her."

"Can't, it's the ladies," replied the male chasers.

The trufflemouzers had all stopped by the overturned table deciding the pasties and pork pies were easier meat than a pork pie on legs.

"Well somebody's got to get her," grated the wizened Houmit.

"She might be having a pee," shouted one of the lads at the bar.

The miserable landlord of The Hungry Houmit, clutching a piece of string pushed his way through the group at the door.

"Out of the piggin way you lot," he grunted. "I'll get her."

Five minutes later he led the now calm animal back into the smoky atmosphere of the bar, with the string about her neck.

"Who's piggin pig is this?" he growled.

"Mine," piped wizened Houmit.

"Well I reckon you owes everybody a pint and somebody get those piggin trufflemouzers out of my pub."

The old man ruefully took out his purse, gave it to the landlord with one hand and took the piece of string with the pig attached with the other, then slumped into the nearest chair.

"Drinks all round," shouted the landlord, for once with a smile on his face.

"And a bag of pork scratchings for the pig," yelled the lad at the bar.

Feeling sorry for the old boy, the young man detached himself from his mates, then went over to his table, after a visit to the gents, his brashness at the bar used to disguise his kind heart. His devilish good looks brought sideways glances from female customers, as he dragged out a chair and plonked himself next to the old man and his pig.

Questioning in a rather too loud voice for the benefit of anyone listening "had a bad day then old pig man?"

The Houmit, who had been wondering if he would get any change from his large round of drinks, looked at the boy through watery eyes.

"Not till I ended up buying you lot ale," he moaned.

The boy knew the old man, who kept a few animals under the trees of a large orchard, in a long valley a few miles on from where he lived with his mother.

"You're Houmit Bramley," stated the lad, "I walk some of the trufflemouzers up as far as your place from time to time."

"Shift up Lukey," shouted the boy's mates, grabbing chairs around the table, several throwing furry hats on top of Luke's and the old man's, which were already on the floor. It was considered rude for any Houmit to wear their furry hats when sitting down.

"The landlord sent this over," said one lad depositing the old man's purse with change, in front of the old chap.

Greatly cheered, the old wizened one asked "where be you lot from then?"

"We all work at the trufflemouzer farm," they sang in unison, already a bit tiddly.

"An' we got off early today to come to the market," piped a long skinny lad with a wart on his nose.

"Where do you lot live then?" enquired pig man.

"We all live at the trufflemouzer farm," came back the chorus.

"Except for Luke, who lives with his ma," piped skinny wart nose.

"Who's your ma boy?" asked the old man jerking the string on the pig, who had got fed up lying down and decided to investigate neighbouring tables.

"She be called Becky," replied Luke, and volunteered, "she ain't quite right in the head so I sleep at home to keep an eye on her when I'm awake," he added as an afterthought. "But she's a lot better now than she ever was."

"What's your last name then."

"Sos," replied Luke, grinning.

"S.O.S." grinned the old pigman dribbling a bit as he took a swig of his ale, "Luke Save Our Souls???"

"Nah, its Duke, Ma only got round to naming me when I was twelve and wanted the minister to call me Lucifer Spawn of Satan, SOS for short, but he didn't want to do that in case it upset the bishop. Ma suggested Lucy for a first name as she didn't think quite proper, the minister said he would settle for Lukey, and suggested Duke for my last name."

Getting fidgety, Luke's mates started picking up their hats and drifting off back to the bar.

Luke raised his pointed eyebrows, patted the pig and got up, picking up his own furry hat, went to the bar and bought a pint of ale then brought it over to the table.

"See you around old pigman," he laughed, turning to join his mates who were now noisily playing darts and trying to impress a couple of young female Houmits.

"Come on lads lets go and have a look across the square," he yelled.

With that the boys and two girls bundled out of the Hungry Houmit shouting goodbye to everyone in general.

Left alone again, and inwardly chuffed that Luke had bought him a drink, the pig man reflected on the lad with the devilish looks and his dippy mother, a scene many years ago jumped from the old mans memory. It was the same time of year as now, in fact it was Mayday.

The market square, unchanged over the last twenty years, was thronged with happy Houmits.

There were stalls selling everything from peas to pilchards, there were races for boys, girls, dogs and ferrets.

That year one of the Houmits had erected a huge scarecrow made to look like their lord and master Ethelfoot, which all the Houmits delighted in throwing vegetables at.

There was a Maypole, and of course there was a parade of maidens, all wanting to be May Queen.

That year there was only ever going to be one girl who would win, Rebecca or Becky the Booful as she was known.

Becky had become an orphan a couple of years earlier, her parents used to drive one of the carts that collected the rubbish at the end of market days, then drive the couple of miles to the big cliff. The carts were backed up to the edge and tipped up so the dregs from the market could fall 200 feet into the sea. On that sad day, her ma, who sat on the back of the cart, had shouted "Whoa."

Her pa, who was at the front, gently coaxing his horse backwards, thought she said "Go!" Horse, cart, rubbish plus Ma and Pa, all went over the edge.

Since then Booful Becky had looked after herself, earning her keep by selling potions that she made from plants and berries, which grew in abundance on the hills around the village.

She stayed in her parent's old hovel, but came into work part-time at the two pubs. The regular advances made to her by the regulars were all rejected, and so far no Houmit had won the heart of the dark haired maiden with the almond eyes and tanned skin.

The judging for May Queen was unanimous and Booful Becky was hoisted on to a platform to be crowned.

All the Houmits were cheering Becky and laughing at the lads throwing rotten vegetables at the scarecrow of Ethelfoot.

Nobody noticed that Ethelfoot, the Baron of Dorset himself, had ridden into the market square.

"First one to knock the scarecrow over gets a date with the May Queen," yelled one of the throwers.

Seething with rage, Ethelfoot spurred his horse through the crowd, sending Houmits, dogs and vegetables flying in all directions.

"That'll be me then," he bellowed, kicking the scarecrow over with an outstretched foot.

"I'll take the prize," he yelled, grabbing Becky and slinging her over his mount's back. Making rude gestures to the confused heap of Houmits, he galloped out of the square and back over the causeway, heading for the mainland and his Manor.

That was the last anybody saw of the Booful Becky, until several years later, when the driver of the mobile fish and chip cart reported that he thought she was living back on Seynorgue, a young boy had come down the path from the direction of her parents' old hovel and ordered two plaice and chips but no vinegar.

The old man finished his drink, picked up his furry hat, and led his pig back down the steps to the cart from which she had escaped a couple of hours earlier.

The market square now only had a few Houmits wandering about, but there was a great deal of noise coming from Burghers Bar across the square, where that afternoon, groups of Burghers had descended much to the annoyance of the locals. Outside the bar Bramley's new friends were involved in a heated argument with some of the Burghers, the two girls standing back looking coy.

The raised voices were almost drowned by the screeching gulls circling over the carts clearing the rubbish.

"Thought it was too good to be true," mused Bramley, successfully loading his pig and setting off home. Until that Mayday twenty years ago the Houmits of Seynorgue had enjoyed a fairly good relationship with their lord and master, but as the Baron's family had got older the relationship had declined, and now, after his death, dealings between Houmits and the Ethels' household had gotten worse and worse.

CHAPTER THREE

Wilful Damage?

The ever increasing family of deathwatch beetles, that were encamped in the oak beams supporting Ethelfoot's bedroom over the Great Hall, were discussing the evening menu, when Mr. Grumblegut took the sheaf of papers from Tar and started to read.

Turning his rear end towards the fireplace, in a loud, if slightly slurred, voice he commenced.

"This is the Last Will and Testament of Ethelfoot, Baron of Dorsetshire, Lord of the Manor and all its lands. Me, Ethelfoot, being of sound mind and round body do, in the event of me being dead, leave my estate and all my personal possessions to…"

Grumblegut, getting theatrical, indicated Ethelfoot's personal possessions, which had been heaved into his bedroom for safe keeping, and started thrusting his stout stick upwards poking the beam of once stout timber, now a honeycomb of tunnels made by the beetles.

It started with a creak, then a crack, then a crash, as the whole ceiling and floor with the contents of Ethelfoot's bedroom, descended on the startled Ethels below.

Grumblegut was knocked backwards and sat on the huge fire. He ignited into a big ball of flame, that only took seconds to reach into Grumblegut's gut, and find all the booze sloshing about inside. BANG went the flame and Grumblegut was no more.

Both the gingers and the wolfhounds were projected across the rubble at a speed unknown to man at that time, ending up in a tangle of legs, arms, fur and tails halfway through the window.

Ethelgay was sandwiched between Bert and Tar in a swearing, screaming tangle, covered in dried mud, soot and bits of wood.

Etheltread lay under a pile of coins and a suit of armour that had come through the ceiling.

Ethelethel and Ethelegs had dived under the stout table, only receiving a joint headache when they collided.

After several minutes the two gingers untangled themselves from the wolfhounds, declaring themselves fit. The dogs also pronounced they were not injured leaping up and licking the two for all they were worth.

Gay, Bert and Tar unsandwiched themselves.

"Good job we weren't by the fire, we could have been a toastie," jibed Bert.

"Anybody hurt?"

"I'm alright," muttered Tar.

"Well I'm not," wailed Gay. "My suit is now completely ruined, and I've got a broken finger nail."

Etheltread pushed off the suit of armour and got painfully to his feet, then promptly fell over, his left leg caving in under his weight.

"Stay there dear," shouted Ethelethel crawling from under the table with Ethellegs.

"Like I'm gunna run over there," grated Tread sarcastically.

Ethelethel picked her way over to Tread who was now clutching his face.

"Take your hands away dear and let's have a look."

Etheltread slowly lowered his hands to reveal a sharp splinter of wood sticking out of his left eye.

"Oh my," exclaimed Ethelethel. "You've been spiked by a bit of the beam, Legs would you like to give me a hand."

"Cor wooden I," replied Ethelegs.

"That's not piggin funny," shouted Tread obviously in great pain.

"Would you like to get hold of that piece of wood and pull it out while I hold his head," instructed Ethelethel.

"Cor wooden I," giggled Legs.

"Will you stop saying that," shouted the enraged Etheltread at his niece.

Grabbing the large splinter Legs gave it a yank, out it came, with the eyeball attached to it like a sweet lolly.

"Doesn't hurt now," muttered Tread starting to drift off. "See if everybody else is alright."

"I'll go and have a look for you," grinned Ethelegs extending her arm and slowly encompassing the room with the eye on a stick.

"I don't think you are being very kind to your uncle," scolded Ethelethel. "Is everybody alright?"

"I've broken a nail," wailed Gay.

"And I've got Ethelete's foot," shouted one of the Gingers.

"Don't be silly boys, is anybody badly hurt?"

"You don't understand," piped the ginger. "I've got Ethelete's foot and I've got her leg as well," the two bits of Ethelete's body were in fact stuck out from under Baron Ethelfoot's huge four poster bed which had come through the ceiling.

"Get over and help him," instructed Ethelethel to Bert and Tar. "You too Ginger II."

"She ought to be able to do it herself," said Legs holding up Etheltread's eye for a better view. "She's always going on about weightlifting and pushups."

"Don't think she can," said Ginger I.

With a grunt and a heave the four Ethels tipped the heavy four poster off the lifeless body of Ethelete.

"She's dead Ma," called Ginger I.

"Oh dear, should we say something," cried Ethelethel.

"Goodbye," they all said.

Ethelete wasn't very popular, except with her hairy athletic friends.

"What shall I do with this, Ma?" called Ethelegs holding up Etheltread's eye on a stick.

"Do you want it," enquired Ethelethel of Etheltread, coming out of his daze.

"No, stick it on the fire."

"Right ho guvnor," chortled Ethelegs, "at least I can say I've seen the grumpy old boss with a twinkle in his eye."

"Go to the kitchen and get me some clean cloths Legs and you boys get Ethelete outside into the new woodshed and start clearing up this mess," instructed Ethelethel in one big breath.

Tar and Bert took one end each of Ethelete and carried her outside, then returned to help the gingers clearing the rubble. Gay busied himself removing bits from his hair and clothing.

Legs returned and helped Ethelethel put a patch on Etheltread's eye.

"Get me two bits of wood boys and we'll make a splint for his leg."

Between them they managed to get Etheltread's leg straight and strap a piece of wood to each side.

"I think we all need a stiff drink," said Tar.

"Especially Ethelete," laughed Ethelegs.

Three hours later the family Ethel retired to the remaining bedrooms or curled up by the fire having consumed all they could.

"Shame about Grumblegut," somebody finally said.

.

CHAPTER FOUR

Greedy Ethels

Next morning the Manor House was woken by the yelling of Etheltread. The previous night's brandy had worn off, he had a dreadful headache, his leg hurt and he had just had a terrible thought.

"Where's the pigging will?" he enquired of each member of the household as they appeared.

"Gone up the chimney with old Grumblegut I s'pose," said Ginger II.

"And my pigging leg hurts," he bellowed at the rest of the group.

"Don't fret dear," cooed Ethelethel.

"The staff will be here in a minute and we'll get this mess sorted out."

The Burghers, who were employed at the Manor, had been given the afternoon off when the will was to be read, and told not to return 'til 8.00a.m. next morning. Etheltread felt he did not want prying Burghers overhearing the reading of the will, or their business would soon be spread all over Dorsetshire.

Most of the Burghers had taken advantage of this unexpected holiday and got well away from the Manor, by going down to Weymouth, out to Seynorgue to spend the afternoon in the pub, or visiting other Burghers employed on the estate surrounding the main house.

Ethelethel as usual took charge, and on a bright May morning the Ethels set to under her instructions. They loaded Etheltread onto one of Bert's carts, and he set off with his elder brother to Dorchester to find a physician, and call on the two remaining Grumbleguts to inform them of the previous day's happenings.

The rest of the menfolk gathered all the valuables which were still scattered over the hall floor, making several trips to one of the empty barns, each one stuffing his purse with gold coins as he went. Eventually they had removed all of the smaller valuable items. They then locked and bolted the doors of the barn securely, just as the first Burghers began to return for work.

That day the Ethels were due to be interviewing peasants, from the surrounding countryside who had applied for jobs as Burghers.

Ethelethel started to flap. "Who's going to interview for the outside jobs, and Berts away, I know he needs more drivers for his buses."

"Don't worry Ma old thing, us Reds will sit in for Tread and Bert," piped up Ginger I holding his and his brother's hands in the air for effect. "The Guvnor's been moaning about us not doing enough, but every time we try, he takes over, now he's not here we'll jolly well show him what we can do."

"Thank you dear that would be a help but I think we should ask Big Mac he knows all the jobs and I will feel happier with him involved," replied Ethelethel without a pause.

Big Mac was of Scottish descent with a huge Scottish accent. He had left his "home" at the age of twelve, both his parents had been wasters and one day after another beating from his father he sneaked out and never looked back.

Following his nose he headed South, and kept going as the weather seemed to improve, from the bleak highland mists that surrounded his old home.

Although only twelve, but already nearly six feet tall, his hard young muscles were already stretching his ragged garb.

He picked up work easily being strong as a young ox, but he had inherited his father's temper, and each job came to an abrupt end after arguments or fisticuffs with his various employers.

He turned up at the Manor aged seventeen. Ethelfoot had employed him and set him to work with the cattle, two weeks later he raised his voice to Ethelfoot who promptly flattened him. For the first time in his life Big Mac apologised, realising he had more than met his match.

That was eight years ago, in which time he grew another seven inches and added several pounds in weight to his already massive frame. He mastered all the outside jobs on the estate, and was now looked upon by the Ethels as a reliable foreman and a handy bodyguard.

Three weeks previously, Big Mac had been despatched with twenty five notices, laboriously prepared in a joint effort by the

Ethels, with their limited knowledge of grammar and writing skills. He was instructed to place one notice in each of the larger villages within the Ethels domain.

He nailed the first notice to an elm tree in the middle of the nearest village's square, then tying his horse to a nearby post he sat down on the grass to watch results.

It wasn't long before a couple of peasants approached the notice, having spotted the huge stranger riding into the square, and keeping a wary watchful eye on him from a safe distance.

"Wot's it say?" muttered peasant one to his mate.

"Dunno, better get the parson."

Off went peasant one to return ten minutes later with the parson and several more villagers.

"Wot's it say parson?" they enquired.

Pulling out the end of a spyglass from his gown, the parson studied the notice which proclaimed after a few mistakes:

SEVERAL POSITIONS FOR STAFF
AT THE GRAND MANOR
ARE AVALBLE AVALBL READY NOW
ANY PEASANTS INTERESTED
COME TO THE SERVANTS GATE
LAST DAY OF MAY
YOU COULD BE A BURGHER

Tucking his spyglass back into his robes the parson turned and addressed his flock, "there are jobs going at the Ethel's Grand Manor if anybody is interested, you have to apply at the servant's gate."

"Wouldn't want to work for them," said peasant one.

"Nor me."

"Or me."

"Me neither," came back a general chorus.

"When do we have to apply," came a voice from the back of the crowd.

"Last day of May," said the parson over his shoulder starting to walk back to his chapel.

Big Mac smiled, untied his horse and rode on to the next village.

His last call was on Seynorgue where a fiery Houmit had torn down the notice, but had been grilled by the surrounding throng as to its contents.

From 6.00 a.m. on the 31st May, a growing rabble of peasants and one Houmit had collected at the servant's gate of the Manor.

Although they distrusted the Ethels and their staff, it was well known that the Burghers enjoyed a better standard of living than the average peasant.

"I'm off," stated Ethelgay, descending into the kitchen with his valise, which he had returned to his bedroom to pack, after helping stow the treasures in the barn.

"You don't need me to talk to staff for the Manor. Gaygear won't run itself, and I've already got enough helpers to be kept on their toes. Berts sending a cart to pick me up early and drive me back to Lyme Regis, let me know when you've got this mess sorted out, and I'll come back to see how much I'm getting." With that Ethelgay flounced out the kitchen door.

"Be a dear go and find Big Mac for me Legs tell him to let the peasants in we will see them about the jobs down in the stables. Are you coming too Tar dear? You might need some more sailors for your boat?" asked Ethelethel all in one breath.

"Right ho Ma," giggled Ethelegs skipping outside gleefully to search for Big Mac who she had always had a crush on.

Out through the yard she saw the door of the barn that had been locked and bolted was now slightly ajar. Creeping up to the building, she peeped inside to see Ethelgay stuffing gold coins into his valise.

"You wicked wooftah," she screeched.

Poor Gay leapt two foot into the air peeing himself on the way down.

"You're stealing our inheritance I'm gonna tell Ma."

"Hhang on dearie," Gay stammered composing himself, dabbing his pantaloons with a silk hanky.

"If I don't get some of this now I'm never going to see it again, with the will gone up the chimney Tread will keep the whole lot for himself when he comes back." Craftily adding, "if you've got any sense you'll grab some for yourself before its all gone, it'll be our little secret. Think of all the pretties you could buy with a few of these," he said holding up two gold coins.

Ethelegs stood open mouthed.

"Tell you what, I'll put some in that milk pail for you, then you can walk down to the dairy and hide it in there. I'm off, my cart is waiting outside the front gate, when I'm gone lock the barn then put the key back under that big stone outside, where we hid it before."

Ethelegs, still open-mouthed, started to nod her head, tiptoeing over to her gay uncle she helped put several handfuls of coins into the pail. Ethelgay breathed a sigh of relief, picking up his valise he gave his niece a most unexpected kiss and hurriedly left.

Legs locked the door and hid the key, then sauntered as well as her shaky legs would allow across the yard. Clutching the bucket with both hands she made her way down to the dairy, where she hid it under some disused rope in the furthest dark corner.

Taking several deep breaths she sat down on a pile of hay, then she started clapping her hands, slowly at first but getting faster and faster, then she started to laugh, softly at first but getting louder and louder.

"What's all the funnies missy," enquired the huge figure framed in the doorway.

"Oh Mac I just fell over and got some tickly hay in my knickers, I was coming to look for you," blushed Legs.

She blurted out the previous days happenings to Big Mac telling him about the collapsed ceiling and the demise of Grumblegut and Ethelete, whose body was in the new woodshed. Then she told him that Ethelethel and the others were on their way to the stable where he was to take the applicants for the jobs.

Etheltar excused himself telling Ma he had more than enough sailors for his boat.

Waiting until the rest of the family had made their way to the stables and were well out of sight, he let himself out of the Grand Manor, and with his rucksack slung over his shoulder, swiftly crossed the yard, retrieved the key from under the boulder and slipped into the barn.

He then proceeded to stuff as many gold coins as possible into his sack, he then slipped out again, relocked the door and replaced the key.

He had rented a horse which he used for transport between the Manor and his boat The Seacow, lying at anchor half a mile out in the bay off the fishing quay on Seynorgue.

Chuckling to himself he rode off, matching the horse fart for fart.

Ethelethel and the two gingers trooped into the stable where Big Mac and Ethelegs were waiting with the pick of the peasants, five male one female plus one Houmit male, the rest of the rabble having been told to clear off.

"Red I and Red II go and sit by Mac on that bale of hay," she stared at her slight brothers, their hair straight and the colour of straw as they seated themselves next to the huge Scotsman with curly hair the colour of pickled beetroot, "you come and sit over here with me Legs you peasants stand in a line there in front of us and don't speak until you are spoken to," instructed Ethelethel all in one big breath.

"Right Mac you know what we want get on with it."

"Any of you lot work with pigs?" asked Mac.

Two large peasants and one small one put their hands up.

"Bullocks," said another peasant.

"Pardon," said Ethelegs.

"Bullocks, I work with bullocks."

"Oh I see," giggled Ethelegs "I thought you were being rude."

"Shut up Legs," chimed in Ginger II "let Mac get on with it."

"You two bigger peasants can have a job at the piggery," Big Mac informed the raggedy pair. "You'll be shown what to do by the Bacon Burghers who work there, you shortarse can work in the Manor with the girl."

The inside staff were generally a weaker but more genteel variety than the Burghers employed on the estate, who had christened them Hammy Burghers.

"Anybody done any building?"

"Me," said the Houmit raising his furry hat, "I used to work for G.B.H. that's General Builders Houmit company," he qualified.

"But every time a job went wrong the bosses used to beat us up."

Out of the frying pan into the fire then thought Mac, adding aloud, "There's a job for you at the Manor, you can help our Wood Burgher replace the ceiling, Bullocks, you can start at the cowshed and the Beef Burghers will show you your jobs. Done any gardening?" Mac asked the last peasant.

"Dun a bit," simpered the mouldy individual scared he wasn't going to get a place. "I've dun a lot of diggin'."

"Got just the job for you then laddie," boomed Mac. "Report to the head Garden Burgher and get a spade, we've got something for you to plant for your first task, it's in the new woodshed, then you will be working in the gardens with the rest of the Veggie Burghers."

"Let me tell them the next bit," Ginger I pleaded feeling that he and his brother hadn't been involved enough.

"Alright dear but get on with it I've got lots of supervising to do back at the house," Ethelethel replied.

Ginger I had heard the speech given by his Father, Ethelfoot, to previous applicants many times and knew it word for word.

"You are on a month's trial," he started. "Outside Burghers all sleep together in upgraded hovels where they are working. Inside Burghers sleep in the male and female servants' quarters up at the house. You will be instructed when to start work and what time you finish." By now he was feeling very important. "Every Burgher works a fourteen hour day but you will get one day a month off."

"Let me do the next bit," chimed in Ginger II not wanting to see his brother get all the glory.

"You will no longer think like peasants, you are trainee Burghers. You do not speak to peasants outside of any matters in the house or on the estate. If you do you'll be beaten and kicked out. Your loyalty is now only to the family Ethel, who you will defend with your lives if necessary. You will be fed and at the end of the month you will receive five shillings wages and your Burgher smock. If you are no good you will be kicked out without any pay. Was that good Ma?" asked Ginger II turning to Ethelethel.

"Lovely dear Mac see these people to where they have to go we are going back to the house," replied Ethelethel.

CHAPTER FIVE

In for repair

Etheltread and Ethelbert were ushered into a physician's house in Dorchester. Etheltread, not in the best of spirits after their journey, was sweating profusely, he clutched a piece of rag to his eye socket and leant heavily on the hazel stick Bert had cut for him on their way.

Tread slumped thankfully into a chair the weedy little man pushed towards him, he was well aware of who his visitors were.

"Can I take that filthy rag from your eye sire?" he enquired.

"No," spat Etheltread.

"In that case let me take a look at your leg."

He moved another chair and gently raised his Lordship's leg to rest on it.

"What are you? Some sort of sadist?" yelled Tread, with such force that the physician jumped back in alarm.

"I cant treat you if you wont let me touch you sire," the little man ventured.

"No you piggin can't," agreed Tread. "Get me a brandy."

The man seemed relieved.

"Of course sire, I won't be a moment it's in the other room." He scuttled out returning after a few moments with a large drink in a round bowl held between both hands. Tread took the proffered bowl and downed the liquid in two great gulps.

"That's more like it doc," Etheltread almost smiled, then passed out.

"Blimey," said Bert, "I've never seen booze hit him like that before."

"He's never had what I put in it before," grinned the physician, "there was enough knockout drops in there to put a horse to sleep, now perhaps I can examine him."

He gently removed the rag from Etheltread's face.

"Oh my," he exclaimed.

Ethelbert explained what had happened while the little chap set to work cleaning the wounded eye socket. A large flagon stood out among the other ointments and potions on a low wooden table. The physician poured some liquid from it into a bowl, then dipped in a clean cloth and proceeded to bathe the repulsive hole which had once contained his lord and master's eye.

"What's that you're using?" asked Bert.

"Gin," smiled the weedy little man, "it'll sting a bit when he comes round, but it should clean any infections, pour yourself a drink if you fancy it," he added. "Promise there's no additives in this one."

Seemingly satisfied with his work, he applied a sweet smelling ointment to the injured place, then bandaged around Etheltread's head, and across the pad he had placed on the empty socket. He moved swiftly and efficiently on to Tread's injured leg, cutting away the strapping which held the two pieces of wood in place.

He stared at the injured leg, twisting his head this way and that, then instructing Bert to take hold of his brother's shoulders, he took hold of Etheltread's ankle and gave it a sharp twist, then a pull. Etheltread let out an almighty snort, but stayed asleep.

"That's better," declared the physician, "but I think he's going to have a limp."

Two more pieces of wood were strapped to Tread's leg, and the little man declared himself satisfied.

"Can you hold his arms sire?" he asked Bert, as Etheltread started to show signs of awakening. "I don't want him ripping off those bandages."

"Probably not," answered Bert doubtfully, "better tie him."

More bandage was produced and the pair bound Etheltread's arms to the side of the chair.

The physician's large ugly patient suddenly shook his head and let out an almighty roar.

"Yeow, my piggin head."

He tried to move.

"Arhh my piggin leg."

The one good eye came fully open and set on the little man.

"I'm going to eat your face," screamed the Baron of Dorsetshire.

"No you ain't brother dear," chimed in Bert. "This bloke has done a good job on you."

"You'll have to leave him here Sire," the physician apologised to Bert.

"How long for," thundered Tread.

"Probably a week."

"Can't you make it any faster?"

"I'll try Sire, but the taxes I have to pay make it impossible to buy all the drugs I need," replied the man getting bolder and taking a verbal side swipe at his lord and master.

"I'll go and see the Grumbleguts, and tell 'em what's happened," said Bert.

"Leave it, I'll do it when I'm better. You'd better go Bert, come back and pick me up next Wednesday," growled Tread.

Bert thankfully took his leave and headed his cart towards his own Manor to the East of Dorchester, making one stop on the way.

CHAPTER SIX

Trufflemouzers

The strain of the famous trufflemouzer had evolved many years before, with the strange mating of a terrier and a wolverine. The owner of the farm, Crufty, had found a litter of ten pups abandoned and cold. Taking them back to his hovel he had reared the pups on warm goats' milk, their recovery and rate of growth was startling and within a month the creatures had become almost fully grown, standing one foot high and measuring two foot from the end of their long snouts to the tip of their bushy tails, with a coarse black top coat and a soft undercoat being slightly lighter in colour.

Crufty became very proud of his little orphans, whose intelligence seemed to match their rate of growth.

So at four weeks old he had led the yapping tribe of nine dogs and one bitch out into the woods.

"Time to see what you lot can do."

Noses pointed in all directions, some in the air, some to the ground, the yapping stopped and off they went.

"S'pose that's the last I'll see of you lot," Crufty said to himself.

After about ten minutes he turned sadly to head back to his hovel, he had become greatly attached to his little furry family. He'd only gone a few steps when he nearly jumped out of his skin. A wild boar crashed out of the thick undergrowth at the side of the path, one trufflemouzer hanging on to its neck, two more attached to each of its hind legs, so close was it to Crufty he was able to whack it hard over the back of its head with the stout cudgel he always carried with him when in the woods. The boar stopped, dead in its tracks, the three trufflemouzers let go of their quarry, jumping up and down excitedly around their master.

"Good boys, that's dinner sorted out for the next few weeks," he praised each one. Still very shaken he sat down, three tongues licking his face and hands.

Three more trufflemouzers appeared from the thicket, two dragging dead rabbits one with a dead rat in his mouth.

"Well done boys," he chortled to even greater excitement from the trufflemouzers. "Where's the rest of them then?" he wondered muttering to himself. "They obviously like me."

One of the boys tugged at his coat as he got up, then looking back over its shoulder headed back into the dense undergrowth.

"Trying to tell me are you," muttered Crufty following the dog, the rest following gleefully in his wake. Knocking the thick bushes aside with his cudgel he pushed his way through until they opened up into a clearing. There under a huge beech tree were his remaining four mouzers digging for all they were worth.

"What you got boys?" he shouted, walking over to the dogs. Four sand encrusted noses lifted out of the dirt at his voice, and at the other end of the four noses, four tails started to wag.

Peering into the hole Crufty exclaimed "Well I'll be!"

At the bottom of the hole were clumps of truffles, the fungi he had occasionally come across before in the forest, but only as single plants.

"Clever boys, that's dinner breakfast and supper sorted out," he laughed.

Reaching down into their diggings he pulled out several of the truffles and filled his pockets.

"We're going to need some help," he addressed the attentive pack. "Follow me."

Off they all trooped back to Crufty's hovel where he hitched his donkey to a small cart, throwing two pannier baskets over her back and slinging a stout coil of rope over his shoulder.

"Back to the woods men," he instructed the dogs. Leading the donkey on a short leash they made their way first to the truffles where he filled the panniers, then to the dead boar where he slung his rope over the branch of a tree, tied it to the hog, and with great effort and determination hauled the carcass on to the cart.

That night Houmit and trufflemouzers dined together on wild pig, Crufty surrounding his steak with truffles fried in butter. The ten dogs were relishing the fresh meat that Crufty had cooked and cut up for them earlier.

That was the first of several hunting trips he had taken into the woods. Over the next few weeks he took many more, but he soon discovered that the truffles turned sour if not used within a couple of days and had to throw the best of his harvest away. The wild boar he and his little hunting machines had caught was skinned then cut up and salted to preserve the meat, along with dozens of rabbits.

The Houmit and his trufflemouzers lived well during the following months, he kept himself to himself, not bothering to go into the market on Tuesdays, where he normally traded some of his livestock and vegetables.

The mouzers loved hunting, and when they weren't in the woods spent their days giving the local rats and mice a torrid time in the hovel's back yard.

The Houmit awoke early one rainy morning sensing something was wrong, nine trufflemouzers were curled up in front of what was left of the previous nights' fire.

The single bitch in the pack had not been herself over the last couple of weeks, not as eager as the rest in the morning, to go flying outside in search of unwary rodents, even refusing her food, but she had developed a craving for goats' milk.

"Jess," he called, a little alarmed.

An answering whimper came from under his bed.

"Whasa matter girl?" he called hanging his head over the edge of the straw mattress and peering into the gloom below. Getting out of the bed he went over to his table where he lit a candle and took it back to inspect Jess. In the soft glow he saw his dog cleaning six pups lying by her side.

Crufty went to the fire and poked the embers into life then threw on some kindling wood, once the flames had taken hold he put on a few of the larger logs that were lying in the hearth. Soon the room started to feel warmer and the glow from the fire added to the Houmit's feeling of wellbeing. He warmed some goats' milk in a pan over the fire, then moved his bed and offered Jess a drink.

She nuzzled her master's hand, then gratefully took a few tired licks at the milk. Leaving the pan close to Jess's head he slipped out to his small barn where he kept the donkey and goats. He found some sacking and took his two big winter coats down from the peg on the back of the barn door, made a brief inspection of his animals, topping up their water and filling their feeding bowls with

43

oats. He then returned, pushed his bed fully back to the adjacent wall, so he could lay the bedding under mum and her new family.

The other trufflemouzers had all come away from the fire to inspect their sister and their new relations.

"Come on you lot, outside," he instructed, opening the door again. The nine mouzers gleefully bundled out into the yard but within five minutes were all scratching at the door, Crufty put down a bowl of fresh water next to the milk and let them in. After a few licks and playful biting of Crufty's ankles they all trooped over to the newborn's bed and lay down around it as if to perform a protective barrier.

During the morning Jess gave birth to four more puppies, although one was stillborn and made no response to her licking or Crufty's rubbing of its small body.

"Only one bitch again," mused Crufty after a detailed inspection of the offspring.

He buried the dead pup at the back of the barn, piling stones onto the small grave so it wouldn't be disturbed.

"Celebration dinner," he called to his dogs, stirring the large black cooking pot that was now always slowly bubbling with pieces of pork, rabbit and various vegetables, at one end of the fireplace.

He dished up nine bowls of stew and put them outside in the yard where it had now stopped raining, the sun warming the earth which gave off a fine steam. Calling the pack away from Jess and her young he instructed them "You stay out here boys, I'll look after her for a while."

He spooned some more stew into a separate bowl, making sure there was more meat than veg, then carried it to Jess and sat with the bowl on his lap while she gently ate. Finally Crufty filled a plate for himself and sat by the fire, the senior mouzers all having returned from their dinner and resumed their positions around Jess and her pups.

The new litter grew at the same startling rate as the first, so after two weeks of making sure Jess and her brood had everything they needed, Crufty got up very early one Tuesday morning and loaded his cart with salted wild boar meat and truffles he had collected in the forest the previous evening.

Letting the goats out into the small paddock at the side of the yard he hitched his donkey to the cart, putting the pups bedding from the hovel on top of the hay used by the outside animals, and calling all the mouzers in from the yard, where the youngsters were helping the older dogs look for stray mice, new smells of the yet unexplored barn were keeping the dogs busy when he shut them in.

Holding back two of the senior mouzers outside, he enticed them up on the cart and set off for the market.

"Hhhaven't ssseen you ffor a while," greeted the stuttering Houmit as Crufty rolled into the village square.

"Wwhats them," pointing to the two mouzers on the top of the cart.

"I calls them trufflemouzers Sidney," Crufty replied keeping well away from Sidney's bad breath.

"Wwhat ddo they ddo then?"

"They are the best little hunting hounds any man could own," Crufty proudly replied. "They catch rats and mice, flush out wild boar and ferret out truffles."

"Ggot any jjobs ffor me today," enquired Sidney, who scraped a living helping out in the market. He had always liked Crufty who, unlike some of the unkind Houmits, addressed him by his proper name, not as Sstuttering Ssid.

"As a matter of fact I have," said Crufty quickly identifying a use for his stammering acquaintance.

"Can you shout loud?"

"Cccourse I can, listen, llloud," he yelled at the top of his voice.

"Stand by the donkey and let the punters know we're selling wild boar meat and truffles," instructed Crufty moving to the other end of the cart, letting down the flap at the back to display his wares, also keeping a safe distance from Sidney's stinking breath.

The market place was rapidly filling up with stalls and carts displaying fruit and veg, fish from the previous days catch, sheep, goats, pigs, cows, poultry live and oven ready, in fact anything that any enterprising Houmit thought could be traded or sold.

Black headed gulls circled silently above, higher still a pair of kites wheeled in the early morning sky.

Rooftop vantage points were taken up by more gulls, with black-eyed ravens and blue-eyed jackdaws squabbling for position in the eaves of lower buildings. Braver herring gulls padded about between stalls and stall holders below.

The gentle summer's morning was shattered by traders arriving late and vying for positions, yelling greetings and curses alike to their competitors.

Stall holders, children ran laughing between the pitches with hoops or playing chase.

A fire had been lit earlier with a pig on the spit, fatty meat causing even more smoke as it dripped into the hot embers.

The stalls selling bread and cheese were doing a good trade satisfying the hunger of the early risers. Both pubs were opening ready to quench thirsts.

A young female Houmit was in tears, ten trays of eggs forming a yellow slimy puddle around her feet.

The fish and chip cart pulled into the space reserved, its rickety chimney puffing out smoke adding to that of the hog roasting fire.

The first customers were trickling in. They and some of the stall holders, seeing Crufty, came over to enquire where he had been for the last few months. The wily Houmit kept them guessing.

"Wait until there's a few more here then me and Sid will let you know," he teased. Pouring some goat's milk for Sidney and himself, he waited and watched the market square come to life.

"Right Sidney give it all you've got."

"Tttruffles wild pppig meat, tttruffles gget 'em while they're fffresh," yelled Sidney. "Ccome and see the fffamous trufflemouzers, bbest bboar meat."

A crowd soon gathered around Crufty's pitch, keeping well away from Sidney's foul breath at the driving end of the cart. The two "famous" trufflemouzers now tied to one of the wheels, were leaping up and down, excited by the noise and colourful throng of people.

"What's a trufflemouzer then Crufty?"

"I'll show you," replied the Houmit unleashing the dogs and crossing his fingers behind his back. "Mice boys," he shouted.

The two mouzers, noses in the air, rushed through the crowd and headed for a large shed-like building on the perimeter of the market square, just this side of the stream where many of the Houmits were relieving themselves. The noise diminished and Houmits strained to see where the two had gone.

Nothing.

The crowd started to get restless and the noise had increased when a yell heralded the return of the hunters, one clutching a dead mouse the other a dead rat, which they deposited at Crufty's feet.

The crowd clapped.

"Thought you said mice, one's a rat," a clever Houmit called.

"Ddon't be ppiggin' ppicky," Sid yelled back, jumping to his employer's defence.

"What else do they do Cwufty?" enquired a middle aged Houmit in a flowery bonnet with a basket on her arm.

"They," proudly indicating to the two mouzers, "are little mean hunting machines. They will keep your hovel clear of rodents. They will find you a wild boar. They will dig up all the truffles you can eat, and they are nice," he added searching for words and petting the two gleeful mouzers.

"I'll show anybody if they would like to come up to my place tomorrow morning, now who wants meat and who wants truffles."

Within an hour Crufty had cleared his cart, jingling coins in his hand he flicked one to Sid.

"Well done Sidney, we are quite a team, come up to my hovel tomorrow, you can help me sell some of these chaps," he gestured towards the pair of mouzers now being fussed by several customers and stall holders alike.

The Houmit bought a few bales of hay which he threw into his cart, then some beef and six chickens contained in a wicker cage, to replace the hens he lost at the start of the year to a hungry fox which had broken into the coup, taking two but killing the rest. Until now he had no money to replace them.

On his way out of the market, he stopped by the young boy selling jams and potions from a large basket, adding to his purchases a jar of blackberry jelly and a tub of special herbs as additives for his cooking pot. The two mouzers made a great fuss of the lad, both jumping up to his waist then rolling on their backs for their tummies to be tickled.

"You obviously make an impression on them," smiled Crufty. "What's your name?"

"Luke," replied the boy, "I love animals wish I could have one of these."

"I've got people coming to my place tomorrow, you're welcome to come along and see the rest of the tribe if your ma and pa don't mind," offered Crufty.

"I'll ask me ma, I know where you live," the boy replied politely.

The donkey cart and its occupants arrived home to excited yapping from the barn, Crufty opened the door and was flattened by the seventeen joyful inmates. He lay flat on the earth and let the dogs swarm all over him, licking and nibbling until they had exhausted their glee. Picking himself up he informed the expectant crowd "beef for tea, but you've got to be on your best behaviour tomorrow, we are having visitors."

He released the chicken into the hen house and secured it for the night. "Bet you'll think twice now foxy," he muttered to himself, "with trufflemouzers on guard."

Emerging from his hovel next morning to a clear blue sky Crufty stared at the small figure stood on his porch.

"Ma says it's alright for me to see the dogs s'long as she knows where I am," stated Luke.

"You'd better go and let 'em out then boyo," laughed the Houmit, who had started to feel a bit cramped in his room, and had decided to just keep the two he had taken to market indoors, but leave the door open, as it was a warm night, giving the pair access to the yard and any unwanted visitors. All the rest he had returned to the barn and bedded them down with the donkey and goats.

The little lad was engulfed by a wave of trufflemouzer dogs and pups all eager to inspect the new face at their homestead.

"Llot of ppiggin' noise," exclaimed Sidney arriving on the scene, "bblimey how many you ggot?"

When the hounds finally lost interest in the two newcomers, Crufty took his visitors into the hovel giving them both chunks of bread and beef with mugs of goats milk while he explained his sales campaign for the morning.

The mouzers busied themselves in the yard taking turns to come in and be petted by the two men and the boy.

Crufty and his pals were coaxing the chicken out into their run when a group of Houmits, two on carts, arrived together, having met on the way from the village.

"Mmorning Bbessie," greeted Sid, to the lady with the flowery hat. "Ddidn't think you would be interested in a ddog."

"Can't get enough wabbits deary," replied Bessie, who had a flourishing business, turning rabbit skins into coats and gloves. "And I weally don't like dealing with Fewwety, he's a nasty piece of work," she added confidentially.

Right on cue Ferrety appeared at the edge of the yard riding a thin morose looking donkey. The weazley little man sold rabbits at market, which he caught all over Seynorgue, netting the many burrows and sending in his ferrets. He was tolerated, but not liked by the Houmits, who knew how he treated his own animals and the methods he used to dispatch the unfortunate rabbits, when they became entangled in his nets.

Clambering off the tired donkey he sidled over to Crufty who was chatting to the rest of the group, who were making friends with the dogs.

"Didn't think you would be interested in trufflemouzers," frowned Crufty at his approach.

"Need dogs to stop the buggers that get away."

"Well they won't be my dogs," declared Crufty. "I've got no time for people who treat creatures the way you do, so you can get back on that poor looking moke and go back to where you come from."

"I'll give you double what you're asking," sneered Ferrety, which was a bit of a surprise to the other Houmits who knew him to be a tight arse as well as all his other delightful traits.

"Not for sale to you, now or ever so go," retaliated Crufty raising his voice.

Ferrety went back to his mount, clambered on and kicked her roughly to get her started.

"You'll be glad of my money when your little venture goes belly up," he shouted over his shoulder as he disappeared from view.

"That applies to anybody," stated Crufty, "if I find any of my dogs are not well cared for, I will come and take them back. If anybody decides they do not want a mouzer after they've bought one, I will buy him back. Right, lets get on Sidney, and Luke get the pups into the barn and shut the door, Jess can come with us today."

Crufty led the group of interested Houmits plus the senior dogs up to the wood, his two helpers carrying sacks bringing up the rear. First to an area with large beech trees.

"Go on then you mouzers find some truffles," he instructed, knowing the area was rich in the delicious fungi, as he had checked it out a couple of days before.

Very soon the several pits beneath the trees revealed the growths, Sid and Luke busied themselves filling the sacks.

"Okey dokey, boys – fetch," shouted Crufty moving with his hunters to the thicker growth surrounding the trees. Noses aloft and to the ground his little pack dived into the brambles and bracken, their coarse coats protecting them from the thorns. Very soon two returned clutching dead mice, then shot off again to rejoin the hunt.

The group of Houmits waited. Fifteen minutes went by and Crufty was starting to worry. Another five minutes then he whistled.

Sidney called, "mmouzers mmouzers."

"Can't understand it," Crufty muttered, his guests were starting to get restless.

After another ten minutes with no dogs appearing, one mentioned he had to get back starting a chorus of agreement.

Feeling deflated and embarrassed Crufty asked Sidney to stay where he was for another half hour, and then led the group back to his homestead.

"Sorry people," he kept repeating, "this has never happened before."

As they approached his hovel it was obvious all was not well, the barn door was now wide open, the chicken were huddled at the end of their run.

"Isn't that Fewwety's donkey tied to your wailings," exclaimed Bessie.

Running now, Crufty and Luke reached the barn where on the floor lay the rabbit catcher surrounded by ten snarling trufflemouzers, the pups huddled into a corner full of hay bales.

The panting group of visitors caught up and took in the scene.

"What for heavens sake is piggin' happening here," yelled Crufty. He called the dogs off and pulled Ferrety to his feet.

"Speak," he commanded, still holding Ferrety's collar.

The terrified man had a large wet patch spreading down his legs.

"Speak," demanded Crufty again.

"Thought I'd come back and get a couple of pups, then this lot appeared," he indicated the senior mouzers.

"Well I'll be," exclaimed one of the gathered Houmits, "Talk about look after your own."

Crufty resisted the urge to ring the neck of the cringing little man as he dragged him over to his sickly donkey.

"Now go," he commanded.

"And ddon't come bback," yelled Sidney, arriving at the scene but not really understanding what was happening.

"The little ones must have cwied out, but we didn't hear it," stated Bessie. "Your twufflemouzers weally are tewwiffic, I weally do want one."

"So do we," shouted the rest.

"Luke, go to the hovel and fetch a flagon of cider," instructed Crufty, "I think we could all do with a drink. Sidney split up those truffles for our guests to take with them."

The Houmits picked out the dogs they wanted, or thought they did, it was in fact the trufflemouzers who picked their new masters and mistresses. Two of the visitors were disappointed, as Crufty refused to sell one of the senior dogs whom he had christened Ben, and of course Jess. But he promised them the pick of the new litter in two weeks time, when they were ready to leave their mother.

Over the next four years the trufflemouzers bred, each time a litter of nine or ten, but always only one bitch.

Crufty was shrewd and refused to sell any of his ladies, also keeping back any dog which took his eye.

Luke had become a regular helper. Sidney called at the homestead at regular intervals and was paid for doing odd jobs around the place.

The hovel had been upgraded and now sported three rooms, the area surrounding the homestead had a stout fence erected, individual runs being contained within.

The Houmit no longer had to sell vegetables in the market to eek out a meagre living, everything in fact was very rosy.

Then on a chilly October morning Crufty arose to be greeted as usual by Jess, but not Ben, the two dogs still holding pride of place in the master's home.

"Get up lazy," he gently coaxed the dog sprawled in front of the hearth. Ben was cold. Crufty felt the chill of the morning eat into his own body which began to shake. He sat back on his bed cuddling Jess unable and not wanting to move.

Sidney arrived, and after making his boss a warm drink, tenderly lifted Ben and carried him to the barn where he wrapped him in clean sacking. The two men were joined by Luke, now a teenager, and the three stood weeping over the grave at the back of the barn.

Worse was to follow, during the next twelve months all of the original litter, except Jess, died, plus three of the second litter, their owners coming to inform Crufty who shared their grief.

"It looks as though they have a maximum of five years," ventured young Luke, one evening after his boss had given away yet another weaned pup to a distressed owner.

"You've got to make a plan guvnor," he instructed, showing wisdom beyond his years. "You can't keep giving dogs away, you'll have nothing left."

The following morning Crufty found Jess under his bed where her first litter had been born, her lovely body already stiff.

Neither Luke nor Sidney could raise their master, who locked himself indoors with his dog for three days. Repeated calls failed to entice Crufty to come out, his only reply, "Go away Jess is dead."

Luke and Sidney were tending the pens when the Houmit appeared holding Jess in his arms.

"I'm ready now," he told the pair, "let's get her buried."

The three once again wept over the small grave at the back of the barn.

Crufty was walking with them to inspect the pens when Bessie, in a new furry bonnet arrived, sitting side-saddle on a fat donkey accompanied by a young mouzer. Sidney went to her and stuttered the latest misfortune.

"I'm weally sowwy Cwufty," comforted the kindly lady, "but I've had an idea."

"See this," she pointed to her hat, "it's part of my first little mouzer. You know they shed their top coats every spwing, then gwow a new one in the autumn weady for the winter, I've collected this fur each time it was shed and made hats, I've got thwee more indoors."

"Bit sick init," exclaimed Luke, always forthright.

"It took a bit of couwage wearing it now he's gone, but I'm glad I did it," replied Bessie. "He's with me all the time now and sevewal other people have asked me to make hats for them fwom their own mouzers' fur."

"That's your answer guvnor," declared Luke.

Crufty had figured, while cradling his dead Jess, the lifespan of the mouzers was a lot less than a normal dog, but there again they matured at twice the rate, therefore their lifespan was a lot less.

Over the next few weeks Crufty and Bessie spent time on market days talking to owners of trufflemouzers, they were both shrewd business people. Crufty cemented his relationship with previous purchasers of the hounds, by offering to replace their dog at half price when their pets went to the big kennels in the sky.

Bessie offered her services as a hat maker and would pay Crufty a commission on the business she did, thus reducing his losses.

As from then, all new customers were advised the average lifespan of the hounds and paid full price.

After weathering that major hiccup the homestead continued to prosper, another building was added, with pens on the ground floor for mothers and pups and a large living area above for the use of increased help, which Crufty had to now fully employ.

Sidney continued to come in odd days, preferring to split his time between the farm and the market. Luke still lived with his Ma but worked full time, now looked upon by the new staff, as one of the bosses.

CHAPTER SEVEN

Inquisitive Houmits

Luke was feeling chirpy as he walked the short distance over the hill to the trufflemouzer farm.

It was a fine morning, the sun already warm on his back. Becky, his ma, had been getting back to her old self over the last few years, the anger and hurt she had felt when Luke was a child were diminishing, she now bestowed the love on the boy that she had been unable to express in his early life. It had been a long time since she had ventured from their hovel, only going up into the woods to collect fruits of the forest with which she made tasty jams and jellies, also ointments and balms which Luke sometimes took down to the market to sell, or exchange for other goods.

This morning she had packed him up some jam rolls ready for his day's work.

Excited yapping and howling greeted Luke as he approached the farm, about fifty young trufflemouzers running to the fence, clamouring for attention.

Crufty himself hearing the excited dogs went to the main gate, letting in the young man whom he had come to regard over the last ten years, as the son he never had.

"Mornin' boss," greeted Luke cheerily. "What's on today?"

"Reckon you and a couple of the lads could give half the hounds a good run and chance to stretch their legs, then do the same later with the rest."

"Good thinkin' guvnor, me Fred and Nobby will go 'smornin'."

Fred the tall skinny lad with a wart on his nose, and Nobby the kennels best darts player, were more than happy to join Luke with a pack of mouzers running excitedly around them.

Leaving three more lads at the farm to look after the rest of the pack, which they would exercise later, Luke, Fred and Nobby set off with a promise to be back by lunchtime.

"Showed those Burghers they couldn't push us around last night," chortled Fred.

Nobby had stood nose to nose with one of the Burghers until he had backed down.

"Yea, didn't Nobby do well," laughed Luke, "let's get a move on we can go and see Bramley and still be back by noon."

Wonderful new smells reached the upturned noses of the exuberant pack, with every step the lads took along the pathway between longer grasses and wild flowers which covered the rolling meadowlands. Some of the scents were rejected, some stored and some had to be investigated. Way up in the clean air, a skylark sang encouragement to the whooping frolicking group below. Higher still, small sheeplike clouds gently moved across the brilliant blue sky. Above all, another must have looked down and smiled down on the beautiful day.

They called the mouzers to heel as they approached a valley covered in white blossom.

"Any old pigmen about," called Luke as they approached.

"Those trufflehounds alright with my animals," shouted back Bramley appearing from the orchard.

"Yea they're used to animals back at the homestead," yelled Nobby.

"C'mon down then, I've got plenty of cider if you boys want a drink."

The lads followed the old wizened Houmit into a barn while the mouzers busied themselves hunting fresh vermin.

Several huge barrels lined one wall, Bramley poured all four a drink from one, then they sat on straw bales, sunlight streaming through large open doors warming the interior.

"How's the pig?" asked Luke.

"Settled in nice, already making eyes at Henry, I've named her Izzy." Henry was a large black boar that ruled Bramley's orchard.

"Didn't expect to see you lot, thought you got into a ruckus last night."

"No problem pigman," boasted Fred, we saw off those Burghers.

"Good on yer boys nobody has had the guts to stand up to those bullies before."

Bramley's little round wife Pippin came into the barn bearing a tray of oatcakes.

"Better have something to soak up that cider boys."

"Thanks missus," said wart nose, "looks like our trufflemouzers have caught a few rabbits while we've been sat here drinking, they'll go good in your stewpot."

After half an hour chit chat and laughter Luke said it was time they were getting back.

"Never been any further than your place Bramley. What's over there?" he enquired, pointing beyond the orchard.

"Never go that way lads, strange country, the only one I know who's been beyond is that little git Ferrety, told me he was a few miles over one night and heard loud moaning, then saw lights dancing in the hills, he don't go there no more and I'm not busting to go and get meself chased by ghosties or piskies."

"Don't blame you," laughed Luke. "You have enough trouble with one pig."

Calling the mouzers, who had now also deposited a pile of dead rats outside the barn, the three took their leave and set off back to the farm.

Pippin dug her husband in the ribs with a fleshy elbow. "I do miss Candy and Brandy," she said.

Slapping his wife playfully on her ample behind, Bramley called after the boys, "tell Crufty I'll be over for a couple of they trufflehounds," as the pair waved farewell.

Candy and Brandy had been two of the first mouzers that Crufty had sold but they had now been gone a year and Bramley hadn't got round to replacing them.

When the three boys returned from their morning walk they related the tale of ghosties and piskies to the other lads at the farm, then during the afternoon when the other half of the kennels were being walked they decided to investigate after work.

Luke went home to check on his ma, then retraced his steps to meet Nobby and their skinny warty nosed pal.

"Where's Fred then?" called Luke to Nobby, who was leaning on the hitching rail outside the main gate, picking his nose.

"Cried off," replied Nobby, inspecting the contents of his fingers. "You know what he's like all mouth and pantaloons. Said Crufty had asked him to keep an eye on that litter born Monday."

Both lads had previously experienced Fred causing arguments or instigating fights, then standing back to let his mates pick up the pieces.

"Oh well nuts to him. You still up for it?"

"Raring to go boss," retorted Nobby, flicking the freshly rolled contents on his fingers at a dandelion.

It was already dusk when the two lads crept back past the barn, where they had earlier been drinking in the warm sunshine. "It's a good job Pigman hasn't got any mouzers," whispered Nobby.

"Yea, we wouldn't have got within a mile without being spotted," breathed his companion. "Fancy a pint while we're here?" he added with a chuckle.

The pair skirted quickly past Bramley's hovel making it to the orchard without raising the occupants. Walking slowly so as not to alarm the few pigs still snuffling around under the trees, getting a late supper before retiring to their huts.

"Wonder if Izzy's moved in with Henry," grinned Nobby, neither of the two animals were in sight.

"Wouldn't be surprised," replied Luke in a louder voice now they were clear of the Houmits home. "She's a girl who's gonna get her man." They both giggled like girls having no others to impress, being at ease in each other's company.

They pushed on over the next low hill as the first owl let the surrounding countryside know it was on the prowl. Thankfully a large moon was rising, to light their way as dusk descended into late evening gloom. Rustling in the long grasses increased as other night creatures commenced their nocturnal activities.

"How much further do you reckon?" asked Nobby starting at a sudden scuffle where a weasel bought the life of an unwary rabbit to an early close.

"Reckon we'll go on for another hour, if we don't see anything then we'll call it quits," replied his mate.

They topped another hill just as a long low moan broke the silence of the moonlit night.

"Boggin' heck what's that?" muttered Nobby.

They stood stock still for a long three minutes neither speaking, no other noises interrupted the stillness.

"Let's go on then," Luke said quietly, "but let's not make any noise."

The pair silently crossed the next valley and crept over another gentle mound, a couple of lights were flickering on the far cliffside, over which a ruddy glow illuminated the rock strewn surface.

Another mile separated the boys from the cliff, the meadowland had now given way to stony ground with large clumps of rushes and coarse grass. They picked their way across to the lea of a long low hill, running from the mound they had just breached to the facing cliff. As they came under its cover a rhythmic metallic clanging cut into the quiet like a knife.

"If that's ghoulies or ghosties," muttered Nobby they're making a helluva noise.

Blending into the background the pair reached the cliff well away from the twinkling lights, just as another loud moan erupted, then ascending the sloping rockface taking care not to dislodge loose stones.

Reaching the top they bent low scuttling across the gravelly surface until it came to an abrupt end, a sheer cliff dropping to a dead calm sea.

Stretching over as far as they dared, they could see the glow emerging from a large cave further along the sea facing cliff wall.

The moonlight and glow from within illuminated a long shiny flat surface covering a third of the entrance, the sea slopping gently into the rest of the eroding archway. A rockfall close to where they lay, stretched out into the sea for about half a mile, beyond the cave another landslip stretched out at an angle forming a natural harbour.

From behind them another low moan echoed back into the countryside.

The clanging suddenly stopped, the boys watched breathlessly as a massive dark figure appeared from the cave and stood on the rough quayside. The thing stretched its arms then threw off a covering draped over its head and the top part of its body, to reveal a black face and a mottled torso, indistinct even in the glow from the cave behind. As they watched it descended several steps cut into the smooth rock then sat at the bottom sloshing seawater over its body. After about five minutes splashing it lifted itself up and slowly re-climbed the shadowy stone staircase.

The pair released pent up breath as the moon illuminated a glistening white human being, its head and back covered in dark hair, its lower face and chest hidden by a bushy black beard.

A clatter of gravel not far from where they lay startled the two, a light appearing followed by someone clutching it on a long pole. Luke motioned to Nobby and they both slid behind a large boulder. The lantern and its bearer thankfully didn't come their way, but continued across the wide ridge then descended towards the cave.

"Enough," whispered Luke.

They crawled back across the ridge and descended the rockface to the gravelly valley. Neither spoke until they'd cleared the mound which obscured the twinkling lights. They sat down under a large bush.

"Reckon there's people working down there," said Nobby, stating the obvious.

Another long moan broke the silence.

"Yea and I reckon that noise is to frighten unwanted visitors," replied Luke. "Them lights are probably where there's sentries and whatever's down there ain't for anybody to see."

Jogging the few miles back, the two quietly skirted the Bramley's place and made it back to the farm where they parted, Nobby letting himself in and Luke continuing, to reach his mother's hovel just after midnight.

CHAPTER EIGHT

Ethelbert

Ignoring his brother's instructions, Ethelbert had left the physicians and gone straight to the solicitors.

He knew the eldest Grumblegut, having been with his father when he was a lad to their offices a couple of times.

He had always liked Grumblegut senior, and the old boy had taken to the boy who was far more respectful than his terrible father, or in fact any of the other siblings, who accompanied Ethelfoot from time to time.

He was ushered into the eldest Grumblegut's office by a secretary.

Shelves around the walls were stacked with books and files, the floor was covered in some neat and some not so neat piles of written papers.

A fire burned merrily in the hearth, either side of which were two comfortable looking chairs.

Old Grumblegut rose from behind a desk and peered over the untidy sprawl of yet more papers.

Bert grinned at the little round man with the beak shaped nose, the little man grinned back.

"Welcome," he said and indicated for Bert to sit in one of the arm chairs coming round the desk and depositing himself in the other.

"What can I do for you young Bert? Goodness you've grown a bit since I last saw you, you were the same height as me last time we met."

"Looks like I kept going, when you stopped," Bert laughed.

Grumblegut chuckled, picked up a small brass bell and shook it till it rang several times. The secretary appeared.

"A drink for my young friend, and one for me I think," instructed Grumblegut.

The secretary disappeared.

"I've got some bad news sir," Ethelbert blurted out. "Your brother has been killed."

"Oh my," the old boy stared in disbelief.

"Oh my," said Grumblegut again, when the tale of his brother's demise was completed.

"So no one has yet seen the Will?" he observed.

A tray appeared, after a knock on the adjoining door with two steaming mugs on it, carried by the secretary. Waiting politely while the pretty girl fussed with a small table, Grumblegut said, "thank you Helen that's all for now, I don't want to be disturbed."

She took her leave smiling at the visitor and her boss.

"My secretary, Helen of Tray," chortled Grumblegut.

"I'm very saddened by the news you have brought me but I hear you've done rather well for yourself. Two gold bars for Blandford Manor was a ridiculously low price." He gave Bert a quizzical look.

Bert stared back, then winked, "You are very welcome to visit us at any time, I'm a wealthy man now, but I am still inquisitive about the will. Are there any copies?"

The little round man looked troubled. "Yes, two," he nodded thoughtfully, "the will must be read with your eldest brother present, but I will tell you the basis of it in confidence, as a friend. Item number five has given me and my brothers some cause for concern, and I would value your opinion, as you are obviously no longer reliant on the legacy."

Arriving back at his own Manor, Ethelbert called a groom and instructed him to take a fresh horse, and ride to the Grand Manor to inform Ethelethel that Baron Etheltread wouldn't be home for tea, or in fact for the next week, as he was being kept under observation by the physician in Dorchester.

Ethelbert then parked his own horse and cart in front of a long trough and dropped the rains allowing the thirsty animal to dip its head. Climbing down from the cart he joined the horse bending down to submerge his dusty face in the cool water, he then turned his mouth upwards under the pump, working the arm to allow a clear steady flow to run over his tongue and down his throat. Refreshed, he strolled across to where a couple more grooms were washing down more carts and coaches of various sizes, pulled up in a neat row.

"Get it unhitched, fellas," he gestured over his shoulder towards his own transport at the water trough.

One of the washers trotted across the yard and led the horse and cart to the line on which they were working, then unhitched the horse which followed him to where, on the far side of the cobbled area a gate gave entrance to a pasture, containing several healthy looking mares.

Bert's own Manor House, smaller than the Grand Manor, was set back from the yard behind some neatly tended flower gardens. The cobbled yard extended into three paths that cut through the garden, then widened out again in front of the house. Taking the smaller right hand walkway he let himself in through the kitchen door.

His wife was busy stirring a large cauldron of rabbit stew as he crept up behind and grabbed her round the waist.

"What's for dinner?"

"Grief Bert," she exclaimed dropping the ladle into the pot.

"Where's everybody?" he enquired.

"I gave cook some time off, her sister and brother came over on a cart from Etheltread's place yesterday morning and asked if she could be excused for the afternoon. Your charming brother had told all his staff to clear off and not come back 'til this morning. I expect she'll be here any time now."

Ethelbert told his wife of the last two days happenings as he sat at their kitchen table, dipping chunks of bread into a bowl of stew.

"So nobody knows who's getting what," he concluded his tale with the meeting at Grumbleguts.

His wife beamed, then reflected "and nobody knows how much we were supposed to be paying back. But the others are going to be hopping mad over this item number five."

The manor house had been bought off his father three years ago, at a knock down price, but with a "gentleman's" agreement between Bert and Ethelfoot that an extra rent would be paid directly to the Baron every two years, Bert's Buses had been set up at the same time.

Ethelbert had seen an opportunity a few years ago, while still single living at the Grand Manor, with the number of stage coaches that crisscrossed their kingdom of Dorsetshire to and from London,

Bristol and Portsmouth, in and out of the West Country. He started to hatch a plan.

He recruited a well known local villain to accompany himself and hold up the London to Exeter stage.

Their first few attempts were disastrous. Bert sat astride his horse one dark night under cover of trees next to the highway. The villain stood in the middle of the road and held up his hand for the coach to stop.

Bert picked up the flattened body as the coach continued into the distance.

A week later the patched up villain took up position, this time mounted on a horse. As a stagecoach, pulled by six horses, thundered towards the pair his horse quickly totted up the opposition, reared and bolted, depositing his rider in the path of the attempted prey.

This time Bert charged out of the bushes to find a mangled corpse.

Not being completely stupid, Ethelbert finally worked out that to have any success stagecoaches would have to be attacked where they were at their most vulnerable.

Recruiting another villain with a small purse of money and the promise of more wealth to come, Ethelbert loaded a horse and cart with implements and provisions he felt would be useful to his plan, then with his new accomplice driving the cart and himself astride his own grey stallion, Spectre, set off to a spot he had marked where the highway was lined by tall trees, and had a steep upward gradient for transport heading towards Exeter.

The coach was due to pass the spot at 5.00p.m. At 3.00p.m. the pair unhitched the horse from the cart and tethered it on a long leash, next to Spectre, well away from the highway, on a patch of grass.

The pair then pulled a couple of axes from the cart and proceeded to attack a tall pine tree. By 4.00p.m. their hacking had produced deep cuts at both sides on the base of the tree.

"Enough for now," said Bert. "Finish it off when I give you a signal."

Bert walked to the very brow of the hill to look out for the coach. Sure enough, after ten minutes, he spotted a plume of dust heading up the road in his direction. Bert waved to the villain.

The sweating horses pulling the coach all breathed sighs of relief as they topped the hill and the going became considerably easier. The coachman cracked his whip and they responded, picking up speed to clear the darker tree lined area which always made them nervous. Their sweat sprayed off them and flew away as a silvery mist, some splashing into the coachman, who being a seasoned driver, had already pulled his scarf round his face and put his head down. Soon they were a speck in the distance.

Bert was still sweating from exertion, having thrown both axes at the unfortunate villain and was now chasing and kicking out at him all at the same time.

They had watched in horror when the pine tree, instead of falling and blocking the highway, had gone backwards and smashed the cart to bits.

The villain, a wiry little chap, who previously made his living as a pick pocket, was wishing he had never given up his career, to accompany this ungrateful git who had promised him untold wealth, grabbed a low branch, and quickly shinned up a high tree, out of reach of his employer's whip.

Bert sat down in the remains of the cart and swore at the villain, the horses, and any unseen wild animals still thick enough to be within hearing distance.

Thoroughly exhausted after an hour, he called to the villain. "'salright you can come down now."

"Promise you won't hit me," came the reply from half way up the tree.

"Yea, get down here."

"Cross your heart and hope to die," from the foliage.

"If you don't get down here now I'll chop the piggin' tree down," shouted Bert, beginning to lose his rag again.

The villain crept down the trunk of the tree and sidled nervously to where Bert was sat.

"Wasn't all my fault guvnor."

Bert picked up an axe, the villain started to retreat, but stopped when he saw his boss attacking another tree.

"Get over here," shouted Bert.

The villain picked up the other axe and got over there.

"Right, this is a practice, we've got to get this to fall where we want it," instructed Ethelbert.

Together they attacked several small trunks away from the road, finally working out which side and where cuts had to be made, to make the tree fall in the direction they required.

Bert made peace with the wiry little man giving him an extra couple of coins for his purse, then loaned him the cart horse and made him promise to meet back at the same spot, same time next week.

As Bert approached the brow of the hill the following week he was relieved to see his accomplice was already there. He had been having doubts on the ride over, as to whether he would ever see his helper again. The chap, who had given his name as Wilf, appeared pleased to see him, Ethelbert had never given his name, always instructing his villainous employees to address him as guvnor.

Wilf had already selected the perfect tree, and made a couple of preliminary cuts low in the trunk with one of the axes they left hidden the previous week.

"Good lad Wilf," called Bert. "We're gonna get it right this week and make some money."

And they did.

The tree crashed across the carriageway, completely blocking any form of passing, its base within the trees on their side of the road, and its tip disappearing amongst the bushes and trees on the other side, at precisely ten minutes before the coach reached the top of the hill.

Head down, urging his straining beasts, the driver was alerted by a shout from his footman as they cleared the brow of the hill and started to pick up a rhythm. Yanking the reins he bought his team to a halt, twenty paces from the obstacle across their path.

The coachman lifting his hat and scratching his balding head, clambered down from his driving seat and stood studying the problem. The footman slid down from his high seat at the rear end of the coach, then walked to the front and stood beside the driver, lifting his hat and scratching his curly black hair. An elderly gentleman poked his head out of the coach to see what was going on.

"You're all going to have to get out and give us a hand shifting this," shouted the footman pointing at the tree.

The elderly gentleman and three more passengers descended from the carriage, muttering amongst themselves about the inefficiency of the coach company.

"Can't help that," retorted the driver, overhearing their remarks. "If you good people want to get to Exeter afore it gets dark, me and him," indicating the footman " are gonna need some help, think yourselves lucky taint rainin'."

The elderly gentleman marched along the tree to where its tip disappeared into the undergrowth.

"Do you carry a hatchet or a chopper?" he called back to the driver.

The footman went to his toolbox under his seat and brandished a small axe.

"Bring it up here man," instructed the old gentleman. "You will have to lop off the top end of this tree at about here," he indicated a point on the trunk before it disappeared between other growth.

Warming to his task the old gentleman shouted at the driver, "You man, get some rope."

Bert and Wilf waited patiently, viewing the proceedings from the cover on their side of the highway. Bert gave Wilf his instructions.

A long hour later, Bert and Wilf stealthily crept from their hiding place, as the driver, footman and passengers started to heave on the rope attached to the, now, free top end of the tree.

They both coaxed the two lead horses of the stage coach, using their bodies as a screen from the activity in the undergrowth, when they had turned them enough, Bert mounted the driver's seat and yelled at the team, cracking the driver's whip, adding to his command. Pulling hard on the right hand rein, the horse and carriage completed its turn, and went back down over the brow of the hill, picking up speed very quickly, before the hot and bothered tree movers grasped what was happening.

Wilf bolted into the thicket and ran to where the two horses were tethered. Leaping on the guvnor's grey with his cart horse on a leash behind, he took off after his master.

They turned off the road, after several miles, into a beech wood, Wilf hanging back to cover any traces left by horses or carriage. Well into the wood a gentle slope led down to a grass fringed lake, and there they stopped.

Dismounting, they linked arms, then went round and round in an impromptu jig, laughing and whooping as they went. Exhausted, they unhitched the team and tethered the six great carriage horses and their own two, on long leashes by the lake. Clambering on top of the carriage, Wilf passed down the luggage, case by case, to Bert. Sitting on the grass they started to undo their prizes, as the first bats of the evening winged over the lake looking for early supper. It was almost dark when they came upon the jackpot. Four previous cases had yielded nothing but clothes, although all of fine quality and could be sold at market. The small red trunk was no different, but when they took out the clothes they found two bars of gold and several purses of coins.

Bert and Wilf slept well that night, one on each bench of the coach with the small red trunk between them, cosy under travelling rugs, left by the departed passengers.

The following day a tired dirty group of six people arrived on the outskirts of Exeter, thanks to a lift by a kindly carter on his way to market. They walked the last two miles and finally arrived dishevelled and angry at the carriage company's yard. They were even more angry, when they discovered nothing had been organised to trace the missing coach.

Three weeks later, the pair of highwaymen, who had by now become firm friends, pulled off the same robbery, but this time on another road. They had bought provisions with the money Wilf got selling most of the clothes to a market trader. They took care when venturing back onto the highway as they narrowly missed being seen by soldiers, obviously hunting for the robbers during the week after their first escapade. Together, they decided, another raid on the same road would be too risky, so they went south and found the ideal spot on the Portsmouth to Exeter highway. Although their journey back to camp took a little longer the robbery went perfectly, an exact copy of the first, on a hill just outside Charmouth.

During their stay by the lake they hadn't been idle, a crude barrier of branches and small tree trunks, now ran along the back of the carriage on the edge of the woods, then turned to form a large U shaped paddock leading to the lake. They had laid timbers between the beech tree's branches, and covered them with rushes from the edge of the water, so the horses could now roam freely within the confines of the fence, down to the gentle beach, and also had cover if the weather turned sour.

By the time they pulled a couple of branches aside to give them access back into the paddock, it was already dark. Parking their new prize carriage along side the first, Wilf jumped down and released the team of four to join the other horses, curious at the new arrivals.

A low moon gave a gentle light to the area, but Ethelbert lit a couple of lanterns hanging on poles outside of their temporary home.

"Leave the goodies 'til morning, I reckon Wilf," said Bert poking the smouldering camp fire into life and adding several more logs.

Wilf grabbed a lantern and clambered up the few steps at the back of the first coach to retrieve a few of the pheasants they had snared earlier in the week, and were now hanging above the footman's seat, tied to a branch well out of reach of foxes. He slung the brace of birds over his shoulder, then selected a large loaf and a flagon of cider from the toolbox under the seat. As he walked by the second coach, he tucked the loaf and cider under his arms, then lifted himself onto the footstep, raising the lantern to inspect the interior of their new acquisition.

Wilf let out a yell and let go of the grab handle and sat down backwards, his fall being softened by a large lump of horse poop.

"There's someone in there guvnor," he yelled.

Bert came running, snatching Wilf's lantern, he too mounted the footstep to peer inside the second carriage. Huddled in the far corner of the rear seat, was a bundle of rags, yanking open the door Bert stepped inside, holding the lantern at arms length, a small dirty face peered out from the rags.

"Who the hell are you?" thundered Bert.

"Aaagh!" yelled back the face.

Bert reached forward to pull aside the cloth being clutched to the face.

"Aaagh!" yelled the face, louder this time.

Starting back, Ethelbert in a softer voice, said. "Tell you what, I'll get out of the carriage then you can come out where we can see you."

"Can't," mumbled the face, lifting its legs to reveal a small pair of feet tied with a rope, then stretching its arms to expose an even tinier pair of hands, also bound.

"Grief fella! Why didn't you call out before?" Ethelbert slipped his hunting knife from its sheath and cut the bonds.

"Not a fella," said the face, rubbing its wrists. "Can't walk yet, my feet are giving too much pain."

Ethelbert stepped out of the carriage and retrieved the flagon of cider from Wilf, then slid it along the floor to the face.

Wilf, scraping horse poop off the back of his breeches, walked with Bert over to the fire.

"What?" he started.

Ethelbert put his finger to his lips and shrugged his shoulders. Silently they loaded the pheasants onto the spit and replaced it over the fire. They both sat staring at the carriage, fiddling with the logs so the birds didn't burn.

"Horses seem happy enough guvnor," ventured Wilf.

"Let's hope we are in a minute," grunted Bert.

Eventually a figure emerged from the carriage, painfully descending onto the step and then the ground. The figure, who had shed some of its rags, made its way slowly across the grass, clutching the flagon of cider.

"Hope you ain't drunk it all," called Wilf.

The face smiled.

"Piggin' heck it's a girl!" exclaimed the bemused little man.

"Course I'm a girl. What did you think I was?"

"Thought we might have collected a phantom, dressed in all those rags."

The girl came to the fireside and dropped on to a large log, handing him the flagon.

"They was takin' me to Exeter, they don't let you have nice clothes if they're gonna hang ya."

"Blimey what yer dun?" exclaimed Wilf.

"Nowhere near as much as you two," retorted the girl. Then went on, seeming relieved to talk, "me pa raised me after me ma ran away with a sailor, he was the master in the shipyard at

Portsmouth, but he fell and broke his neck, so I was kicked out of his house by the docks. They caught me stealing food from a warehouse, one of the blokes got fresh with me, when they were taking me in, so I hit him with a lump of chain, it didn't do him much good, serves him right, filthy beast. They locked me in Portsmouth jail, then yesterday, they told me I was being taken to Exeter for public hanging."

"Blimey," said Wilf again.

"Aren't you the least bit frightened of us?" asked Bert, joining in the conversation for the first time.

"If you think you're gunna die tomorrow, there ain't much left to be frightened of," answered the girl sullenly.

"Well it looks as if you will have two partners on the gallows if we get caught. You'd better stay with us 'til we decide what to do," Ethelbert stated. "This is Wilf and you can call me guvnor, same as he."

"What's yer real name then?" asked the girl.

"That's not for you," Bert glared. "All you need to know is, I'm the boss and what I say goes, no argument. Now what do we call you?"

"Mikki," replied the girl.

"That's a bloke's name," laughed Wilf.

"Taint to, tis short for Michaela which Dad told me came from a foreign ship, but I likes Mikki."

"Mikki it is then," said Bert. "Now how's those birds doing Wilf, and give me that cider afore you gulp the lot."

The three sat around the blazing logs sharing out the pheasant and bread while passing the flagon between them. They swapped stories, the two highway robbers boasting of their achievements for the first time, as they had nothing to lose, wishing to impress, as all males are wont to do when in female company, leaving out the early disasters before they perfected the robberies.

"Can I get myself clean before we sleep?" asked Mikki.

"Help yourself," said Bert pointing to the lake. "Me and Wilf are sleeping in the first wagon and we promise not to look while you bathe. Don't we Wilf?"

"Tell you what, there's still a few clothes in that trunk under our carriage, I'll get em out and stick them in the other wagon for you, we'll probably find something better tomorrow when we unload this lot," Wilf indicated the untouched spoils loaded on top of the second coach.

Next morning Bert and Wilf arose to find Mikki gone.

"Ungrateful little cow," stormed Ethelbert.

"Now we could be in big trouble."

"Thought she was alright guv, never trust a woman s'what I say."

Bert had run over to Spectre and was slinging his saddle across the horses back, yelling at Wilf, "We're going to have to get out of here fast."

"No we ain't," the wiry villain replied pointing to the reeds at the edge of the lake from where Mikki emerged, twisting her long fair hair, wringing out water, wearing a pair of breeches and a blouse both about five sizes too big for her.

"Mornin' boys," she called cheerily. "What's all the shouting about? I've just been for a swim."

"Blimey guv," stammered Wilf, looking at the girl with a clean face in baggy clothes that didn't disguise her female form.

"Yea blimey," agreed the guv.

"Thought you'd gorn," Wilf beamed.

"I'll get some breakfast while you get freshened up if you show me where you keep the provisions," Mikki replied with a very feminine chuckle.

The pair returned to the camp fire having taken more trouble than they have for weeks with their appearances.

Two platters were already set out with fried eggs and mushrooms on toast.

"Aren't you having some?" asked Ethelbert.

"Never eat in the mornin, just drink, there's some warm milk here with a drop of brandy in it."

"Blimey missey keep this up and you can stay," grinned Wilf.

Mikki was delighted when she glanced at the guvnor and he gave her a sly wink.

They got the boxes and trunks, also six heavy sacks down from the second coach and prised them open. The trunks only contained clothes, but at least Mikki was able to find two pairs of breeches and several blouses, more to her size. There was also a jacket and a pair of long riding boots which fitted her to a tee. Two large cases were stacked with wine, the bottles separated by straw packing. Another was full of large round cheeses. The sacks all contained oats and flour, which was more than useful as they had just eaten their last loaf. Mikki declared she could make bread with the flour, also some oat cakes, and the rest of the oats could be used as different fodder for the horses, currently dining on grass.

Wilf, a little away from the other two, had been struggling to open a heavy wooden brass bound case. "What's this?" he exclaimed, holding up a pistol then tipping it up and peering down the wrong end of the barrel.

"Don't do that," yelled Mikki. "You'll be blowing your brains out."

"What's it do then? I ain't never seen anything like this afore," replied Wilf lowering the gun.

Bert stood watching the pair, grinning, his brother Etheltar owned a similar pistol but he had never seen it used.

"Let's have a look then," said Mikki going over to the wooden chest.

Inside were twelve pistols, laid out in two trays of six, one under the other. Beneath the two trays of firearms, the chest was divided into several compartments, with one end being occupied by a separate large tin box. One compartment contained cleaning rods for the pistols, another, ladles for making the round lead bullets and another with about a hundred bullets already prepared, the last compartment was full of flints. The tin box held gunpowder. Inside the lid of the chest, a brass plate proclaimed the makers name, underneath which was the address ending in Italy.

"My Pa had one like this," stated Mikki, taking the gun from Wilf, holding it up and studying it, then extending her arm and pointing it at a knot hole in a tree. "He showed me how to use it, in case I ever needed to."

Very few of the pistols had filtered into Britain and were still a rarity. The only manufacturers being in the Mediterranean.

"Let's have a go then," said Wilf excitedly.

Mikki checked the firearm over then primed and loaded it.

"Let's have a go then," babbled Wilf again grabbing the pistol. Bang, the gun went off throwing the startled little chap on to his backside, Zing went the ball of metal as it glanced off the hub on the wheel of the first coach, whiz as the bullet flew past Ethelbert's left ear and disappeared into the distance.

"You stupid idiot," yelled Bert grabbing a long piece of wood and charging at the frightened Wilf now shaking where he sat.

"Stoppit guv," screamed Mikki, bringing the enraged Ethelbert to a halt in mid swing of his stick.

"S'sorry boss," stammered the trembling Wilf.

"I should piggin well think so stupid sod, you nearly killed me."

"Calm down boys and I'll teach you all that me Pa taught me," Mikki soothed the pair.

She spent the next hour showing them the workings of the pistol, how to load and prime the piece, how much powder to use, explaining what would happen if they didn't get the quantity right. She also explained the ladles, and how to make leaden bullets tailored to the bore of the gun. Next she showed them how to clean and oil the barrel and the mechanism. Finally she demonstrated how it should be fired.

They nailed a large round tin tray to a stout beech tree, and stood back twelve or so paces. Wilf, having recovered from his scare, was excited again and insisted on going first. Extending his arm and taking careful aim at the eye level tray. He snatched at the trigger, bang went the gun, nothing happened.

"Missed," chortled Ethelbert. A rook from the top branches fell dead at the base of the tree.

"No I ain't!" exclaimed the elated Wilf, jumping up and down.

"You're s'posed to be hitting that," Mikki and Bert shouted together, clutching each other in fits of laughter, pointing at the tray.

Mikki reloaded and handed the pistol to Ethelbert who took careful aim, gently squeezed the trigger and fired, clipping the very edge of the tray.

"Well done guv," praised Wilf. "Now let's see what you can do missy?"

Mikki again reloaded, then fired, hitting the target not too far from the centre.

"Think we all need a bit of practice," said Mikki, placing the weapon down by the side of the chest.

The last box contained cans of green ship's paint and several brushes.

"Not so good as last time guv," muttered Wilf. "But more fun."

"At least we can eat for a while before we have to go out and buy food," replied Ethelbert. "You could shoot some rooks."

"What did you plan to do with the carriages?" enquired Mikki.

"Hadn't really thought about it, we only went for what they were carrying, s'pose they'll have to stay here when we finally leave this place," mused Bert.

"No they won't," said Mikki excitedly. "You can make more money, carriages like this used to fetch a pretty penny at the Portsmouth auctions. Me and Dad used to do some of the repairs on the ships and that paint will cover anything, I'll do it," she finished quite out of breath.

"Well well she gets better and better," grinned Wilf.

The two carriages sported their owners' colours, one brown the other yellow both with red wheels and carriage poles to which the teams of horses were attached.

"If you think you can make a good job of it," Ethelbert eventually replied. "There will have to be no distinguishing marks or we will all hang."

"Next time you go out find me some black paint and I'll make them look like they've just been built," Mikki retorted gleefully, visualising the job she was going to do on them.

The next few days were the best the two outlaws had spent in the woods. The warm Spring days were filled with laughter and cheeky banter between them and the girl.

The first yellow of daffodils and primroses, which scattered the green banks of the lake was coming to an end, to be replaced by brilliant white bushes of blackthorn. The woodland was also slowly being reborn, a few birch trees already showing green, and new leaves on the beech trees pushing off the old withered brown ones that had clung on through winter.

More wildlife came to the water, every day a heron chose new positions round the lake, then stood like a statue until its long neck and beak shot downwards to grab a fish. They saw a pair of kingfishers flashing back and forth to a hole in one of the sandy banks. Every evening deer came to the edge of the lake to drink gently from its waters. An orchestra of bird song rang out every morning from the woods behind them, as if to welcome the warm days of summer ahead.

The horses were making short work of the grass in front of the two carriages, so every day Bert or Wilf led them to the far end of the lake, where a large meadow, encompassed by blackthorn and brambles, provided fresh lush grazing.

Mikki spent her days rubbing down the coaches, ready for painting, using coarse sand from the shore on pieces of rag. Any odd knocks or marks she attacked with one of the files or other implements kept on board each of the coaches, used to tend to the horse's hooves.

Their larder was supplemented by rabbits, which were abundant in a warren half way along the lake, but their general food supplies were getting short, and it was decided Wilf should ride out to one of the local markets.

While he was away the friendship between Bert and Mikki became stronger, and each evening they sat side by side talking, sometimes far into the night.

Mikki came up with an idea of how to make the robberies neater and quicker, which appealed to Bert, and together they thrashed out the finer points, Bert, well aware of the first pathetic attempts by himself and Wilf.

The little man returned after four days, but instead of riding, he sat on a cart loaded with goodies, which the horse was pulling.

"Bought it for a song," he gleefully proclaimed.

The three cheerfully unloaded the cart, Bert and Mikki exclaiming how well Wilf had done with each different food item they came across, which would give them a variety in their diet.

He had also purchased several bags of different fodder as treats for the horses. Behind the cart, tied by two pieces of rope, were two goats which would provide them with fresh milk.

The delighted Wilf, in turn, marvelled at the two gleaming coaches, which Mikki had finished painting that morning, and from under the seat of the cart proudly produced two cans of black paint and some more brushes.

Beaming, Bert heaped more praise on their small companion, then added, "come and sit down Wilf and we will tell you our news."

The trio sat together on a large log, passing a fresh flagon of cider that Wilf had purchased, between them, while Bert and Mikki excitedly related the scheme they had hatched while he was away.

"So we need to buy two more horses," concluded Ethelbert.

"And we all need to practice with the pistols," added Mikki.

Late spring moved into early summer as the Exeter to London return coach slowed to negotiate a large pothole in the highway, filled with overnight rain, which had now turned to a light mist rising from the warm ground in the early morning. Successfully rounding the obstacle, the coachman encouraged his team to a trot, then yanked the reins back and applied the long wooden handbrake, connected to one of the front wheels.

"Wish he'd make up his mind," muttered the piebald mare to her mate in the trace next to her at the rear of the team. She then stood trembling as a loud crack rang out directly in front of them, followed by a bellowed command.

"Halt."

The driver and coachman peered in disbelief at the large sack with legs astride a grey horse in front of them. The sack held up a smoking pistol in one gloved hand, the other held another pistol trained on the coachman.

Either side of the carriage two more sacks materialised out of the mist, both on horseback, and both carrying weapons now pointed at the footman and the rudely awoken passengers, who had been trying to snooze after their early start.

"Everybody out," commanded a sack pointing its firearm inside the coach.

"Throw down the luggage," shouted the other sack with the pistol on the footman.

"No," said the footman.

Bang, went the sack's pistol, taking off the footman's cropped hat.

"Throw down the luggage."

"Yes," said the footman.

"Take off all your valuables," said the sack on the other side of the coach to the bewildered travellers, now stood huddled by the footstep.

"Throw them down there." The sack indicated a patch of gravel.

Several rings and coins landed on the ground.

"Any more?" enquired the sack.

No answer.

Bang, went one of the sack's pistols. Several more pieces of jewellery and purses joined the rest.

The footman meanwhile had thrown down the boxes and trunks from the top of the coach to the ground.

Both sacks held up their hands, the sack on the grey horse at the front of the coach shouted "You can get back in now." Then to the coachman, as the last traveller closed the door, "on your way," moving the grey to one side and adding, "have a good trip."

The three followed the coach for about a mile then turned and galloped back to the scene of the robbery. Whipping off the sacks as they dismounted Bert, Wilf and Mikki all sweating profusely raised their clenched fists in unison, and shouted "Yessss."

Wilf ran to a copse at the side of the road and reappeared a few minutes later driving the horse and cart. Swiftly the three loaded the scattered luggage.

"We've got the rest, let's go," said Bert taking the reins of Wilf's mount.

It was a while before the trio pulled thankfully into their hideout, having had to take extra time concealing hoof prints and cart tracks in the soft ground.

They unhitched the cart, then Bert and Wilf remounted and led Mikki's new mount, the small cart horse, and the ten carriage horses from their overnight paddock, along the side of the lake to the pasture at the other end, where the horses gleefully cantered among the lush grasses.

"Pleased with our two new mounts," said Wilf, indicating the pair they had bought for Mikki and himself.

"Didn't flinch," agreed Bert, "mind you we gave them enough practice."

Prior to the robbery the trio had rehearsed it in fine detail, using one of their carriages as a substitute for the intended victim, shouting commands at imaginary coachmen, footmen and passengers, then firing the pistols at appropriate times to get the horses used to the sound.

Mikki kept coming up with, "what if?" and they rehearsed what they would do, hopefully covering all eventualities. The sacks had been her idea, as they would be coming into closer contact with their prey. To the already opened sacks they made holes for their eyes and arms.

"The eye holes in my sack need to be bigger," said Wilf, "I could only see out of one of them."

"You only need one now you can shoot straight," Ethelbert and his little companion dissolved into fits of laughter.

"What's got you two going," grinned Mikki, who was already dishing out a stew that had been left simmering.

"Wilf said he can only see out of one eye hole," chortled Bert.

"Well he only needs one now he can shoot proper," replied Mikki.

"That's what the guvnor said." Wilf dissolved into fits of laughter again. Bert and Mikki clutched at each other to stop falling over, as they whooped with glee high on their success. Mikki planted a big kiss on the surprised Bert's nose.

That summer the trio executed nine more robberies, also taking in the Bristol to Exeter road as well as the other two routes.

Between them they had amassed a large fortune as well as another carriage and four, when one of the passengers and the footman had attempted to put up a fight, they had both been shot in their legs and then left with no transport as a lesson to others.

On their last attack they had to flee for their lives, Wilf abandoning the horse and cart for his own mount, when a troop of soldiers appeared at full gallop heavily armed with muskets, following the footman giving a long blast on the brass coach horn as he clambered back into his seat.

Since then Ethelbert had become very withdrawn, spending long hours by the lakeside staring out over the water. When Mikki or Wilf tried to include him in their conversation, his answers were short, with none of the usual banter that had gone before.

"Tell you what," said Wilf one evening, attempting to lighten the mood. "Let's all ride over to Blandford, it's the annual horse fair this week."

"What a good idea," chimed in Mikki, "I think we could all do with a break and let off a bit of steam."

Ethelbert responded, "yea let's do it, I'm getting fed up with living out here in the woods." Perking up, he added, "we need to dress as gentry, so no one would suspect we are really three sacks," he finally laughed.

Raiding the several trunks of clothes, still untouched from previous robberies, they delighted in selecting fine garments and dressing as dandies of the day. It was decided that Mikki should also dress as a young nobleman, as it would be quite out of fashion for a lady to be seen not sitting side saddle, riding at any more than a gentle trot.

Insuring all the other horses were content in the meadow, the three set off before dawn on their own mounts, and rode into Blandford next morning, passing through on the way the large Blandford estate, now unoccupied.

Within Ethelfoot's domain were several such estates and Manor Houses, occupied by Lords of the Manor. Each responsible for his own lands and serfs, that lived and worked upon them. These Lords in turn, came under the duress of Ethelefoot Baron of Dorset, each year collecting taxes, half of which was then payable to the Baron.

A year or so ago the Lord of Blandford, who had been a constant thorn in Ethelfoot's side, refused to pay his dues. The Lord was an uncontrollable gambler, and had in fact lost most of the money in bad wagers.

Ethelfoot, accompanied by Etheltread, Ethelbert and the two Reds, had ridden to the Manor and accosted him. After a tremendous argument he and Ethelfoot had fought, Ethelfoot finally running him through with his sword.

The staff were dismissed, and the Lady of the Manor, who had locked herself in her boudoir, smashed Ethelfoot in the face with a warming pan still full of last nights coals, when he broke down her door, then made her escape back to London, her original home.

As the trio approached the horse fair, Ethelbert's mood had changed completely from the misery guts he had been during the last few weeks, yelling and laughing with Mikki and Wilf as they galloped the last few miles.

A large notice was displayed on the wall in the tavern where they first made their way, on entering the town's square.

"Wonder what that says?" Wilf muttered.

"Grand auction," read Mikki. "Sale of valuable Coaching Inn and all its contents, plus Coaching business currently providing transport from Exeter to London, Bristol and Portsmouth as well as several carriages. Viewing 5th October, Auction 6th October all must be sold, White Hart Exeter."

"Always fancied running a pub," said Wilf.

"No reason why you shouldn't," replied Ethelbert, as they took their seats by the window, waiting to be served.

"That would fit in nicely with what I have in mind," he added in a murmur.

"What's that boss?" asked Mikki squeezing his arm.

Ethelbert decided it was time to tell all to his partners in crime. Leaning over the table so his face was close to Wilf and gently pulling Mikki towards him, he stated," I'm Ethelbert, third son of Ethelfoot, Baron of Dorset."

"Well I'll be," exclaimed Wilf. "Always thought there was a resemblance to that lot."

"Morning Sire," greeted the landlord bustling up to their table. "What can I get you gentlemen?"

They ordered their breakfast and the landlord bustled off, bowing slightly towards Ethelbert as he went.

"Looks like I told you just in time," grinned Bert. "I've been wondering what to do over these last few days, and this morning it has all become clear. I'm going to buy Blandford Manor off my old chap, and you Wilf, can set yourself up as landlord at that tavern in Exeter. Between us we will run the coach service."

Wilf's face broke into a huge smile. "You sure you're one of that lot guv? Everybody says they're all pigs."

Mikki still with her head forward over the table started to softly cry.

"Wassa matter lovely?" asked Wilf.

"That'll be the end of us then," sniffed Mikki. "And I've really enjoyed being with you two."

"Doesn't have to be," said Bert gently. "How about marrying me and becoming Lady Michaela?"

Mikki threw her arms around him.

"Don't kiss me," Bert said hastily. "Remember you're a bloke."

As they sat at the table in the window of the pub in Blandford during the first week in September, it felt like Christmas Day.

"We need to buy a small carriage and pair," Wilf ventured. "Something more befitting to a Lord and Lady."

"And I can show my husband/guvnor that he hasn't really married a bloke," chortled Mikki.

The trio wandered happily out into the square, taking in all the sites, sounds and smells of the thriving horse fair.

Just before lunch they found exactly what they were looking for, a light carriage with a leather half hood, to which was hitched two young grey mares. "Your Spectre is going to like those," grinned Wilf, referring to the guvnor's grey stallion.

After another bite to eat at the Inn the three cheerfully made their way back to the hideout in the wood. Mikki delighted in driving the carriage while her future husband led her own mount.

Next day, now that his mind was clear, Ethelbert set off early, giving Mikki a smacker on the lips and Wilf a friendly hug.

Spectre carried two large saddle bags as well as his master. As he rode up the driveway to the Grand Manor the two Gingers came out to meet him, greeting him excitedly and bombarding him with questions.

"Tell you more later," their favourite brother laughed. "Where's the old man?"

The pairs' faces fell and pointed towards the stables. Bert nudged Spectre and trotted round to the rear of the building, the horses' hooves silent on the peat pathway.

His father was crouched behind a gooseberry bush, about to leap out on an unsuspecting maid busily hanging out washing.

"Mornin' guvnor," he yelled.

Ethelfoot's head shot up scratching his nose on the prickles. The startled maid turned to see the old man leering at her, screamed, dropped the washing, and fled back into the house.

"Where the piggin hell've you been," shouted Ethelfoot.

"Making my fortune guv," Bert peered down at his randy old git of a father.

"Piffle," shouted the Baron of Dorsetshire. "You'll never have enough to furnish a piggin hovel."

He and Bert had never seen eye to eye, and he was enraged being caught in his present position by the son he hadn't seen for nearly a year.

"I want to buy Blandford Manor," stated Ethelbert.

"With what?" sneered his charming Father.

Ethelbert reached behind him taking a gold bar out of one of the saddle bags, which he dropped to the ground in front of his Pater.

Ethelfoot stared in disbelief. "Where did you get that?"

"Mind your business Pa and I'll mind mine," replied Ethelbert, enjoying himself.

By now the large round Baron of Dorset had recovered his composure. "That'll get you in but I still want piggin rent."

"No I want to buy it. How much?" demanded Bert.

"Another nine of those," sneered his delightful Daddy. "No wait," he added before Ethelbert could reply, stroking his greying beard. "I'll do a deal with you boy, you can have Blandford Manor and all that goes with it, including the piggin title, for two gold bars."

"What's the catch?" Bert asked warily, still taken aback from the amount the old man had asked for, which would have made a serious dent in his wealth.

"You pay me one more bar each year for the next eight years, which we will agree on a separate document, strictly between me and you."

Ethelbert reached into his other pannier, took out another gold bar, dropping it next to the first.

"Deal," he said holding out his hand, but still slightly puzzled by his father's seeming generosity.

"And, you are responsible for collecting taxes from your piggin serfs each year. And, I don't want the same shenanigans as I had from the last piggin idiot," the old chap added, referring to the last Lord of Blandford whose life he had bought to a cutting end.

From the taxes collected by each estate, half was paid to the Baron who in turn paid the Monarchy a yearly set fee from his Lands in Dorsetshire. Ethelfoot was also required to pass on half of any sale of estates to the King or Queen of the time. His deal with Ethelbert would save him four gold bars.

"Come on boy lets go into the house and let the family know who's the new Lord of Blandford."

Etheltread was the only person present in the great hall not to offer his congratulations, the rest of the Ethel's with the exception of Etheltar who was away at sea and Ethelgay, who was running his shop, were delighted to hear of their brother's good fortune, when the Baron proudly announced the new Lord of Blandford.

Ethelfoot now treated his son as his favourite, proclaiming to the family how well his boy had done, stating, "He's a chip off the old block."

"Not piggin' likely," muttered Ethelbert under his breath.

The Gingers bombarded him with questions as to how he had made his fortune. Bert glibly lied, telling tales of dealings and good fortune in Bristol and London.

Ethelethel rushed back and forth from the kitchen with food and drink, each time making sure Ethelbert was served first. Ethelegs squeezed up to her big brother, who promised she should be the first to visit his new home. Ethelete marched across the hall and extended her muscular hairy arm shaking hands with Bert offering congratulations.

Etheltread hardly able to conceal his emotions, got up and stormed out of the gathering, that was treating his younger brother as if he were the main man.

Finally Ethelbert broke away, saying he had more business to attend to.

Ethelfoot took him aside as he bid his farewells, saying that he would instruct Grumblegut solicitors to draw up deeds for the Blandford estate, proclaiming Bert the new Lord of the Manor. And that he and Ethelbert would concoct their own agreement for the rest of the money.

Ethelbert rode back into the camp by the lake, shouting. "Got it, its' ours."

The next week was filled with activity as the outlaws broke camp.

First, they rode to the new home and inspected the purchase. Twenty rooms, mostly in good repair and far more pleasing on the eye than Bert's old family dwelling. Each room furnished with exotic rugs, chairs and sofas.

Outside there were barns, and best of all, a stable block, for twenty four horses. They rode and walked the boundary, which was in need of attention in several places, they estimated the estate of grass and woodland covered about five hundred acres.

Two huge stone stags sat on top of the arched entrance way. Mikki turned as they rode back to the lake and said, "look after the house boys we'll be back in a trice."

They then made two journeys, first with the small carriage and one of the coaches into which were bundled the goats, then the other two stage coaches loaded with spoils from their robberies.

The three coaches now sported several new coats of green paint, having black wheels and carriage poles.

The last day by the lake was spent in covering any traces that the site had been occupied.

They finally slept in the Manor on the sixth night, wonderfully comfortable after the cramped coaches.

Mikki prepared a notice which they displayed at the friendly tavern in Blandford, advertising for staff. The following week they employed a cook and two maids, then three estate workers and two grooms, the groundsmen coming in each day, the grooms taking it in turn to sleep over the stables every other week, so they could still have time in their own homes.

Leaving the Manor under the watchful eye of the stags, the three journeyed to Exeter on the 4th October. Bert and Mikki in the leather hooded carriage, Mikki now resplendent in fine female attire. Wilf and Bert dressed as gentlemen, Wilf on horseback.

They booked into the White Hart coaching inn that night, which was still being run by receivers, prior to the auction in two days time.

The walls in the pub were covered in notices advertising the forthcoming sale, there were also several posters stating: Wanted dead or alive the sack gang. Another was worded: Reward for information leading to the arrest of highwaymen, known as the sack gang, it went on to list the various robberies and where they had taken place.

Sitting in the bar that evening the three placed themselves so they could hear the general chatter. They overheard that the White Hart was being sold due to a massive drop in trade since the robberies began, being the main staging point for coaches leaving and arriving in Exeter. They also heard the carriage companies were selling up for the same reason, also the lawsuits that had been raised against them by disgruntled travellers.

Ethelbert and Michaela were married next day at Exeter Cathedral, Bert's new bride looking gorgeous in a dress she had packed specially for the occasion. The excited Wilf showered them in rice as they left the ceremony. They returned to the tavern to celebrate. In the yard at the rear, a group of children, one with a bag on his head, were playing their new game of get the sack. They then had a guided tour of the premises and viewed the stagecoaches and horses which had been polished and groomed, to be included in the next day's sale.

Finally the three retired to their rooms, Wilf to his own, Lord and Lady Blandford to a suite, where their luggage had been transferred from the singles they occupied on the previous night.

"Come on gentlemen you can do better than that," sighed the auctioneer to the miserable turnout to the carriage auction, as another pathetic bid was half heartedly tendered.

The Mayor of Exeter who was in attendance, worried by the loss of trade within the city, called, "We guarantee the buyer a monopoly on the routes."

A large white-haired gentleman who stood at the bar already tipsy on cider, shouted "we guarantee that the buyer will soon get the sack," then dissolved into guffaws of laughter accompanied by his attendant cronies.

Another bid was put up from the floor.

"There is a reserve gentlemen," grumbled the auctioneer.

"How much?" shouted the tipsy one.

"You know I can't divulge that sir," called back the exasperated dealer. "If that's your best gentlemen we will have to call it no sale," looking round the room.

Ethelbert signalled the man and topped the previous offer by one hundred guineas.

"Sold!" shouted the auctioneer banging down his gavel.

A few more people had packed into the room for the sale of the tavern.

The bidding started briskly, with several locals having grand ideas but no cash to match.

"I'm taking no more bids of ten," the auctioneer called getting annoyed again. "Minimum increase fifty guineas."

Two punters raised the stake.

"Three hundred!" called the first.

"Three fifty!" called the second after a while.

"Four hundred!" called the first.

The auctioneer looked to the second bidder, no response. "Going once, four hundred guineas for a fine coaching inn and all the stock."

"And no customers!" yelled the tipsy one.

"Five hundred!" shouted Wilf, resplendent in silk frock coat, riding breaches and leather boots. "I'll bring my own customers!" he called to the chap at the bar, acknowledging him with his silver tipped walking cane.

"At five hundred guineas," called the auctioneer. "Going twice." A long pause. "Sold to the fine looking gent with the fine looking cane. Well done sir I hope you will be happy."

The heckler at the bar started to clap, and soon the whole pub joined in.

"Drinks all round!" yelled Wilf as the hubbub subsided. The party went on well into the night.

"I suppose we can call that half and half," Bert shouted into his little friend's ear, and keeping his arm firmly round his new bride's waist.

"Clever guv," Wilf laughed, as the pair had both paid just under half the amount they expected to.

They let it be known that they would see the staff of the inn plus coachmen, footmen and grooms the following afternoon in Lord and Lady Blandford's suite.

Only one coachman gave Ethelbert a quizzical look, but soon beamed with pleasure to find that he could have his old job back, and a small increase to his salary.

The carriages were taken to the local coachmakers and Mikki supervised the new painting job, insuring they matched the same shade of green as the ones she had painted herself. She also organised new posters for the bar and various meeting points in Exeter advertising the new owners Bert's Green Buses.

The pair finally returned to their mansion with promises to return in a couple of months, leaving Wilf happy as a dog with two tails, pulling pints and supervising the coach firm for his old guvnor.

Needless to say, as coaches started regular journeys again without being attacked, travellers returned, and soon both businesses were doing a thriving trade.

Ethelbert and Mikki were blissfully happy in an unaccustomed Manor, the other coaches were brought out of the barn, they also purchased several smaller carts for shorter journeys, establishing new routes and depots across Dorset.

Ethelbert took Mikki to the Grand Manor with him and introduced her to the rest of the family, when Grumblegut sent word that the deeds to Blandford Manor were ready for signing. They stayed for the night. That evening Ethelbert and the Baron also signed the other agreement, which they painfully put together themselves.

They visited Wilf every two or three months as promised. When they inquired if any questions had been asked as to why it was safe to travel, and the coaches were always on time, Wilf replied: "I just tell 'em these coaches belong to Lord and Lady Blandford and they guarantee no holdups."

CHAPTER NINE

Ethelgay

Ethelgay completed a tiresome journey back to Lyme Regis in the middle of the afternoon, aboard the cart he had ordered from Ethelbert, now wishing he had paid extra for a coach, which would have been faster and cleaner.

Feeling an absolute sight, he instructed the driver to deposit him at the back entrance to his shop, where there was also a door to his living accommodation above, not wishing to encounter any of his employees until he had washed and changed.

Creeping up the stairs, that ran beside the shop, he couldn't resist a peep through the spyhole, that was knocked out so he could watch and listen to proceedings without it being known.

The shop was unoccupied, but all the stock looked neat and tidy and the place looked fairly clean. He was about to continue up the rickety stairs when the bell over the shop door rattled, then rang to announce a customer.

Louis, the main singer in the boy band, which made up Ethelgay's staff, appeared from the stockroom. The band, which so far had little success, had named themselves The Schmoes, and he had become known as Louis the Schmoe.

"I'm looking for thomething in thilk," stated the customer. "I thee you've got theveral bloutheth in the window."

Louis, a good looking chap, with a honed six foot body, was never short of girlfriends, as well as his looks they took to his friendly, cheerful personality, also his wicked sense of humour.

"Thertainly thir," replied Louis, quick to spot an opportunity for some fun.

"I hope you're not taking the pith out of my lithp," frowned the customer.

"Thertainly not thir, I've talked like thith for years," Louis quickly retorted.

Ethelgay could see the other members of the boy band hiding behind the stockroom door, all shaking with repressed mirth, so as not to alarm the customer.

Frankie, who played the fiddle, and also arranged their music, another good looking lad, but of smaller, stockier stature with close cropped hair, Richard, who hated being called Dick, and Marcus, who always carried a few days growth on his face, were both of dark complexion, in contrast to Louis and Frankie's fair skin, but both attractive boys in their own way.

"Thmockth?" asked the customer. "I would like to thee what colourth you've got in thtock."

"I'm not quite thure what colour thmockth are in thtock, thir."

Ethelgay could see that Louis was straining to keep a straight face, and craned forward to see some of the new summer stock he hadn't seen himself yet. Unfortunately the customer and Louis moved out of range of his peephole, so he continued up the staircase, glad to deposit his heavy valise of gold coins in the living room over the shop.

He thankfully stripped off his soiled clothes in the large bedroom to the rear of the living area, then washed his hot smelly body in cold water, which he poured from the pretty jug, into the pretty bowl, on the ornate washstand. He threw the dirty water out of the window, into the alley at the rear of the shop, then repeated the process with fresh water, but this time adding scented oils. Starting to feel considerably better, he rubbed himself dry with a cotton sheet, then powdered all his important little places, and dabbed eau de cologne at strategic points on his person. He selected a powder blue blouse and a pair of white pantaloons from his extensive wardrobe, a pair of fine leather Moroccan sandals completed the attire, and Gay was now feeling ready to take on the world, as he combed and brushed his hair, studying the gorgeous person in the gilded mirror above the washstand.

Before descending to the shop he opened the valise and dug his hands into the glittering mass of coins, letting them run slowly back through his fingers. By now he was feeling thoroughly elated, reflecting on what he had done. There was enough money to keep him in splendour for a very long time, also with the death of Ethelfoot, and the burning of the Will he doubted if Etheltread would ever know that he still owed a considerable sum, which he had borrowed from his father to set up the business, choosing to leave his uncouth family for the more genteel settings of Lyme Regis.

The shop bell tinkled, and Louis bounded out from the stockroom once more.

"Afternoon sir, lovely day," he greeted the figure which had turned its back to close the door.

"Got any thilk bloutheth?" enquired Ethelgay turning to face him.

"Aw hello boss," Louis reddened realising that his earlier playacting had been rumbled.

"Did he buy anything then?" asked Gay.

"Yea, a blouth and two thmockth," grinned Louis, knowing that his boss would forgive almost anything as long as he made a sale.

"You look exceedingly dapper if I might say so," added Louis, using all his charm to avoid possible retribution.

The other three came bounding out of the stockroom.

"How's trade been?" Ethelgay asked in general, his eyes darting round the premises.

"Not good boss," replied Richard, holding up the bucket from below the counter into which they deposited the takings. He tipped the contents onto the counter top for inspection.

"More than not good it seems," said Gay, looking at the meagre pile of coins, wondering how many had found their way into his assistant's pockets.

"Let's have a look at the new stock."

Marcus retrieved some boxes from the rear stockroom, and Frankie indicated several items he had displayed, using his artistic talent, in the corner by the window where the light would show off the colours to their best effect. Marcus deposited several boxes on the shop floor, and took off the lids to reveal the stock which had arrived while Gay was away.

"Nothing wrong with these," murmured Gay, pleased with his selections and designs.

Each year, before Christmas, Ethelgay closed the shop for a month and went to London, where he studied the in vogue fashions, spending the festive time with way-out friends in the capital. In the New Year he travelled back to Bristol, where he selected rolls of silk, cotton, linen, sackcloth, calico and velvet, that would be sent to various tailors and seamstresses in his own area. When he returned to the shop, he reopened with a winter sale of last years unsold stock, and spent his spare time designing and copying out bits he had seen, sending the drawings to his outworkers ready for the new season.

"We just ain't getting the punters in boss," stated Louis. "Looks like it might be a bad year."

Ethelgays previous high spirits were starting to fade with the gloomy forecast, then Louis added: "Me and the boys have come up with a bit of an idea."

"Go on then," said Gay, depressed by his failing business venture, but greatly consoled by the thought of his new found wealth upstairs, thinking, perhaps I'll close it down.

"Me and the boys ain't getting any gigs, boss," stated Louis.

"You and us needs a gimmick boss," put in Richard.

"If you give us some time off each day and supply us with new outfits we will go and play our music on the promenade, and model the clothes," stated Frankie, adding, "we can have a big sign made saying: Clothes supplied by Gay Gear.

"We bought one of them dulcimers and I've made it louder by altering the innards," said Marcus proudly, adding "bet you'd like to have a go on it."

Ethelgay's youth had not been spent as his brothers, hunting and playing boisterous games, preferring to wile away the hours learning to read, and play the harpsichord left at the Manor by one of his father's mistresses, who had taught him the basics, before she was discarded for something younger and prettier. The reading had been a problem, and he only managed a few basic words, but he had taken to the music like a duck to water. He had his own harpsichord in his quarters above the shop, and spent most evenings having a tinkle.

The boys beckoned Ethelgay, and trooped out into the rear stockroom where the instrument stood, now repainted in garish colours.

"We've been practising out here in the evenings, Gayboss," declared Louis, " and Frankie's been writing new pieces trying to change our sound, but none of us is good enough on that," he pointed to the keyboard.

"Show us how it's done, bossman," they all encouraged.

Ethelgay gently fingered a chord. The sound produced was nothing like the gentle perfect notes given out by his own instrument, instead a harsh metallic clang. Gay started, then went into a fast minuet which sounded nothing like anyone had heard before, but was certainly not displeasing.

Together the boys shouted, "More! More! More!" when he finished, clapping their hands and stamping their feet.

"That's what we need, Gayboss," shouted Louis above the din. "Why don't you join us?"

"Yea join us," shouted Richard and Marcus together.

"We could make our own brand of music," Frankie added excitedly.

Ethelgay was taken aback. "You want me to play in your band?"

"Yes boss."

"Please boss."

"Go on boss," came back the replies.

Gay scratched his cheek, secret envy he had felt whilst watching performing minstrels during his visits to London, started to surface.

"You're a boy band, I'm ten years older than all of you."

"Don't matter if you're good boss," stated Frankie.

"You don't look ten years older than us," added Richard.

Ethelgay was sold, the last compliment hitting the bullseye of his ego.

"Alright, we'll give it a try, but no way am I putting myself out in front of potential customers, until we're good enough."

"Hooray!" the boys clapped and stamped their feet again.

The next few weeks were some of the most enjoyable Ethelgay had known. Every evening the five rehearsed, the dulcimer was tinkered with and fine tuned until he was satisfied. Marcus and Louis constructed a wooden rack that would house three extra drums, when Frankie suggested that a louder beat would enhance their music.

Gay spent many hours with Frankie, writing fresh pieces which would suit their style of play. Until now, the only popular songs heard played by travelling minstrels, consisted of, hey nonnie nonnie with lots of fol de rols.

Their sound was certainly different. But would it appeal to the general public?

Finally, on a warm Tuesday evening in July, they were ready. Pulling a large handcart on which was mounted the dulcimer, with the drums and their stands piled around it, the five all sporting different new outfits each had selected from the shop, trundled on to the Cobb as the promenade in Lyme Regis was known, and set up for their first public gig.

With the sea behind them they unfurled a large banner and attached it to the railings at the top of the steps leading to the beach. Bold lettering proclaimed "THE SCHMOES. ALL OUTFITS SUPPLIED BY GAY GEAR".

The four drums were unloaded and mounted on their rack, it was decided they should go next to the dulcimer that would stay mounted on the handcart.

Richard, resplendent in a dark blue smock, went behind the set and gave them an exploratory roll.

From an open upstairs window facing on to the promenade, a crone screeched, "is it war?"

"No love," shouted back Richard, "We're a band."

"I'll shut my window if its sand," called the crone, "piggin stuff blows everywhere."

"No we're a band," yelled Richard.

"Who?" enquired the crone.

"Aw, nuts," muttered Richard, and gave an extra loud roll on his drums.

Several more faces appeared at windows, and evening strollers stopped, inquisitive as to what was going on.

Ethelgay climbed on to the hand cart, wearing a pink frockcoat with gold brocade, a white ruffle blouse and tight white breeches, on his feet were white leather shoes with gold buckles. He had tied his hair in a ponytail with a black ribbon.

Marcus and Frankie on fiddles took up their positions in front, both wearing dark green blouses with black breeches and riding boots.

Louis came and stood between the pair holding a megaphone, similar to those used on ships for hailing. His fine figure was decked in a short smock open to the middle of his chest, and worn loose over light purple velvet breeches, with black shining buckled shoes. His head was covered by a wide brimmed floppy purple hat with a couple of peacock feathers for added effect.

Richard kept a drum roll going, then Ethelgay chanted, "One, two, three, four."

All five joined in singing the first ditty which only included backing from the dulcimer and drums.

"Gay gear gay gear,

Gay gear is why we're here

Gay gear gay gear,

Gay gear is over here."

They pointed towards the shop.

"There'll be no fuss

To dress like us

Gay gear Gay gear,

Gay gear is why we're here.

Gay gear Gay gear,

Gay gear is over here."

They pointed towards the shop again.

"If you want clothes

That look like those."

Gay and Richard pointed to each other. Louis put down the megaphone and pointed, using both hands, to Frankie and Marcus on either side of him, Marcus and Frankie both pointed to Louis, who retrieved the megaphone for the final.

"Gay gear, gay gear gay gear gay gear."

The watchers laughed nervously.

"What did they say?" screeched the crone.

A chap under her window called up, "gay gear is over here," and pointed as the group had, in the direction of the shop.

"Oh, I knew that," replied the crone, and promptly shut the window.

Ethelgay went into the fast minuet he had played that first evening with the boys, this time with a drum backing and fiddle accompaniment, Louis strumming a Lute. Next, they went into a lively song by Louis with musical backing, and the two boys at the front putting their heads together for a harmonised chorus.

The few people watching, had now become several people watching. Every window behind them now had heads sticking out.

Somebody whistled. Then the crowd started to clap.

"More!" came a shout from the back.

"More! More! More!" shouted the rest.

Richard started a drumbeat that sounded like horses hooves. Louis crouched as if he was holding the reins to a team of horses and sang.

"The London stage came over the hill
Hoorah hoorah!
The London stage came over the hill
Hoorah hoorah!
The three sack robbers they sat quite still
They all jumped out with a mighty shout
Ready for the kill!"

The drumbeat stopped.

"Halt!" shouted Ethelgay.

Richard Frankie and Marcus pulled sacking over their heads and then to a new drumbeat chanted.

"We are the sack gang sack gang sack gang
Try to catch us if you can."

Gay went into quick tempo on the dulcimer. Frankie and Marcus made rude gestures to Louis, and ran round the back of the cart and grandstand with Louis in pursuit.

They repeated the whole thing, this time with the crowd clapping, laughing and joining in. Fifteen times the song and the antics were repeated, the crowd of people watching cheering and singing at the tops of their voices. Finally, Louis looked to Ethelgay in desperation, struggling to catch his breath.

Although nothing had been heard of the sack gang for a couple of years, their exploits were still a major topic of conversation, whenever a group of people got together.

Richard stopped drumming and Gay came in with another quick piece on the dulcimer. Some of the watchers now started dancing to the new number.

The boys then did a couple more songs before going into their opening ditty, this time as a finale.

When they'd finished the gay gear jingle, Louis shouted to the crowd, "Thank you very much people, I'd like to introduce Frankie and Marcus on the fiddles," the boys raised their hands and then played a few bars of a fast jig. The crowd shouted and cheered.

"We've got Richard on the drums." The crowd whistled and clapped, Richard replied with a short drum solo.

"On the dulcimer, we have the boss." The response was deafening, people yelling whistling clapping and waving. Ethelgay, deliriously happy, stood at the instrument and his fingers flew over the keys.

When the noise died down a couple of the girls in the front called, "and who are you?"

"Me? I'm Louis, Louis the Schmoe. And we are the Schmoes. Hope to see you all here same time next week. Thank you and good night."

More applause, then a voice shouted, "Sack gang!" quickly followed by more calls, "sack gang sack gang!"

So once again the five went into the sack song, until completely exhausted they shouted "Enough!"

Many willing hands helped them load the drum kit and pull the cart the few hundred yards back to the shop, then push it through the double doors in to the stock room. Then after many pats on the back and general hand shaking, the five said goodnight and sank into the stockrooms soft chairs, elated with their evenings work.

Ethelgay produced a large flagon of wine and five beakers which he filled and handed round, still standing, he raised his own beaker, "to The Schmoes, you're on your way."

"The Schmoes!" came the reply.

"They loved us," laughed Richard, who very seldom looked happy.

"You were great on the drums Dick," Louis retorted grinning wickedly.

"Don't call me Dick," Richard spat back, starting to pull an angry face, but immediately changed it back again into a smile.

"You were all terrific," Gay raised his beaker to the four again.

"Couldn't have done it without you boss," Marcus came back. "They've never heard a dulcimer like that."

"To the boss!" Frankie raised his fist over his head and punched the air.

"To the boss!" they all shouted.

They noisily consumed a couple more large flagons before the boys changed back into their own clothes, then happily staggered out of the double doors to find their lodgings a few yards up the street.

"Who's opening up tomorrow?" Gay called after them.

"Don't worry boss, we'll do it," Frankie called over his shoulder. "You can have a lie in after that performance."

Gay let himself out and locked the doors, then re-entered through the door to his private abode and climbed the rickety stairs.

Lighting two ornate candles he stood and preened himself in front of the gilded mirror.

"You're a star," he told the dazzling figure looking back at him, "and you're already rich. Wonder if it will do anything for business?"

He folded his clothes carefully and sank down happily into his goosedown mattress.

Ethelgay was awoken next morning by the sound of laughter, he got up and walked into his sitting room, the sun was already strong through the front window and he judged it must already be after 10.00 a.m., the hour which the shop opened for business.

The sounds of mirth were louder, coming up through the floorboards. Ethelgay went back into his bedroom and pulled on a pair of pantaloons, then crept downstairs to his spyhole.

There were about a dozen people in the shop all chattering amongst themselves, and with Frankie and Louis who were in attendance. Gay hurried back to his bedroom and finished dressing. Satisfied, after a brief study of himself in the mirror, he flounced down the staircase and made his entrance into the shop through the stockroom. He stood at the stockroom door arms out wide, and called, "Good morning everybody welcome to Gay Gear."

All faces turned towards him, everyone started to clap, then they all came over to him holding out their hands in greeting.

Ethelgay was bombarded with questions.

"How do you get that noise to come out of your dulcimer?

"Where did you find those songs?"

"Where's the other two?"

Gay answered each question in turn, taking time with each individual.

The bell over the shop door announced the arrival of more customers.

Louis and Frankie were surrounded by younger females. "I want one of those short smocks you were wearing last night for my boyfriend," a pretty girl fluttered her eyelids at Louis.

"So do I," said another young thing.

"We want a smock like your drummer wore," an older lady called above the hubbub to Ethelgay, clutching her reticent husband's sleeve.

An old boy who had been swept up by the crowd coming into the shop, asked, "have you got any mackerel?"

"No Dad," Frankie chuckled. "You want the fish shop down the road."

"Frankie," called an attractive dark haired maiden, "I'd like to see what your green blouse looks like on me."

"Do you want him wearing it at the time?" Louis, overhearing, called back in a loud voice. Everybody laughed. The attractive dark haired wench flushed and dropped her head.

"Course you can my lovely," said Frankie, taking her hand and leading her to a counter, from under which he produced a box of silk blouses.

The chit chat and the banter went on all morning, more importantly, so did the sales. Customers came and went, many stayed and were still in the shop when Marcus and Richard arrived just after lunch.

"Told them we'd cover this morning boss," Louis whispered.

"What time do you call this then?" asked Gay looking stern.

Richard started to lose his colour, eyes hardening. Marcus, started to go back out.

"Ladies and gentlemen welcome our other fiddle player and drummer," laughed Ethelgay.

Once again the crowd of customers broke into spontaneous clapping and cheering.

The two boys, realising their boss had been fooling, broke into beams of delight and were soon surrounded by admiring fans.

And so it went on. Sales that week were beyond any expectation. Each day Ethelgay singled out each boy and gave them a bonus. Every evening they tried out something new with their music, perfecting the pieces they were not happy with.

Their success continued, even increased, over the next two weeks.

Every Tuesday evening, excited followers pushed the handcart, loaded now with even more gear, down to the promenade, where the Schmoes played to the ever increasing group of excited fans.

Each Wednesday, the shop was opened by the exhausted boys, until Frankie suggested that they moved their night to a Saturday. Reasoning that although they would lose the impact, which generated large sales in the shop on a Wednesday, there would be even more people about, and at least it would give them all a chance to have a rest on the Sunday, when Gay Gear closed for the day. Thankfully, they all agreed. The following Tuesday at the end of the act, which now contained even more audience participation, with songs using the words "Do the" and "Follow the leader" Louis announced they would not be appearing on the following Tuesday, to huge groans of disappointment and shouts of: "We want the Schmoes!" Then adding, "But we will be here on Saturday," to mighty cheers and more shouts of – "Long live the Schmoes!"

"God bless the Schmoes!"

"Schmoes, Schmoes, Schmoes!"

Late on Saturday afternoon there were already people stood outside the stockroom door, when they wheeled out the handcart. Everyone wanted to do something, anyone who couldn't find a bit of the cart to pull or push, took the other boy's instruments, proudly marching down to the seafront.

The group, for every performance, completely changed their dress, so as to show off more offerings from Gay Gear.

Arriving on the Cobb in a noisy throng, the fans started to help unload the drum kit and unravel the banner to go on the railings.

A large overweight woman, with an overpainted face, marched up to Ethelgay. "Why don't you set up your group further along there?" she demanded, pointing down the esplanade.

"Why?" enquired Gay.

"Because I want you to play in front of my tavern," she stated.

"No," said Richard and Marcus together. "You told us to get out a couple of months ago and we were barred."

The two boys had queried the price of her ale, then moaned about how long they had been kept waiting on a Sunday evening, when the Mermaid and Winkle had been busy with visitors, and the price of a pint had suddenly increased.

"Well you're not barred now," puffed their stout adversary.

"No," said Marcus and Richard again, who had been regular customers.

"No," came cries from the people already leaning out of their open windows.

Mrs. Scraggett was joined by her husband and one of her large spotty daughters, who worked behind the bar of the large thatched tavern.

"Please boys," the daughter simpered in a far friendlier tone.

"We can't disappoint these people," Gay knew that several of the window gazers had been customers over the last weeks.

The Scraggetts were the largest family in Lyme Regis, as well as the tavern they owned several other retail outlets, run by other members of the family.

Mr. Scraggett, a nice chap, but ruled, as were the rest of their tribe, by his painted wife, offered a compromise. "Play here for a couple of hours boys then come along to us, we'll make it worth your while."

Mrs. Scraggett glared at her husband.

"How much?" demanded Richard.

Mr. Scraggett looked to his wife.

"Two sovereigns," she ventured.

"Have a nice evening," said Marcus, and continued tying up the banner.

Mrs. Scraggett looking perplexed, volunteered "four."

"Eight," said Marcus and Richard together, "and free drinks while we are playing."

Mrs. Scraggett scowled, "That's exorbitant," she moaned.

Her husband and daughter whispered in her ear.

"Be in front of the Mermaid in two hours then," she conceded.

"Money first," grinned Richard, chuffed with their bartering success.

"Money first," agreed the three, and retreated back along the promenade, the large spotty daughter looking over her shoulder smiling at the boys.

The Schmoes did a two hour stint, the new song written that week proving a success. Then Louis called out, "if you want any more, we'll be at the Mermaid and Winkle for the rest of the evening."

The five strolled along the front, their ever growing number of fans, shifting and setting up their equipment.

Richard and Marcus sauntered into the tavern. "Evening Mrs. Scraggett, Mr. Scraggett," Marcus said nonchalantly.

The other three followed them in. "Just getting set up," said Richard, "then we'll put some more customers in your boozer."

Mrs. Scraggett grimaced, considering her establishment far superior to any boozer.

"What's your pleasure afore you start, boys?" asked Mr. Scraggett.

They gave him their order, which Mr. Scraggett placed on a tray, then put eight sovereigns next to the frothy ale. Thirsty after their first session, the contents of the tankards were downed in a very short time.

"C'mon then you two," said Louis quietly to Richard and Marcus, you've won your battle, "now let's give the customers what they want."

At 11.p.m. the group were still bashing out tunes, the glow from within the Mermaid, and lanterns placed outside, illuminating their act. Inside and outside the overflowing tavern, customers were singing and clapping.

Mrs. Scraggett came out bearing a tray containing more jugs of ale, various pies, plus bread, ham, cheese and pickle. "Best night we've had for ages," she said positively beaming, during a break in the music. "Give them another couple of tunes boys, then finish when you are ready."

The couple of tunes turned into another dozen, before once again the exhausted group called enough.

"Same again next week, chaps?" enquired Mr. Scraggett, as the helpers loaded the cart.

"And we will double your fee," chimed in Mrs. Scraggett.

Her husband looked at her aghast; he had never known his wife give away anything, especially money.

"I've already counted some of tonight's takings darling," she murmured in his ear.

"How are we going to split eight sovereigns?" asked Richard, as the five, arms linked, danced merrily back along the darkened seafront, following their equipment being transported back to the shop by revellers.

"Two each to you boys, you've earned it," Gay laughed.

"That's not fair on you boss," came back the general reply.

"There'll be more, just you wait and see, it's your band and you deserve every penny."

"Thanks boss," said Louis, "but it's now our band, we are the five Schmoes."

Mrs. Scraggett sat straight up in bed, awoken by some forgotten nightmare. Sweat filled the valleys between rolls of flesh, her husband lay on his back, snoring peacefully beside her. A warm breeze ruffled her pretty curtains at the open window, which gave a view of the promenade and sea beyond. Moonlight cast silver streaks over her fine boudoir furniture.

Whatever was wrong? Her sleep-crowded brain demanded an answer. Slowly, her head cleared. What had she done? You've given away money, her mind told her.

Slowly, the previous evening's events trickled back, she shook her husband, who rolled onto his side but continued snoring after a couple of grunts.

"I've given away money I didn't need to," she muttered to herself. The thought was almost too much to bear.

"I've offered to pay extra, when I could have got away with less."

Her heavy rouge now felt sticky as she put her hands to her face, the sweat creeping up and tickling the top of her head.

That fop and his accomplices had duped her. They seduced me with their wild music and made me vulnerable, her mind started to offer excuses, not taking into consideration the amount of gin she had consumed, during the course of the evening. Upstarts, coming into my town and setting up business.

She had already missed owning another business, which those other upstarts Berts Buses, had bought from under her nose. The livery stables at the rear of the town had changed hands before she even realised it was up for sale. Bert's Buses were now running a profitable service to and from other towns in the area. As well as hiring out horses, with carts if needed, on a self drive-ride basis.

Her eldest daughter ran a wet fish shop, and was now experimenting with fried fish and chips. Mrs. Scraggett had always been annoyed when she saw her customers at the quayside, buying fish fresh from the boats instead of from the shop.

"I've got the best tavern in Dorset," she said to herself. "Boozer indeed!"

The two youngest daughters, both spotty, looked after a small shop, selling boiled sweeties, which they made on the premises.

The trade that fop was doing had turned Mrs. Scraggett green with envy.

Got it, shouted her brain.

Mrs. Scraggett rolled out of bed and deposited her ample backside on the potty, emptying her bladder. Easing herself up she waddled to the window, still dripping, then emptied the contents into the street below.

I'll buy the fop out. The answer screamed at her.

"I'll buy it before he gets too big for his boots, next thing, he'll be opening up something else. All that money going into his pocket should be mine," she muttered to herself.

By now her usually good business brain was consumed by the thought of owning Gay Gear.

The next week sped by for the Schmoes, after resting on Sunday.

Monday was the busiest in the shop yet, all five kept going by the constant stream of customers and well wishers. Mrs. Scraggett stood outside for an hour and watched "her money" disappearing into the coffers of Gay gear. Then unable to stand it any longer, marched into the shop and called to Gay, eventually extracting him from customers all ready to part with cash.

Confidentially she whispered, "if you ever think of selling your little shop, I might be interested."

Gay, somewhat taken aback, thought for a moment, then replied quietly, "I'm not really interested in selling at the moment Mrs. Scraggett, as you can see we're taking too much money."

Early on Tuesday, Louis and Frankie hired a horse and cart, and took a trip out of town to the windmill, where they bought five hundred flour sacks for a penny each, then delivered them to the local tannery with instructions.

They returned to the shop to find the other three stretched to the limit by excited customers. Gay proudly announced that the landlord from a pub called the Otter Inn on the road to Exeter, had been in and booked the group for the Saturday after next.

Mrs. Scraggett walked by twice, taking in the numbers of customers each time, and doing mental arithmetic of how much money she could make.

Wednesday, Ethelgay hired a horse and visited his outworkers, with orders for more stock. When he returned, the boys gleefully informed him that landlords from taverns in Axminster and Bridport had been to the shop and made bookings for the Schmoes to appear at their inns.

During his ride, he thought over Mrs. Scraggett's offer. He was comfortably off from the money he had stolen, having sat down and counted seven hundred and thirty six gold sovereigns, when his valise was emptied out. Over the last few weeks, the shop takings had pushed that amount up to almost a thousand. He didn't owe anybody, always paying for his goods on order, and his outworkers in advance, to keep them happy.

Gay Gear had been bought to get him away from his gruesome family, and he still felt certain, anything that he had owed the old man, which would have been written in the will, had now gone up safely in smoke. Although he had enjoyed the shop work for the first few years, he now found it tiresome, having to open and close at certain times, with not much free time to himself, always at the beck and call of staff and customers alike.

But what about the staff? The boys were earning more than he or they had ever thought possible. He was paying all four weekly bonuses to match their soaring sales, and it looked as if they would now be picking up even more money, with the success of the band.

Riding back along the coast road, he passed a magnificent mansion, which looked out to sea across a small bay. Hung on the gate was a sign proclaiming For Sale.

Ethelgay rode on, then turned back and rode through the open iron gates. A middle aged lady was tending overgrown flower beds, that bordered an overgrown lawn in front of the house.

"Afternoon ma'am," he docked his tri-cornered hat to the woman, as she straightened warily at the sound of his arrival.

"Good afternoon young man what can I do for you," came the reply, in a cultured voice far from the gentle Dorset accent.

Gay judged the woman to be in her mid forties and still retained some of the beauty that had obviously graced her younger days.

"Saw your sign ma'am," he stated dismounting. "Why do you want to sell such a lovely house?"

"I don't," replied the lady, "but I find it is getting more difficult to maintain since my husband died."

"I'm so sorry," said Ethelgay, then easily adding, "can I be of any help?"

"You can if you've got five hundred guineas to spare," came the quick response.

"May I have a look round?" said Gay completely unruffled.

"Only if you've got that sort of money," the lady ventured, "I didn't think anyone round here was that rich, only the Lord of the Manor and that Baron of Dorset, who appears to be trying to keep everyone else poor."

"Ma'am I can assure you I am a wealthy man," Ethelgay replied. "Now if you would be good enough to let me view your lovely home I'd be obliged, as I have another property in mind," he lied.

The woman feeling surer that this was no time waster, and she was possibly about to lose the sale, graciously walked over to the oaken front door and beckoned. Ethelgay immediately fell in love with the place, taking in its massive oak beamed drawing room, with leaded windows, giving views on to more lawns and the ocean beyond. He made complimentary remarks on their way up the large open staircase, to the eight bedrooms above, but didn't let his excitement show, so as to retain his bargaining powers.

He learned that the lady's husband had been a ship owner in London, with a fleet trading in the new worlds. Also that he had been considerably older than his wife, and decided to retire to the country five years previously, but had died suddenly two years ago.

"What about the furniture?" he enquired, referring to the many splendid pieces on show, obviously of foreign descent.

"Included in the price," stated the lady, who gave her name as Mrs. Veronique, "as long as I don't have to haggle."

They returned to the drawing room, which he could see would need work done, then she led him outside on to lawns, also in dire need of attention, which sloped to a small cliff, with steps down to a sandy beach. Skirting round the building, a large stableblock came into view at the side of the house, its only occupant being a small trap, the horse for which grazed peacefully in a meadow beyond.

"I'll return with an answer within a week, after I've seen the other property," he lied, hardly able to contain his excitement, he had never seen anything that he wanted as much as this house.

Mrs. Scraggett had inspected Gay Gear from the outside, during her weekly inspection of her other retail outlets. Once again seeing a shop full of customers.

Thursday, during a rare quiet spell, a coach drew up outside Gay Gear. A fat man in a powdered wig with a large chain around his neck stepped out, then entered the shop accompanied by two lackies.

"I'm the Mayor of Exeter," he announced. "I hear excellent things about your band, the Schmoes," he offered.

"Thank you Mr. Mayor," replied Ethelgay, quite accustomed to facing dignity from his days at the Manor.

"I'm going to book you for the county fair, to be held in Exeter's Cathedral Square."

"We're honoured your honour," grinned Louis.

"How much?" asked Richard, coming straight to the point as usual.

"We thought two hundred guineas," said the Mayor.

Frankie and Marcus, who had been listening intently behind the stockroom door, both fell down flat on a pile of empty boxes. "Two hundred guineas," they mouthed to each other.

Richard, keeping a very straight face, said "we'd have to stay for a couple of nights."

The Mayor smiled and replied "we will put you up in the best tavern in the city, all expenses paid."

"All expenses paid," mouthed Frankie and Marcus to each other.

"We would need transport," Gay interjected.

"We will send a couple of coaches for you," the Mayor answered promptly.

"Hope we don't run into the sack robbers then," Louis laughed.

"That," said the Mayor, "is a sore point. I'll see you there."

With that the Mayor started out of the shop, then stopped to look at a velvet frock coat. "Try that if I may," he nodded to Louis.

"I'll get you one out of the stockroom Mr. Mayor," said Louis, sticking his head through the stockroom door and indicating to the pair within, to find something larger.

The Mayor was delighted with the extra extra large coat that fitted his ample figure perfectly, and insisted on wearing it out, leaving one of the flunkies to pay, and confirm the date of the booking, he called, "farewell". The other flunky trolling out of the shop to open the carriage door for His Worship.

Mrs. Scraggett stood on the other side of the street, had twice almost fallen on her podgy face, craning her neck to see what was going on within the premises, exceedingly jealous that the fop had been visited by dignitary, which as far as she was aware had never graced any of her places. This was too much.

Knowing that she was doing wrong, she once again entered Gay Gear. Ethelgay ushered her into the stockroom.

A good sign? she wondered.

"Thought any more about my offer?" she stated without preamble.

"To be truthful, I haven't," lied Gay.

"I thought two hundred and fifty guineas," said Mrs. Scraggett, "which is twice what the place is worth."

"I think you'll have to rethink," Gay frowned, crossing his fingers behind his back, as it was a very fair price.

Mrs. Scraggett, realising she had met her match, scowled and stomped out of the shop, banging the door behind her.

That evening, before the boys went back to their lodgings, Ethelgay produced a flagon of cider, and asked them to accompany him for the first time to the living room upstairs. When they were all sat comfortably, each with an ornate chalice full of frothy apple juice, Gay related what had occurred over the previous few days. Without divulging any of the prices, he told them of Mrs. Scraggett's interest in the shop, and raptured over the house he had found.

"Go for it Gay boss," Louis immediately replied.

"Yea go for it boss," the others agreed.

Frankie was the only one to look a trifle doubtful.

"How much did the old cow offer you for the business?" asked Richard, forthright as ever.

Frankie said "I've enjoyed these last few weeks boss, it seems a shame to let it go."

"We're certainly not going to let the band go boys," Ethelgay assured. Then added his winning line "if you want to, you can all live at the new place, there's plenty of room for us all to have our privacy, and I shall need help getting the grounds back into shape. We can spend more time on our music, and the Schmoes will be the talk of the West Country."

"Alright boss," they cheered.

"How much did the old cow offer you for the business?" Richard asked again.

"Two hundred and fifty if you must know, Dick," said Ethelgay, annoyed.

"Tell her five hundred, and please don't call me Dick, boss," Richard glared.

All the boys agreed not to breathe a word of their discussion, and they would play as arranged at the Mermaid and Winkle on Saturday, but go straight there without performing on the esplanade first.

Friday, Frankie and Louis once again hired the small horse and cart from Berts Buses Depot, then picked up the flour sacks they had left at the tannery. That afternoon the sacks were displayed in the window of the shop, with a notice, Frankie had produced.

COME AND BE A SACKMAN WITH THE SCHMOES.
MERMAID AND WINKLE THIS SATURDAY.

The sacks, all different colours which the tannery had dyed them, now had eyeholes and an opening for the wearers mouth.

They sold forty nine that afternoon at sixpence each, then another hundred and thirty three the next day.

"We're going to have to close early," stated Ethelgay on Saturday afternoon. "I need a rest before we play tonight."

They eventually closed at 3.00p.m. The four boys stretched out in the stockroom, Gay retired upstairs to collapse on his goosedown.

They only got a couple of hours however. By 6.00p.m. a racket at the stockroom doors announced the arrival of their fans, many already wearing flour sacks, covering their heads and shoulders.

People turned up from miles around, for that night at the Mermaid and Winkle. Their first audience from further along the

Cobb, although disappointed at not getting a free show, joining in the fun and spending money in Mrs. Scraggett's tavern.

The sack song was a riot which went on for over an hour, and they sold another fifty or so sacks, during a break in the performance, which Marcus had thoughtfully put on the cart.

For the first time they all wore similar outfits, different coloured waistcoats over white ruffled blouses, tight black pantaloons and shiny black riding boots.

Mrs. Scraggett's fat fingers grasped coin after coin from customers caught up in the carnival atmosphere.

When the final customers had either left or been thrown out, she invited the group to come in for a nightcap.

Frankie and Richard escorted the fans back to the shop and stored the gear, then returned to the inn.

Mr. and Mrs. Scraggett sat next to each other at a large round table, with the boss and the other two boys facing them. Their spotty daughter had plonked herself next to Louis. They pulled up chairs and took grateful swigs at the tankards already waiting for them.

"Tuck in boys," said Mr. Scraggett, gesturing towards the large platter of cold meat, bread and pickles in the middle of the table.

"We will book you again next Saturday," stated Mrs. Scraggett.

"'fraid we're already spoken for, for the next two weeks," replied Marcus, relishing in watching their plump hostess squirm.

"Well I've got another business deal with your boss young man," she retorted starchily. "And I assumed you would be playing here."

"We've come to no arrangement yet ma'am," said Gay, politely adding "you know you shouldn't assume."

Richard was loving watching the old biddy squirm, and interrupted "by the way boss, I forgot to mention that chap from Bristol called in again the other day, when you were out, said he'd see you next week."

"Wish you'd told me that before, Dick," replied Gay, giving Richard a wink away from the Scraggetts, realising the little rogue was pushing the sale.

"Don't call me Dick, boss," Richard looked angrily at Gay, but then returned the wink, once again out of sight of the Scraggetts.

"What business are we talking about ma'am?" asked Gay, turning back to the large landlady. "As far as I'm aware, no deal has been struck yet, whatever's to be said, can be said in front of my lads."

Mr. Scraggett fingered his tankard nervously. The spotty daughter edged closer to Louis, who eased further away.

"I've offered you a good price for Gay Gear," said Mrs. Scraggett. "You said you would think about it," she added, lying.

"You're not gonna sell Gay Gear boss," chimed in the boys, all looking shocked.

"Mrs. Scraggett has made an offer for the business," said Ethelgay, "but I haven't yet given her offer any consideration."

"How much boss?" enquired Richard after a long silence. "Gay Gear's got to be worth a thousand guineas now it's taken off."

Mrs. Scraggett looked ashen.

"I think you are a little over estimating our worth," smiled Gay, leaving the painted lady a chance to come back.

"I've offered two fifty," stated Mrs. Scraggett, "which is far more than it's worth."

"No it's not," said the boys in unison.

"That's an insult," said Marcus.

"All right boys," said Mr. Scraggett, trying to lighten the mood. "If you owned Gay Gear, how much would you accept for it?"

"Why are we letting staff get involved?" snapped his wife.

"Mr. Ethelgay appears to want to include his chaps, after all, its their jobs we're talking about as well," said Mr. Scraggett stoutly to his domineering wife.

The four boys and Ethelgay got up and walked to the other end of the bar, out of earshot of the straining Scraggetts.

"Who's this chap coming back to see me Richard?" grinned Gay.

"There ain't nobody boss, but its got the old trout worried," Richard whispered.

"How much then boys?"

"What we said boss, five hundred," Richard answered for the rest, "but try her on seven fifty."

Back at the table Mr. Scraggett was now getting increasingly annoyed with his greedy wife.

"We are going to have to pay more than two fifty if you really want it," he told her.

"Course I want it, they're making a fortune that should be ours. Who's this other man coming back to see the fop? Before we know it Scraggett, we will have bigger business moving into our town, and I told you, they've now got dignitary using the place," Mrs. Scraggett replied pouting.

"You've got anything to say Beatrice?" She reached across the table and poked her large spotty daughter.

"Sorry Ma, wasn't listening." Beatrice had been gazing coweyed at Louis, imagining unimaginable things.

"Oh what's the use," Mrs. Scraggetts voice rose. "You try and do things for your family and they just aren't interested."

Mrs. Scraggett had never done that much for her family, just using them as cheap labour in her establishments. The only person Mrs. Scraggett had ever really been interested in, was Mrs. Scraggett.

"Sounds like we've got her rattled Gay boss," said Louis.

Ethelgay flounced back to the table, followed by the boys.

"I've decided I will sell, if the price is right," he announced.

Mrs. Scraggett was elated.

"Seven fifty," said Gay.

Mrs. Scraggett was deflated.

"That's ridiculous," she scoffed. "I'll pay six hundred and not a penny more."

"You're a hard business woman Mrs. Scraggett." Gay rubbed his forefinger down his nose. "Alright six hundred it is."

Mrs Scraggett beamed.

"Plus stock," Richard demanded.

Mrs. Scraggett scowled. "All right, plus stock," she agreed.

"Thank goodness for that," Mr. Scraggett breathed a long sigh, knowing his pushy wife would be happy for a while now, and perhaps give him some peace. "Let's drink to it."

He went behind the bar and refilled everybody's tankard.

"To the new owners of Gay Gear!" toasted Ethelgay towards the Scraggetts.

They spent the next hour discussing the niceties of the deal. It was agreed that the new owners would move in on Tuesday in two weeks time, after the band had played in Exeter. The Schmoes would play at the Mermaid and Winkle once a month for the same fee, for the next six months, dates to be decided.

It was almost dawn when the five left the tavern, none showing any emotion. The spotty daughter stood in the doorway as they left, so they all had to squeeze past her ample bosom.

When they were well along the lightening promenade, Gay turned to the boys, his face radiant.

"Thank you lads, you were brilliant."

"What a coup boss," said Frankie. "You've just sold Gay Gear for five times what it's worth."

"I'll make sure all four of you see some of the profit," Gay chuckled.

They all linked arms and went into a crazy dance, whooping and yelling, until a couple of upstairs windows were thrown open, rudely awoken residents angrily shouting at the group to keep the noise down.

They all lay in until way past noon on Sunday. On Monday, Gay invited Richard to accompany him. So they once again hired a pony and trap from Berts Buses livery stable, which Ethelgay drove to Mrs. Veronique's house overlooking the sea. Filling him in with financial details on the way.

Introducing Dick by his proper name. "This is Mr. Richard Rose, my financial advisor," then on the spur of the moment, "from the Roseland Peninsular in Cornwall."

Once again Gay was conducted around the mansion, this time with Richard in tow. At the end of the tour, Richard, who had dressed for the occasion, addressed Mrs. Veronique in an official voice.

"Mr. Gay was correct when he informed me that he had found a beautiful property, but I feel with the amount of repair that needs to be completed, I would only value it at four hundred guineas."

"Did Mr. Gay tell you that the furniture was included?" Mrs. Veronique bristled somewhat.

"To be fair ma'am, he did not. In that case I would suggest a deal at four fifty."

Mrs. Veronique walked away, then turned and offered her outstretched hand.

"I will need a deposit," she stated.

The deal was struck. Gay produced a hundred sovereigns as a statement of his good intent.

They arranged that Mrs. Veronique would vacate the house within two weeks, giving her time to move her personal possessions, to a cottage she had been looking at in Lyme.

On the way back Richard apologised, slipping easily back into his local accent. "Couldn't go any lower boss, the place is magnificent, worth seven hundred and fifty guineas of anybody's money."

"You were terrific Dick," grinned Gay. "If the band ever fails I can see where your future lies."

"Don't call me Dick, boss," Richard grinned back.

The gig at the Otter Inn on the following Saturday, was another huge success. During the week Frankie had composed another audience participation song:

It's Otter Inn than out

It's Otter Inn than out

E I addio, it's Otter Inn than out.

Groups from the audience took it in turns to stand in the huge doorway of the pub, jumping back and forth, in and out of the bar all singing along.

The landlord was delighted with the band's performance and added a couple more sovereigns to their fee, booking them to appear again in two months' time.

Sales continued at a startling rate during the next week, until the close of business on Wednesday. Prompt on Thursday morning, two of Bert's Buses pulled up outside the shop, also one of Berts carts hitched to a pair of horses. The band's clothes were loaded into the first coach by two excited fans, who had insisted on becoming the group's gofers. The pair then loaded the cart with the musical instruments, plus all the other paraphernalia which was now part of the act.

The Schmoes piled into the first carriage, leaving a notice in the window of the shop.

FRIDAY SATURDAY AND SUNDAY

THE SCHMOES

ARE APPEARING AT

THE COUNTY FAIR EXETER

Gay Gear will reopen Tuesday under new management.

The Cathedral courtyard and lawns were already decked in banners, when they arrived in Exeter just after lunchtime. Workmen were busy constructing several stages and arranging seating. Several large tents had been erected around the area for the sale of refreshments.

Stall holders had already knobbled prime positions on roads either side of the square for the sale of: clothes, furniture, costume jewellery, dubious looking bottles of potions, and farming implements. One displaying several types of cooking utensils had already attracted a crowd, its trader telling them their food would taste better cooked in one of his pots. All seemed prepared to camp out until the fair finished on Sunday.

The Mayor, accompanied by several hangers on, came over to greet the boys, proudly showing them round the site of the forthcoming festivities, asking them which of the stages would suit their act.

He then escorted them into the plush tavern set on the edge of the square, an alleyway beside it leading on to Exeter's bustling High Street.

The gofers were shown the rooms which the boys would occupy, and duly carried their clothes and cases to each. A stable area was to be used for the storage of the rest of the gear, and the gofers were informed they could bed down there, so as to keep a close eye on the equipment.

The Mayor, over goblets of wine served in the tapestry lined bar of the tavern, informed the Schmoes that their first performance was required at teatime on Friday, then again later in the evening and the same on Saturday and Sunday.

After an hours idle chatter, His Worship excused himself, having many other important things which required his important attention, before proceedings commenced on the morrow.

The five took the opportunity to explore Exeter, which after two bad years, was once again a hive of business. The four boys, were amazed at the size and variety of the shops, also the amount of people which thronged the thoroughfares. They walked around the old stone walls which had been built by the Romans many years before, then took another stroll around the cathedral square. They checked on their equipment and the two gofers, Gay giving each some money for food and ale, before returning to the hostelry, where they were waited on through the evening with fine food and wines.

Friday morning dawned bright and clear. The Mayor declared Exeter's Autumn Fair officially open.

By now there were even more stalls crowding into any vacant spaces around the cathedral. Fresh produce was now displayed. The two butchers' pitches festooned in chicken, ducks, pheasants, hares and rabbits, all hung over and around their counters. A fishmonger was spending more time beating off defiant hungry seagulls than serving his customers, one lucky gull dodging his flying arms, and making off with a live eel, then having to avoid other raiders intent on stealing the prize.

Several greengrocers were doing a roaring trade with locally grown vegetables. Another displayed exotic fruits, which the five hadn't seen before, offering reticent lookers a taste of what he called: bannanies, pinyapples, oranges, grapers and melloons.

Several jugglers wandered through the increasing throng of people, tossing balls and clubs as they went. A fire eater amazed the watchers by sucking in real fire from the ends of blazing torches, then blowing flames from his mouth. People on stilts peered down on the excited throng. Bonneted maidens offered sweet morsels from trays they carried in front of them, supported with ribbons around their necks.

On one of the stages a string quartet was already playing gentle music, to a few older folk sat in front of them. As the quartet finished their repertoire, the cathedral bells rang out, then another group of minstrels took their place.

By the time the boys returned to the tavern, for lunchtime refreshment, the square was a mass of people. Peasants in drab smocks, mixing with brightly clothed dandies. Street urchins running between smart gentle folk, and hags wearing nothing but rags.

The babble from excited voices gave Frankie cause for concern.

"I don't think anybody's going to hear us boss, with all this racket going on."

"Don't worry Frankie boy," Louis replied cheerily. "Time we get on, they will probably be too drunk to care."

The Mayor, resplendent in scarlet cloak with fur trimming, bustled into the tavern.

"All set you Schmoes?" his ruddy face beaming with the success of it all.

"All set Your Worship," replied Gay, as the portly gent shook hands with other well wishers. He then bustled out again and Frankie followed him, speaking to him briefly in the doorway.

"What's that about?" nosed Richard.

"Wait and see," Frankie replied importantly.

When the Schmoes mounted the stage already set up with instruments, proudly guarded by the two gofers, the crowd seemed larger and noisier than ever. Louis whispered to the pair, who disappeared into the throng.

The platform they had selected, backed onto the cathedral, huge buttresses either side stretched well out on to the paved frontage. A group of musicians further along the lawn played a final minuet, and received a smattering of applause, when they finished the piece.

"We've gotta wait 'til they peal the bells," said Marcus nervously.

"Wait and listen," Frankie confided.

Then, instead of a peal, came a single bong, from the belfries largest inhabitant, when its echoes had died another bong followed, then four more.

The noisy crowd had ceased its chatter, looking to the cathedral wondering what was going on.

"Go for it Louis," instructed Frankie.

"Hello Exeter, we are the Schmoes!" Louis bellowed through the megaphone, the sound being helped by the wall of the cathedral behind, and the buttresses to the side.

"Hello Schmoes!" came back the reply from the two gofers.

"You can do better than that!" yelled Louis.

"Hello Exeter!"

"Hello Schmoes!" a few others joined the gofers in reply.

"We ain't going to play until we hear from you!" shouted Louis.

The Mayor and his cronies looked somewhat frightened.

"Hello Exeter!" all five bellowed at the tops of their voices.

"Hello Schmoes!" came back a louder reply.

"Get on with it," grumbled a large white haired chap, clutching a flagon of cider.

And they did.

Ethelgay, looking stunning in frockcoat, hammered out the first notes of a very fast piece they had rehearsed. The besmocked Richard joined in after two bars, beating out a rhythm on the drums. Another two bars and in came the trio, all in glittering waistcoats, loose blouses and tight breeches. Frankie and Marcus on fiddles, and Louis on a lute, which had been tampered with to give it a harsher sound.

They finished their short introductory number, and Louis yelled through the megaphone to the astonished gathering. "Now here's a song especially for the Mayor." Away they went into the sackman song, this time the two gofers donned on coloured sacks to be chased by Marcus. The crowd roared with laughter and were soon joining in.

From then on they could do no wrong, their attentive audience listening to the new sound, and participating in the frivolities.

The gofers pulled out the remaining coloured sacks from where they had been stored earlier under the stage, and soon were doing a roaring trade at one shilling each.

At the end of two hours the cathedral bells pealed out, and the sweating quintet climbed down off the stage to a standing ovation. The Mayor was waiting for them, when they finally made it, followed by admirers, back into the lounge bar of the tavern. His large round face crinkled into a large round smile, "there you go boys," he announced, filling goblets from a large flagon of sparkling wine. "You deserve every drop of that."

The crowd pushed into the bar, demanding to be told what time the Schmoes were reappearing. The Mayor hauled his bulky frame on to a chair, and shouted above the din. "Listen for the six bells, in about four hours, now be good citizens and let them have a rest."

Not a chance. More people were trying to get into the tavern, a chant starting, "We want the Schmoes!"

They eventually struggled free an hour before they were due to reappear. The night was still warm, so they changed, this time all wearing loose three quarter length different coloured smocks, over their favourite tight pantaloons and riding boots. This time with an added touch that Ethelgay had dreamed up, face paint.

The four boys sported black and red lines and zig zags on their cheeks and foreheads, Gay wore rouge, lipstick and heavy eye makeup. Louis grabbed his large brimmed hat with peacock feathers, as they once again descended into the excited throng.

Six bells rang out from the cathedral tower. The crowd parted allowing them access to the tavern door, as each band member went through the doorway they were lifted shoulder high by the people gathered outside, unable to get in.

"We want the Schmoes!" came a chant from the direction of the stage.

"We've got the Schmoes!" their transporters chanted back, ferrying them towards the bandstand. A mighty cheer went up, each time one of the five were deposited on the platform. They took up their positions in front of the cheering, laughing, chanting fair goers.

Louis held up his hand, a hush descended, "Well met Exeter!" he yelled through the megaphone.

"Well met Schmoes!" came back the deafening response.

Once again the boys went through their routine, this time it seemed with the whole of the audience wanting to take part, under the glow of five thousand lanterns, which illuminated the spectacle.

And so it went on. The performances on Saturday and Sunday drawing in even more excited revellers. They received bookings from the Mayors of Plymouth and Barnstaple, both guests of their hosts. Reservations were placed by a dozen or so more landlords of local taverns, some offering cash in advance to secure the Schmoes, who were undoubtedly the hit of the show.

The coloured sacks were completely sold out and were now being sold on by enterprising partygoers at three times the price.

Ethelgay retained the services of the two coaches and one cart, when they returned to Lyme on Monday, employing the drivers to transport his own furniture and trinkets to the mansion.

On Tuesday morning, a gathering of Scraggetts presented themselves at the shop by 6.00a.m. then between them and Gay staff, agreed the prices for all the various items which made up the stock of Gay Gear.

The five made a somewhat sad departure from the place which had given them a start, leaving the new owners to open at 10.a.m.

The boys helped Gay load a heavy locked casket full of money into the carriage, which had waited for them, each one richer by fifty sovereigns that their appreciative master had given them. The boys were absolutely thrilled when they drove through the iron gates leading up to the huge house.

"Told you so," said Richard, feeling very important.

All had come from peasant families, and had never dreamed of living in a place such as this. The other coach and cart were already there, and had started unloading. Mrs. Veronique was waiting in her pony and trap with two small dogs and her ancient part time gardener in attendance. He was to take Mrs. Veronique to her new cottage, then return with the outfit which had been included in the sale, and continue in his post as part time groundsman. Gay paid the sad lady the balance of what he owed her, then escorted her to the gate as she could no longer hold back the tears. He then turned and minced back up the drive, to his new house and new life.

CHAPTER TEN

Etheltar The Boy

The farm cat raised its taut body slowly, still concealed by buttercups and kingcups, which bordered the large pond. Eyes fixed on the mother duck lying contentedly on the warm bank, her brood of eight ducklings pecking at small morsels in the short grass around her. It had taken the cat twenty minutes to reach the point for its final attack, gingerly creeping on its belly, taking care not to rustle the yellow flowers above its head. Now it had selected its victim. The quivering body became still, but the tail continued to swish back and forth. The cat broke cover and sped, having to run the last few yards in the open.

Instantly alert, the duck screeched at her offspring, but too late for the smallest of her brood, which the cat had selected, and had been the slowest to react.

The cat sprang the final six feet, pinning the small bundle of yellow down with outstretched claws.

Across the short stretch of water, a podgy child aged seven or eight, jumped to his feet and clapped with delight at the kill. He had been on a small hillock busily smashing grasshoppers that jumped onto a mossy boulder, with a small rock he still clutched in his chubby fingers. He had managed to count five before his powers of arithmetic left him stranded, he guessed it must have been a hundred when he spotted the cat going into the flowers, and watched its progress from his vantage point.

Bored now, he wandered back across the field to home, leaving the gate swinging wide as he crossed the cobbles outside the cowshed. Someone inside was giggling. He crept along the wooden wall and climbed onto a pile of dried muck, raked from within. Peering through the slats he could see the back of a large Beefburgher at the opposite wall, the fingers and hands of someone draped around his neck. The face of the someone came into view, and he recognised the Hammyburgher maid, who had been entrusted with the care of the family's newest offspring.

He watched for five minutes, but nothing seemed to be happening, just giggling from the maid, and mutterings from the Burgher.

Bored once again, he slid down off the muck. Several large bins containing feed were backed against the wall of the shed, nestled in the shade between them was the cart which had been made by one of the Woodburghers, to transport the various babies, produced over the years by his daddy and one of his several mummies, who came and went at regular intervals.

He lifted the white muslin which covered the cart and peered at his newest brother, busy attempting to suck his toe. The cloth fluttered in the gentle breeze which suddenly picked up dust and straw from the cobbles, reminding him of the fishing boats he had seen, when accompanying his father to the quayside on Seynourgue.

The boy replaced the cloth and lifted the single metal bar, which acted as a handle for the cart. Pulling it slowly across the cobbles so the wooden wheels shouldn't make a noise, he went back through the gate into the field, bumped across the track made by the cows, the baby gurgling contentedly at its shaky ride.

At the edge of the pond he cut two sticks from a willow tree, with the knife he had stolen from his elder brother, then lashed them together to form a cross, with a piece of twine he always kept in his pocket for emergencies.

He wedged the mast for his "boat" erect at the end of the cart with some stones, then impaled the muslin sheet on the protruding ends of the sticks.

Satisfied with his efforts, he wheeled the cart into the water and gave it a shove, so the wheels came clear of the gravelly bottom and the craft floated serenely out onto the pond, it's sail fluttering in the light breeze.

The baby was still gurgling contentedly, when a piercing scream reached him from the other side of the field.

He was still enjoying his boat, when a posse of shouting screaming people and barking dogs came up behind him ten minutes later. His father pushed passed him, running into the water, followed by the Beefburgher he had seen in the cowshed earlier. The baby's mother staggered to the waters edge, grasping his elder brother and sister's hands.

The Hammyburgher maid followed with two more of the house servants.

The large dogs, three wolfhounds and one greyhound, were running up and down the water's edge barking excitedly. They were the only ones who seemed pleased to see him.

The baby started whimpering, as the pond water which had seeped through the joins in the wooden cart, had now soaked into his bedding.

His Father was about to grab the makeshift craft, when the Burgher slipped on the muddy bottom and grabbed his master's coat to save himself, but only succeeded in pulling him down as well, both collapsing in a plume of water.

The baby's mother screamed, as the little boat rocked dangerously on the waves the pair created. Letting go of the boys sister, she took a swipe at him with her free hand. Her screams were now matched by the baby, as the carriage tilted and let in more water.

The sodden Burgher was the first to regain his feet, and take the final couple of strides to lift the bedraggled infant from its sinking ship.

The boy had received the odd slap for misbehaving, but that afternoon he had his first thrashing. His mother had disappeared into the house cuddling her baby, accompanied by scurrying maids, when his father dragged him roughly into the woodshed and seated himself on the large round base of a tree trunk, which was used as a chopping block, stretched the young Etheltar across his lap and ripped down his breaches. His father had long gone, when the boy got to his feet still sobbing, angrily breaking the stick into several pieces which had been used to beat his bare bum.

Etheltar, now aged ten, had spent a profitable morning by the pond, skewering frogs with a spear he had furnished from a hazelnut tree. His ugly little fat face contorting into an evil grin, each time the sharpened stick went through a fat, bloated body. Now his stomach reminded him it was nearly dinner time, so he stuffed his pockets with several of his victims, picked up the stone jar, which he had filled with spawn, and made his way back to the house.

He entered through the kitchen door, so he could go up the back staircase to his bedroom, to hide his prizes. It was unusual to find the kitchen empty, cook was nowhere to be seen, and he had passed the scullery maids on his way in.

Dinner was obviously about to be served, as the large black cauldron, containing a mishmash of meat and vegetables, had been taken off the fire, and was stood on the stone floor by the entrance to the dining room, ready to be taken in for the family to help themselves. Another large bowl of whey, sprinkled with currants, was on the stout kitchen table, and would be served as a cold pudding, one of the family's favourites. The watery substance looked very much like the frog spawn he had collected. Glancing round to ensure that nobody had come in, he emptied his stone jar into the bowl and gave it a bit of a stir with the wooden spoon, which had been used earlier to mix the substance. Still nobody around, he stared at the black cauldron. He could hear the family assembling in the dining room. Three frogs' corpses were soon out of sight in the cauldron, as he pushed them down to the bottom with his spear. He dodged up the back staircase as the cook appeared.

Young Etheltar entered the dining room, coming down the main stairs to join the rest of the family, as cook proudly plonked the large cauldron in the centre of the table.

His father and the latest mummy were busy talking, the rest of the kids chattered amongst themselves, with his eldest brother Tread, as usual, acting as the boss. The newest mummy continued talking as she ladled out the stew.

"Why aren't you eating, boy?" his father enquired.

"I've got tummy ache," he lied. "Could I just have some bread and cheese?"

"No you piggin can't, either eat that or piggin go without," shouted his unsympathetic daddy. "Give me some more of that, woman," he added, poking his wife with his spoon.

The dutiful new mummy started to ladle some more stew from the cauldron, then she screamed, dropped the ladle and fainted.

"What the piggin heck's up with you," Ethelfoot's voice rose again, getting up and peering in the cauldron. "There's a piggin frog in here!" he shouted.

"Cook!" at the top of his voice.

The children were all standing up looking in the cooking pot when cook bustled in redfaced from the kitchen.

"There's a piggin frog in the piggin stew!" yelled Ethelfoot. "How's it piggin happened?"

"Must have jumped in when I left it on the floor," the frightened woman replied.

"Well there must have been a herd of piggin frogs, there's two more in here," thundered Foot.

"Don't know Sire, honest, don't know," the cook started to snivel.

"Well I'm still piggin hungry. What's for pudding?"

"I'll take this away and get it, it's your favourite," answered the cook, in an attempt to appease her master.

The newest mummy got to her feet and excused herself, saying she wanted to be sick.

"Well you can piggin stay and dish up my piggin pudding first," commanded her loving husband.

Cook returned and placed the bowl of currants and whey on the table. The newest mummy picked out the wooden spoon to dish up, then screamed, "Something's moving in the pudding," and promptly fainted again.

Stupid cow, thought Ethelfoot, time I got rid of her.

The children clambered round the bowl.

"Yeth Daddy thomething's moving," exclaimed Ethelete, aged six.

"Cook!" bellowed Ethelfoot again.

The poor woman was already on her way, having heard the mistress screaming again. Gingerly poking the spoon into the bowl, produced movement from the spawn, hidden by the whey.

"Them's tadpoles," she started.

"And I s'pose they piggin jumped in the piggin pudding!" yelled the Baron of Dorset.

One by one faces turned accusingly towards the young Etheltar. His father's eyes fixed him with a stony stare. Unable to bluff it out, the boy did the only sensible thing, got up and ran.

His father found him hiding in the woodshed, which was handy, as he was already in place for the second major thrashing of his young life.

The family were all indoors, none of the outdoor Burghers were around to annoy, having snuck off to various hidey holes to keep out of the rain, which was beating on to the cobbles outside of the woodshed.

The boy, now fast approaching his teens' was incredibly bored. Bored with sitting indoors with the family, bored with not being able to roam the estate, bored with sitting in the woodshed.

He fingered the purse he had stolen from the newest mother's room, and thought of ways to spend the money.

Some of his puppy fat had given way to young muscles, but his still full face was now producing spots, which made him even uglier.

He amused himself for a while catching flies, that were now getting dopey in the cooler autumn days. Many fat harvest spiders had weaved their traps between the upright supports and beams of the roof.

He invented a new game, which he christened the spider and the fly. Clutching a large green insect in his still chubby hands, he stood on a line he had drawn in the sawdust, about three foot from a web, then hurled the winged missile at the target. The fly regained its senses within a fingers length of the sticky silk strands and applied its airbreaks, stopping in midair, then soaring above the trap.

The boy made a mark in the dust, below the crude picture of a fly.

Soon he returned to his footmark clutching a shiny bluebottle in his grubby palm. Taking careful aim he threw at the centre of the web, currently unoccupied, its minder hunched in the angle of the wood at one corner. This time the fly was too slow and twanged into the net, it started to struggle but the trap held firm. The motley brown hairy body charged from its hiding place and sank grateful fangs into the prize. The fly continued to squirm, but soon became still as the spider sucked precious juices from its intestines until it was sated, then proceeded to spin its victim into a silken shroud.

The boy made a mark in the dust under a round circle with legs, which he had drawn to indicate the spider.

He caught an even larger bluebottle, and went to a web he had spotted with an even larger spider sat in the middle. Carefully marking a line on the ground exactly the same as the distance from the first target, he launched the insect with all his might, the effort causing him to let off a mighty fart, which exploded from his fat bottom. The fly went straight through the lower strands of the web, giving the spider some cause for concern over its craftsmanship.

The boy stood for a while, sniffing the horrible smell he had created with pleasure, then made another mark below the drawing of a fly.

His makeshift scoreboard registered, flies five spiders two, when he spied a wasp. Problem, how to get the wasp into the web without being stung. He searched for ten minutes before he found what he wanted, a stone jar and a thin slice of wood. During the hunt he stumbled over a tinder box, left by an errant Burgher. Trapping the wasp in the jar he slid the wooden cover across the open top, then went to the largest web and the largest spider he had seen. Shaking the jar produced an angry buzzing from within. He stood inches from the massive web, pointed the container, and pulled away the cover. The yellow and black inhabitant, still dizzy from too much apple juice, staggered out into the centre strands, which were weaved much tighter than those on the perimeter. Its struggles only entangled it more, as its hairy adversary crept cautiously towards it then scuttled the last few inches to embrace its prey. The wasp reacted by shooting out its pointed sting, twisting its body to try and get a strike. The spider danced warily around the insect until its jaws clamped around the wasps head, its struggles became weaker, then finally its body stopped moving all together.

Young Etheltar left the spider wrapping up the corpse, which would provide its supper later in the day. He picked up his new find and sat down on a pile of logs. He emptied the small amount of tinder onto more shavings, then struck the flint on the steel to produce a spark. After three attempts, his little mound ignited, and he quickly added more shavings. Soon steady flames danced from the little fire and the boy added larger sticks.

Outside the heavy rain had become a gentle patter on the cobbles. The boy peered out the woodshed door and saw his elder brother talking to one of the Burghers, who was leading his Father's favourite hunter out of the stable. Wondering what was going on he ran down to join the pair, as the rain ceased altogether.

"Father told me to get his horse ready as soon as the rain stopped," Etheltread informed him.

"Is he going hunting? Can we go?" The boy's boredom lifted with the thought of an ensuing chase.

"Dunno 'bout you. Father said I could go, as I will be Baron of Dorset one day and you will still be nothing." His brother pulled himself to his full height and sneered at Tar, who was several inches shorter than himself, but a good deal stockier. He then stuck out his tongue and turned to continue talking to the Burgher.

The younger boy leapt on his back and bit his ear, it was a couple of minutes before Etheltread was able to release his hold, then swing a punch at his fat nose. The pair were brought up suddenly by the Burgher yelling, "The woodshed's on fire!"

The two boys stopped their scuffle and looked up the yard. Sure enough a cloud of smoke and steam was coming out of the woodshed door, and off the rush covered roof, then they saw the first flames flickering through the wooden slats which made up the walls.

The three tore across the yard, leaving the hunter standing by the stable door wondering what was happening.

"Fire!" yelled the Burgher and Etheltread, racing to the water trough, grabbing a bucket each from the side of the drinking place and submerging them into the water. "Fire! fire!" the Burgher yelled again.

Flames were pushing through the roof as the Baron of Dorset who had been dozing by his own fire, stumbled from the house, pulling on a jacket.

"The piggin woodshed's on fire," he yelled, cleverly stating the obvious.

In the short time it took him to reach the water trough, the whole roof was a mass of flames. Several more Burghers came running from all directions, and the family appeared from the house followed by barking hounds.

Everyone pitched in, some ran to the stables and the dairy to grab more buckets, then formed a chain from the water trough to the woodshed. The Baron, his eldest son and the Burgher who had been preparing his horse in the forefront, throwing water on the blaze from buckets which had been passed down the line.

It took an hour before the flames were no more. The Burgher, who was operating the pump over the water trough, collapsed over the arm. The line of bucket passers sat down on the still damp cobbles.

The sooty Baron surveyed the remains of the woodshed and muttered, "How did that piggin happen?"

Etheltread pointed at Tar "he was in the woodshed Pa."

There was no escaping the accusing finger. Tar bolted down the yard and leapt onto a pile of straw, then onto his Father's surprised horse, kicked it into a trot, then a gallop, and disappeared across the grassland which bordered the stables.

CHAPTER ELEVEN

Etheltar the Man

Etheltar stood at the wheel of the Sea Cow and watched for a breeze to stir the main sail, which hung limp from the mast. They had been becalmed now for more than three weeks off the Azores, on a return trip from the Barbary Coast, at the top end of Africa where they had traded, buying spices, silks and cotton, which were now stored in the hold and would be sold at a small profit, when they finally made it back to Bristol.

The boy was now a young man of twenty two years, and was as at home on the deck of a ship, as he was on horseback. His puppy fat had all gone to leave a muscular frame, his previously cruel features now sported several days growth around the chin, and his face had mellowed.

His father had caught up with him four days after the woodshed fire, when a message was sent to the Grand Manor from the landlord of the Burgher Bar on Seynorgue, stating that his son was slumped in a corner, drunk as a skunk and would his Lordship please come and get him.

The young Etheltar had been loaded onto a cart and driven back to the family home by one of the Burghers. The Baron, who had been more concerned over his favourite hunter, was for once gracious enough to thank the landlord, who had insured that the horse had been fed and watered over the last three days.

The scars on the boys back and legs had still not healed, after the thrashing with the buckle end of his father's belt, when the door to the bare room in which he had been locked was opened by Ethelethel, his elder sister by one year.

"Papa says you are to go to your room and put all your clothes in this," she dropped a cloth bag in the doorway, "then come down."

His father was dressed for travel, when he descended in to the great hall. Without a word he indicated for the boy to follow him, and marched out into the yard where the family's coach was waiting, a Burgher at the reins of the team of four. Still not speaking, the Baron opened the door of the carriage and poked the boy to get in, the door was shut and Ethelfoot climbed up next to the Burgher.

Tar stared stonily at the family, which had assembled at the entrance to the Manor, then turned away as the coach rumbled across the cobbles onto the drive leading away from his home.

It was hours before the boy was awakened by shouts and sounds unfamiliar to him. He peered out to see they had pulled up on a quayside which he did not recognise. His Father opened the door and silently indicated he should get out, then led him up a gangplank onto a large sailing vessel, which the carriage was parked beside.

A very large elderly man with red hair and a stained red beard greeted the Baron as they stepped aboard. He saw his Father hand the man a purse before disappearing from view, leaving him with another sailor who had different coloured eyes looking in different directions. He was escorted to a cubby hole no bigger than the dining room table back at the Manor, the sailor pushed his head down none too gently, then placed his booted foot onto Tar's rear end and propelled him into the tiny space. The door slammed shut behind him, leaving him in complete darkness. Fumbling awkwardly around he discovered what seemed to be a pitcher of water and a platter with a lump of something on it.

The movement of the floor jerked him awake from a fitful slumber. He sat up and drank from the pitcher, then fumbled around to locate the food, something moved under his fingers when he picked it up and he dropped it in horror. The confined space and movement of the ship caused him to throw up and he lay for what seemed like days feeling decidedly unwell, with the stench of vomit filling the small airless hole. At last the low door opened revealing a pair of legs, a bucket and a scrubbing brush.

"Out," a voice commanded.

He emerged shakily, the sailor who had imprisoned him pointed to the brush and bucket.

"Clear up yer filf, bring it up on deck and empty it over the side," the gruff voice commanded.

He blinked in the daylight as he mounted the steps on to the deck, and screwed up his eyes against the sunlight. Several sailors stood around looking at him as he made his way to the rail of the ship, then burst into raucous laughter as he emptied his slops over the side, and received most of them back, splattering onto his face and body in the breeze, as the ship galloped along under billowing sails.

The sailor with the strange eyes surveyed the lad, then handed him another bucket full of sea water. "Go and finish yer job below, lad," he grunted.

After several trips up and down to his temporary prison and washing it out, the sailor accompanied him back to the deck, declaring himself satisfied.

"Bring the boy over here with us, Google," called a fellow with rings in his ears and nose.

Some of the crew were gathered round four barrels, sitting on wooden crates.

"Here boy, want some food?" the ringed sailor shoved a dish with what looked like they used to feed the pigs back at the Grand Manor, across one of the barrels. Tentatively he dipped a spoon into the muck and tasted it, he found that if he didn't sniff as he ate and swallowed the whole spoonful, it wasn't too terrible.

The first months aboard the vessel were something worse than he had ever imagined, but gradually the boy mastered the tasks he was given, his young body hardening in the salt air as the ship zipped along.

The captain hardly ever acknowledged the boy, but he was now accepted by the rough bunch which made up the crew.

Over the course of the next four years Etheltar learnt and liked the shipboard duties. He learnt the configuration of various sail settings, as the weather changed. How to sail with the wind and against. He was on deck in calm and storm.

As his knowledge grew, he found he could predict the weather, and found himself calling out orders, to shorten or lengthen sail, to take full advantage of the wind before it arrived. He stood with the helmsman and was now trusted to take the wheel himself. Most of all he enjoyed working in the rigging, a great sense of adventure tinged with fear, when up in the top masts with the ship's deck rolling sixty feet below the maze of ropes.

One afternoon, the skipper, who now included Tar in conversation, when he was sober, told him to report to his cabin, in the aft of the ship.

"Know anything about navigation?" he asked, as Tar stepped over the threshold and marvelled at the luxury the captain surrounded himself with, most unlike the cramped quarters occupied by the crew.

"No skipper, but I'd like to learn," the boy even surprised himself, with his new thirst for knowledge.

Over the next three years Etheltar was summoned to the aft cabin on odd afternoons, and poured over charts and maps, with compass, compasses and rule, learning the art of navigation.

Every day now he took the sun shots at noon, to plot the vessel's position, within a few nautical miles, working out complex calculations on a piece of slate, as the old skipper was seldom in a fit state.

This last voyage he had argued strongly with his red headed captain, over the purchases which were now in the hold. The last two trips had given poor returns on the silk cotton and spices, they had to pay more each time they bought, and the selling price in Bristol continued to drop.

The crew, like their master, relied on a good profit to earn their pay, and were becoming increasingly aggressive towards the old man, seeing the sailors on other ships employed in less savoury trades, with far more money than them, to spend in the taverns of Bristol and vice dens of Tangiers.

Google, who had been so named to match his eyes, came and stood by him, one eye looking at Tar the other somewhere else.

"Nuffin doin then Eff," Google looked disconcertedly at the drooping canvas. "Me and the boys is getting' well sick wiv this."

The delay meant the rations put on board in Tangiers, were running short and the fresh water was now covered with a green slime. A hatchway below the pair was thrust open, the old man stumbled on to the lower deck.

"Wind, I need wind," he shouted in slurred tones.

"I'll give you wind," muttered Etheltar, and produced a long rumbling fart.

"You carn arf fart Eff," Google chuckled with admiration.

Frog came bouncing along the lower deck and promptly fell over the captain who staggered backwards, just as he hopped passed on his single leg.

"Look where you're going, oaf," the skipper swung an arm at Frog as he scrambled to his foot, but had to grab a piece of rigging to stop himself falling over. Frog hopped on to where ever it was he was going.

The captain belched loudly, turned and stuck his head back through the hatchway, aimed to grasp the rope support, missed, and went face first down the wooden steps leading to his cabin.

"Always close the hatch after you, captain," called Tar.

"Good job it ain't rough, Eff," muttered Google conspiratorially, "a bloke could go over the side fallin' abaht like that."

The rest of the crew were either lounging in the shade under one of the mizzen sails they had taken down and stretched above the deck, or dangling from ropes hung over the sides of the ship, lowering themselves in and out of the shimmering water, in vain efforts to escape the oppressive heat.

A shoal of sardines, a mile wide, broke the surface in thousands of shiny flashes, pursued by about twenty excited dolphins, the surface settled back into an unbroken mirror, reflecting the burning rays from above.

Ringer came and joined the pair at the wheel, devoid of much of his jewellery, but with livid red holes in his ears and nose where it had been.

"Ad to take me cowin rings off," he stated "they was grillin me 'ead."

"Well don't go in the water," laughed Google, looking at him and Tar at the same time. "You'll cowin sink wiv all them 'oles."

Thankfully the sun finally disappeared below the horizon, the scorching decks cooled enough for the crew to discard their boots, and once more walk barefoot.

The only person to sleep below for the last fortnight, was the captain. His spacious cabin sheltered from the heat by the two upper decks, and the large lattice windows flung wide open, in the aft end of the Sea Cow. The crews quarters were almost airless and stank of urine. The small portholes provided little relief to the cramped sleeping compartment. Now the men curled up where ever they could on deck, grabbing anything soft, to make their sleep more comfortable.

Six more days went by in similar fashion, until early on the twenty third morning after becoming becalmed, Tar, as usual, was on the upper deck, sprawled under a canvas he had draped over the wheel. He was startled awake as his makeshift canopy twitched, he sniffed the air, and scrambled out, looking up at the sails which were also fluttering. He dashed to the aft rail, sure enough the sea was now showing ripples. A white cloud crested the distant horizon, in the early morning sky behind the Sea Cow.

"Wind!" he yelled.

The already stirring crew were jerked fully awake by bellowed orders from Tar and Google, shinning up the rigging to unfurl the top sail on the main mast, and out on the rat ropes along the spars, releasing the mizzen sails fore and aft.

The captain struggled onto deck, still sporting a scarred face from his fall down the companionway.

"What's happening?" he yelled, his befuddled mind struggling to take in all the activity around and above him.

"We got wind skipper!" one of the crew yelled back, dashing past him.

Tar stared alternately at the cloud, then the sails, then the sea. Yes, the cloud was getting bigger. Yes, the sails were filling. Yes, the sea was chopping up and yes they started to move.

The Sea Cow, like some prehistoric monster waking from its slumber, seemed to shake herself as she picked up speed, the sails above her head and back starting to fill.

They made it back to Bristol after a further twenty days. Their intended five of six week journey, taking well over three months.

The cargo was unloaded, the captain informed the gathered crew that they had twenty one days shore leave, before disappearing to his cabin, to make a start on the fresh supply of booze which had come aboard. He left Tar to pay out even smaller purses than the crew had collected on their previous voyage.

Tar and Google had overseen the emptying of stale water barrels, and refilled two of the twenty, so as to provide fresh drinking water for them and the two crew members stricken with scurvy, and unable to move from their bunks, for the first week. Both now fully recovered, had taken off to join their mates, in one of the many taverns which lined the waterfront. They had also purchased fresh fruit, meat and bread which they consumed each day with relish, after the long days of only dry biscuits and maggoty cheese. The captain came on deck occasionally and took some of the vittles, plus jugs of water back to his cabin.

At the end of the second week in dock, most of the crew had already returned to the ship, having spent all their pay drinking and gambling. Google invited Tar to join him going ashore, and the pair left Ringer, now completely reringed, in charge of the vessel. He took him to a tavern at the end of the quayside, where he introduced him to his twin brother, Boogle. Google and Boogle were identical apart from their eyes. Instead of eyes looking outwards, Boogles's eyes looked inwards, and instead of one blue left and one brown right, Boogle had one blue right and one brown left. Tar learnt that Boogle had been first mate on a slave ship for ten years. He had made a mint of money, until it was shipwrecked off Land's End two years ago, drowning every man apart from himself, and the four other unsavoury looking characters he currently sat drinking with.

Tar enjoyed the next few days, his new acquaintants acting as guides to the worst places in Bristol. The group consumed gallons of ale, ate mountains of pies, had two fights with other revellers and soon picked up several dubious females, who escorted them on their tour. Google and Tar returned to the ship at the end of the twenty one days shore leave, to muster the crew and lay in provisions for the next intended voyage. The captain, sober for once, stood at the head of the gangplank as the pair staggered back onto the Sea Cow.

"And where the helluv you been?" he demanded of Tar.

"Having a week off, after running your piggin ship for the last four months," Tar bristled, shaking off the effects of the last few days.

"Get down to my cabin now." The old man turned his back on Tar, and stomped down the companionway.

The crew listened intently to the shouts that emitted from below, curses and threats, topped with much banging clattering and breaking of glass, for well over half an hour, until there was silence.

Tar reappeared on deck. "Well that's sorted that out," he stated to the men gathered around the hatchway. "All shipshape, Ringer? Let's get this trip under way."

"Still ten men short Eff, don't fink they'll be joining us."

"Right, you and me sort out provisions, then get water barrels stored. Google round me up more crew, I want your brother and his mates, you can tell them the pay for this voyage will be double what the lads got last time."

The Sea Cow sailed out of Bristol five days later, with a full complement of crew and better vittles than any of the men had seen before, on a ship setting out on a six week voyage.

Three days out of port in very rough seas Google muttered, "you can't do it all yourself Eff, let me see if the old man's fit to give you a break." Google returned to the poop deck where Tar was yelling orders to crew members, scuttling about on the pitching slippery boards, his weird eyes weirder than ever.

"He's dead Eff, and he pongs somefing rotten!"

"'Spect he does," replied Eff nonchalantly. "I killed him in Bristol, we'll get rid of him tonight before he stinks the whole ship out."

Google's one eye looked at Tar in admiration, the other followed the antics of Frog, trying to keep his balance on one leg.

Another two days, and the violence of the seas coming out of the Bristol Channel, had settled to a gentle swell. With a steady breeze behind her the Sea Cow raced towards her destination.

Tar took over the old mans cabin and called Google, Ringer and Boogle in for a conference.

"So, how you gunna make this trip pay more money?" they all wanted to know.

"The prices in Tangiers will still be cowing ridiculous," moaned Ringer.

"We ain't going to Tangiers boys, we're going to Casablanca."

He then instructed each man what he wanted of them when at sea and when they were docked. He also told them how much they could expect to earn as trusted mates, which would be twice that of the crew. During their time ashore, Boogle had told Tar of the town further down the same coastline which dealt in human traffic, and the money a ship could make, "if the deals wuz dun right."

The crew of the Sea Cow took to their new skipper who was hard but fair, they also worked well under Google, Ringer and Boogle when Tar was not on deck.

They docked in Casablanca after only thirty seven days at sea, fair winds carrying the Sea Cow swiftly, with all sails unfurled.

Tar gave the crew an advance on their expected earnings. He had found a secret compartment at the bottom of a large sea trunk in the old skipper's cabin, stuffed with gold coins. He had Google assemble the men on deck after they had anchored, a mile out. Unknown ports presented unknown dangers and Tar felt safer with water all around the Sea Cow, rather than being tied up to the quay. Already bum boats were jostling round the ship, offering fresh fruit, meat and booze.

"Alright fellers!" he yelled. "We're gonna be here for at least two weeks. You can all have a week's shore leave, the long boats will ferry you backwards and forwards to the Cow. I'm leaving Google and Ringer in charge, decide amongst yourselves who wants which week and sort it out with them. Those on board will still be under orders, no more booze than the daily ration is allowed."

"Boo!" shouted the crew.

"When you're on shore leave you can get drunk as skunks," he continued.

"Hooray!" shouted the crew.

"Any man caught inebriated while on duty will be put ashore and left. Up to you lads," he finished. Most of the "lads" were twice his age.

An hour later Google, Boogle and Ringer reported to him in his cabin.

"All sorted Eff," stated Google. "I'm doing the first week aboard."

"Keep a firm grip then, don't let any of the locals aboard. Boogle, you and me is going ashore."

Boogle led Tar through twisted smelly streets and unkempt buildings, to a part of town away from the docks. Beggars and street urchins pleaded for money. Every dark doorway was suddenly occupied, by a male or female, demanding they entered and partook of the delights offered within.

"Just ignore 'em Eff and keep walking," Tar's bosseyed companion noticed his skipper fingering the sword strapped to his side.

As they moved further away from the sea, trees were more evident amongst the now scattered houses. They arrived in a large square, on the far side of which, was a massive stockade, behind which they could see the start of the jungle. Over the top of the stockade bold lettering pronounced: SLAVES R US.

They crossed the square and Boogle pulled on a heavy chain, suspended at the side of two high wooden gates. From within the stockade a bell clanged.

A few moments passed before one of the gates was swung open by an extremely large Arab in a turban, with a livid scar down the right hand side of his pock marked face.

"Boogle, me ol' mate, thought you wuz brown bread," he greeted in perfect cockney rhyming slang.

"Whatcher Turd, how's business?" Tar's squiffy eyed mate and the Arab hugged each other.

"This is me new skipper," he introduced Etheltar. "But we calls him Eff. Eff, this is Turd, he's been boss of this place forever."

"Pleased to meet you Turd, hope we can do business," the Arab took Tar's outstretched hand in his massive fist, whilst gesturing to the several large cages along the sides of the compound as he led them in.

On one side, a sign over the single long cage covering the complete wall proclaimed: PICK YOUR OWN. On the other side, three smaller cages carried individual signs stating over each; JOB LOT. GOOD DEAL. CHEAP. To the rear of the stockade another pair of huge gates led out into the untamed land beyond, over which a sign stated; CATCH YOUR OWN PAY AT GATE. Tar reflected, Turd obviously liked to label all his own possessions.

The Arab and Boogle were consumed in conversation, so Etheltar wandered around the stockade peering into each of the cages.

The long cage, he estimated, held about a hundred men women and children of varying colours, from light brown to very black. Most of the adults were quite young, the children ranged from about eight years upwards. Most cowered away as he approached the bars, but a few of the younger bucks stood their ground and stared at him aggressively. Large bowls contained water and other smaller bowls were heaped together, obviously for the captive's food. To the rear of the cages an opening led into a covered area, which he presumed was used for sleeping.

The "job lot" cage had a slate attached to it with the number 38 scratched on its surface. He counted five young females, with smaller children and babies, several males, who looked older than those in the long enclosure.

The enclosure with the sign "good deal" above it, had a slate which was marked 30, and contained a mixture similar to the previous cage.

The last, which proclaimed "cheap," that was marked with the number 46, held older women and men, a couple of which appeared to be very ancient. One of these wore a necklace of small bones and held a nobly stick, which was pointed at Tar on his approach. The wizened little old man emitted strange clicking noises, he wore a dirty loin cloth tied around his waist. All the rest of the captives were completely naked.

Tar mooched back across the dusty central yard deep in thought. He stuck his head into the doorway of the hut he had seen Boogle and Turd disappear into earlier.

"Come in me ol' sparrer, take wine with us," the massive Arab stood up, greeting him in a strange mixture of arabic etiquette and friendly east end of London banter.

A bare wooden table was set with various dishes which were unknown to Etheltar. Turd and Boogle already had large pottery bowls containing wine in front of them. As he sat down, an extremely pretty black girl hastened to his side, placing a bowl in front of him, which she filled to the brim from a large stone pitcher.

The three ate a delightful meal, the large Arab proving to be the perfect host, entertaining them with tales from the jungle and desert, where slave hunts had taken place over the last years. He invited Tar and Boogle to remain as his guests, leading them out of the stockade across the square. They followed him through large iron gates, set in a high wall, which surrounded one of the most beautiful buildings Tar had ever seen.

"My home is yours, honoured brothers," he informed them. "Anyfink yer want jus' say."

The girl who had waited on Tar walked behind them with a couple of attractive females, as they approached the massive doors of the palace the girls scuttled ahead, and by the time Turd had ushered them into a sumptuous marble floored room, three times the size of the Great Hall back at the Grand Manor, they were already busy placing more fruit in already overflowing bowls on gilt tables, which stood by each of the lavish silk chairs and settees, which were scattered around the room.

The three girls were giggling amongst themselves, as Turd pointed out the treasures he had collected over the years, which were hung stacked and displayed in alcoves around the walls of the room. Paintings from Italy, rugs from Turkey, gold and silver ornaments from the near and far East.

Each girl deposited herself daintily on one of the settees, having placed a pitcher of wine and two goblets next to the bowls of fruit .

They looked dutifully at their master.

"Which one do yer fancy Eff?" the large Arab asked grinning from pockmarked ear to pockmarked ear.

For the first time in a very long time, the captain of the Sea Cow who had led his crew through mighty seas and raging storms, was flustered. He looked enquiringly at Boogle trying to cover his embarrassment.

"Take yer pick boss, you're the 'onoured guest, it's the custom."

Etheltar closed his eyes, he mustn't let them know its was going to be the first time he had spent a night with a girl. He opened his eyes wide, blinked, then went and sat next to the girl who had served him in the stockade.

"Good on yer Eff," chortled Boogle, rushing to another settee.

Turd puffed out his chest and beamed, the third girl got up and ran to him, he caught her as she approached and slung her over one of his massive shoulders, then marched to the nearest seat, turned her smartly across his knee, and whacked her across her bottom with the palm of his hand.

"Pour me some wine me darlin'," he demanded, releasing the giggling maiden.

Boogles partner released herself from arms which already encircled her, she and Tars maiden then tended to pouring out the drinks.

Turd stood up, raised his goblet and boomed, "a toast to my new friends and the business we're gonna do." He then tilted the goblet and knocked back the liquid in one gulp.

Boogle stood and followed suit. Not wishing to be outdone, Tar did the same, then promptly sat down, his head spinning.

"What in heavens name is this brew?" he managed to ask, picking each word carefully, as his mouth didn't seem to want to coincide with his brain.

"Special passion potion me old mucker, it'll prepare you for the next course," Turd beamed.

Tar saw each girl was also sipping from their own drinking vessels, before he could stop her his partner had refilled his goblet.

A heady perfume from golden incense burners mingled with the encroaching night, the girls musty scent was strong now, as she snuggled closer.

Tar could see a low sickle moon through the fine grills which covered the arched windows. His body had a wonderful relaxation about it now, which he had never experienced before. Each time he blinked the twilight seemed to blend into different gentle colours.

Turd and Boogle were both engrossed with their partners when Tars maiden took him gently by the hand and guided him toward a wide marble staircase which led off the room and up to an inner gallery above.

Next morning when Tar awoke, he was alone, he swiftly dressed and descended the staircase to the great marble floored room, where Turd and Boogle were already seated, eating a variety of fruit and nuts from silver trays set before them.

"Mornin' captain," greeted Turd.

"Enjoyed yourself last night guvnor?" enquired Boogle with a grin.

"Never better," Etheltar replied, with the confidence now, that he had lacked the previous evening.

"Come over 'ere and tuck in, oh 'onoured guest," Turd shifted along the settee making room for Tar.

And so it continued for five sumptuous days and nights, Tar and Boogle living like kings.

Each morning the pair and their host arose late, descending from their grand bedrooms to bathe in the natural rock lined pool, fed by an underground stream in the courtyard to the rear of the building. They spent afternoons lazing in the shade cast by cultivated plants and minarets, which graced the roof of Turd's palace. Brightly coloured birds fluttered between the trees beyond the grounds, monkeys danced along the high walls, deftly catching titbits thrown to them.

They were attended by slaves, skilled in the graces rich families would expect from servants, and clothed accordingly. Turd informed them that his palace was used as a training ground for the best of his captives, overseen by an elderly married couple of white haired negroes, both of whom spoke English. Tar's host advised him all the house slaves were for sale, but at premium prices, and although they, and the pick your own slaves, would cost more than the job lots, he could expect higher returns for the younger attractive men and women, when they were sold in Britain. Boogle agreed, having been caught on the previous trip, when his skipper had gone to another trader, who specialised in a buy one get one free policy, and had lost over half the stock on the return journey.

"You've gotta treat 'em right Eff, taint no good if they dies on the way 'ome," he informed his attentive skipper.

On the fifth day, Tar made his choices. He took ten of the house slaves which had taken his attention, then selected forty from the pick your own cage.

He chose: 25 jet black negro bucks, 8 jet black negro maidens, 7 lighter skinned maidens.

It was arranged that Turd would deliver the captives to the quayside, and the Sea Cow would shift her moorings for two days, to pull up along side in one week's time.

The ship sat gracefully at anchor, as the pair returned in the longboat and boarded the scrubbed deck, where some of the crew were sat repairing one of her sails.

Google and Ringer had done a good job in command, the two cargo holds now had stout wooden covers, constructed by the ships carpenter, which could be used instead of the usual watertight ones, when conditions allowed.

"Well done gentlemen," Tar greeted the pair. "Any problems?"

"Only one Eff, caught one of the new blokes pinchin rum, we've already 'ad 'im flogged," replied Google.

"That'll do me," said Etheltar. "Your turn now, go and enjoy Casablanca. Don't get too drunk, we're bringing the Cow into the quayside in a weeks time, I'll need you both to load the cargo."

The next week was spent with Tar and Boogle supervising the loading of extra rations, and more water barrels, which made up part of the ballast.

Turd, and three other large Arabs, led four lines of slaves chained to each other by their ankles, on to the dock, where the Sea Cow was now moored. Tar and Boogle inspected the purchases, and declared themselves satisfied, then Tar led Turd aboard and down to his cabin, leaving his trusted mates to load the stock.

"Nice doin' business wiv yer honoured captain," said Turd in his strange mixture, as he took his leave an hour later, clutching a large bag of money.

"Same goes for me Turd, look forward to seeing you again." Tar once again subjected himself to the mighty Arab's vice like hand shake, as he stepped down the gangplank.

"Cargo is secure below!" called Boogle.

"Long boats ready Eff!" called Ringer.

"Two crews gorn missin'!" called Google.

"And they can stay missin'," called back Tar. "Untie fore and aft, longboats take the strain."

The Sea Cow slid gently away from the dock, attached by ropes to the longboats, which steered her out into deeper water.

The male and female slaves had been separated, and stored in the two holds.

"Don't want no 'anky panky on the way across," Boogle whispered confidentially in Tar's ear.

Although they remained chained, their conditions in the holds were not much worse than those of the crew. Straw pallets had been provided for their sleep. Each day the captives, from the forward hold, were led up in two tethered lines and allowed to stay on deck for three hours, while two of the party were released and given buckets to wash out their smelly compartment. They were then led back down and the hatch secured, before the aft hold was opened and the same procedure followed.

The Sea Cow made it back into Portsmouth after fifty five days, only one storm had marred their voyage when the watertight hatches had to replace the wooden grills. Stormy seas lashed the ship for three days and nights, before a worried Tar allowed his bemused prisoners once more on deck.

One of the dusky females had died and two of the young bucks were seriously ill. Tar instructed they should be released and remain on the poop deck. After two days the younger of the two rushed to the side of the ship and leapt into the waves, never to be seen again, the other recovered after a week and was returned below.

Portsmouth was the nearest port for their particular goods, unless they sailed into the English Channel and up the Thames directly to London. One of the largest slave trading businesses retained a warehouse in the docks, and ran a regular service to various parts of the country.

"Come back an see me s'afternoon my luvver," the large round blonde haired man instructed Tar, after the lines had been led ashore, already opening the odd bucks mouth with a grimy thumb and peering inside.

"Seen better," he announced on Tar and Boogle's return.

"Not many you ain't Jimbo," retorted Boogle, who seemed to know everybody.

"I could go to a thousand," stated Jimbo.

"Sure you could," said Boogle attempting to look him straight in the eye. "'An one day ships might not need sails, fifteen hundred."

They all laughed.

"You ain't in Africy now Boogle I ain't bartering."

Big Jim stood his ground.

"Looks like we've gotta sail to Lunnon Eff, better get the stock back aboard."

Tar tried not to look dismayed.

"Alright you bosseyed git, twelve hundred," Jimbo chuckled.

"I fought that's what you fought all along," Boogle grabbed Tar's arm and deposited his hand in big Jims to complete the deal.

"So give me a breakdown on what you expect to pay for each," Tar wanted to know as he loosened his grip.

"I reckon on fifty guineas for house trained, twenty for other bucks and fifteen for maids," the large blonde man ventured after a long pause. "But don't hold me to it, and they've gotta be in good nick."

The pair returned to the Sea Cow and its expectant crew, where Tar instructed his three mates to inform the men they would have two weeks shore leave, and their pay would be ready in two hours. He then returned to the aft cabin with a large bag of coin.

After scratching his head and scratching a slate with figures, he called for Ringer to come down to his cabin, together they came up with what they considered fair. He had already found out that for similar voyages, crews usually picked up twelve to fourteen sovereigns. He called up to Google and Boogle to come down to the cabin, then told them what he proposed.

"That," the three agreed, "was the best purses any ship ad ad and everyone wuz gunna be cowin appy."

One by one the crew filed into Tar's cabin and made their marks against their names, on the list that had been prepared by the unusually literate Ringer.

Each man picked up twenty sovereigns and the three mates collected forty. Tar told each one that the two sovereigns he had advanced them in Casablanca could be counted as a bonus.

He then instructed his three mates that, he required the ship to be manned by one of them, and six or seven of the crew over the next twenty one days. They would stay in dock for the next month, during which, the Sea Cow would be restocked with food and water and any repairs taken care of.

"Same rules as when we were moored in Africa boys, but those on board can have a double ration of rum, I'll leave the rest to you."

"Fanks Eff, don't fink anyone's gunna let you down wiv pay like that," said Google as the three took their leave.

Etheltar sank gratefully on to the large comfy bunk and reflected on the very profitable voyage. The last trip under the command of the old skipper, running cloth and spices, the crew had only picked up six sovereigns after a miserable voyage.

He reckoned that he had made around five hundred guineas, which, after restocking and repairs, would leave him well over four hundred.

The Sea Cow put to sea after thirty two days in Portsmouth harbour, a very complete and very ready crew were eager for the next trip.

They cruised up the Solent and stayed well in sight of the southern English coast for three days. As they changed to a southwesterly course on the mark, which was the tip of Seynourg, a shout from the crow's nest alerted Tar.

"What's up matey?" shouted up Etheltar.

"Dunno skipper, better come and take a look."

Tar was agile for a big man and soon joined the lookout in the large canvas bucket, near the top of the main mast. Swinging his glass in the direction his crew man was pointing, a very old craft came into focus, seemingly floating in a large lagoon, separated from the sea by rockfalls from the cliffs on the land at either side, but accessible through a gap in the fallen boulders.

Tar shinned down the rigging and ordered the crew to drop anchor, then lower a longboat, which he boarded with Google and Ringer, leaving Boogle in charge.

The boat slid through the opening into calm water encompassed by the natural harbour walls.

"Its one of they old Viking ships Eff," stated Ringer, as they tied up to the rotting hulk.

Tar and Ringer climbed aboard treading gingerly on the old timbers. The single mast had long gone, snapped off at the base. Several holes in the decking gave sight into the hold, which contained about two foot of dirty sea water.

An aft cabin above deck was surprisingly sound and dry. Old furs and leathers piled in a corner crumbled at their touch. The first of three large wooden chests revealed swords, axes and shields, all usable with a little attention. The second, helmets, with strange horns poking out at different angles, also other horns which produced rounded notes when blown into by Ringer. The third and smallest chest had a stout lock which they broke away with one of the axes. Golden crucifixes, jewelled silver and gold chalices, ornate swords and daggers were scattered within, between them, gold coins, rubies, emeralds and diamonds, twinkled in the sudden light.

"Grief, looks like the gods is smiling on us Eff," uttered Ringer, sticking his hands into the treasure in disbelief.

"This, Ringer, will remain between you and me and the other two," Etheltar's generosity to his crew on the last voyage didn't stretch this far. "Leave it for now, we'll collect it later, when there aren't so many eyes." The cabins only other occupant was a long gently curved horn, twice the length of a man's body and nearly as thick.

They returned on deck and went forrard to inspect the fearsome figurehead at the prow of the ship. It was a beast neither of them knew and remained almost intact, carved from one huge piece of wood. The face of a cow but with a far wider snout was adorned with two massive antlers, but unlike those of deer, the horns had large flat areas, big as uneven dinner plates, with several points on each. The head of the fearsome creature must have overseen many a journey and many a raid in years gone by.

The pair climbed down into the longboat and Etheltar pointed to the large black hole at the base of the cliffs.

"Let's go and have a look lads," he instructed the eight oarsmen.

To one side of the opening, a long flat ledge of rock, washed by the sea, formed a natural quayside. They rowed through the arched entrance. The ledge continued above the heads of the oarsmen in the great gloomy tunnel, but Tar, stood in the prow, could make out the shiny surface, its depth into the rough rock was, in some places, as narrow as a man laid flat, but in others, the back of the ledge faded into the gloom.

They rowed for a long five minutes, the going easy in the calm water. The roof of the tunnel, in some places, almost touchable, in others, disappearing into darkness. Slowly the gloom lightened, a further twenty strokes and the tunnel opened into a huge domed cave, as high as a cathedral, but twice as wide and four times as long. Daylight spilled onto the clear blue water from three holes at the back of the cave, high in the "cathedral's" dome, adding to the sense that this was a special place.

The longboat ran aground on the long gently sloping beach of firm white sand, which ran from the rear wall of the cave, and some way around the side, opposite to the ledge, which now came to an end.

The walls and the roof of white rock could now be clearly seen, surrounding the great inland lake of crystal clear blue water.

At several places along the walls, water trickled down, at one point falling gently over an outjutting slab, to form a small waterfall.

"It's bootiful!" exclaimed Ringer.

"Yes," agreed his skipper. "It's bootiful," and in that moment knew what he wanted to do.

Tar and the crew of the Sea Cow spent a whole week exploring the great cave, "the quayside," and ledge with lanterns, which revealed several smaller caves, of different sizes and depths, sinking into the rockface.

The three openings high at the rear of the dome, were inaccessible from within, so Tar and two of the crew searched the rockface facing the sea, finding a point which provided ample hand and footholds. At the top they crossed a wide ridge, then descended the other side, to find three large holes sunk into the stony surface. Two of the holes were higher than a man, and they walked gingerly along several paces, until they could look down into the cave below. The third hole, the smaller of the two crew members, crawled into, and reported back after fifteen minutes that it had become higher and was the other opening which they had viewed from the beach in the cave below.

The Viking ship was towed into the tunnel, then moored securely to the ledge, a suitable distance in, well out of sight from the ocean beyond.

Tar figured that the entrance to the lagoon from the sea had only recently been opened up by a heavy storm, and that the galley had, up to that point, been hidden from view.

Two longboats gently eased the Sea Cow through the gap, at the height of a spring tide. Crew men with long poles testing the depth every few strokes of the oars. Tar breathed a great sigh of relief as the ship cleared the entrance, and the bottom of the lagoon was untouchable, even with two poles tied together.

The Sea Cow was far too tall to fit into the tunnel but was moored safely at the quayside. Tar called all the crew together on deck.

"I want this place," he informed them. "I want Ringer and three men to stand guard, for the weeks it takes us to complete this voyage. We will leave you with food and weapons, but above all, I want it to remain unknown to anyone but us, so the weapons are a last resort. You'll all share in the profits of this trip."

Frog hopped forward, followed by two of his buddies.

"What 'appens if you don't make it back Eff?" asked Ringer doubtfully.

"If we aren't back in six months you can consider yourselves lucky you ain't lying on the bottom of the ocean with us, and are relieved of your duties," Tar replied laughing.

That night, he and Ringer, removed the chest of Viking plunder to his cabin on the Sea Cow. The next morning, she eased out gently from her mooring on the top of the tide.

CHAPTER TWELVE

Vikings End

As Etheltar rode back to join the Sea Cow, after the attempted reading of his Father's will ten years later, he was in high spirits. The gold coins he'd stolen from the woodshed, safe in his rucksack, slung in front of him, where he could touch it.

He had always got a kick out of bettering his elder brother, and this was the best yet. He also considered his lifestyle to be far superior to that of Etheltread, though it still galled him, to remember his brother's smug face when he had been despatched from the family home all those years ago.

It had taken eight years to achieve his own "Shangrila," which he had envisaged the first time he had walked up the beach from the inland lake.

Since then, the Sea Cow had made thirteen voyages back and forth to Casablanca.

The last five trips she had been skippered by Ringer, who he had, over the last few years, instructed in the art of navigation. Google and Boogle were unable to grasp the complex calculations, and remained as trusted mates.

While he was away at sea, artisans had constructed his own "Palace" which faced onto Moose Pool at Vikings End, by which the lake and cave were now known.

Stonemasons, carpenters and metal workers, had been employed and paid more money each month than they could have earned in a year, in return for their workmanship and vows of silence. When each of the artisans tasks were finished they were offered the chance to stay on to look after the general maintenance of Vikings End or leave and return to their homes, those choosing the latter were murdered before they got very far.

After the first tentative dips into the slave market the Sea Cow had been subjected to considerable alterations, carpenters were busy day and night constructing extra "accommodation" wherever they could. Etheltar increased his crew and was now buying up to a hundred poor wretches each trip.

Now, only untrained bucks and maidens were purchased from Turd, the best of each bunch being taught in servant skills by his own pair of negro retainers, Alf and Lilly, both of whom could now speak English, as well as several African languages.

Tar reckoned to train these captives within a year, then sell them on, smartly attired, and ready for the rich houses of Britain. Those that didn't shape up, were moved on, but were all in good condition after spending time at Vikings End before being sold. All of his slaves now commanded the very best price. Over the years, several had tried to escape, their bodies now hung as grizzly reminders to the rest, halfway along the entrance tunnel.

The Sea Cow now started her voyages by taking conditioned slaves to either Bristol or Portsmouth to be sold. She then continued her voyage to Casablanca the money from the sales being used to purchase fresh stock.

Two cannons, mounted on swivels hidden in the boulders of the outer harbour wall, faced out to sea. The tunnels, which supplied light and air into the cave, were always manned by armed guards, equipped with muskets and Viking horns, to warn of any intruders. The long horn they had found in the galley, was now supported by rocks in the largest of the three tunnels, and was blown every so often at night, emitting a long low mournful note, which was enough to scare the pants off anyone getting too near.

Inside the cavern, deserving crew members were employed as guards, and allowed to miss seatrips partaking in the delights of Vikings End.

The Viking ship, with the fiercesome figurehead of an animal, which Ringer had discovered was called a Moose, was stilled moored at the quayside. Carpenters had enjoyed renovating the craft on odd days, when not fully employed within the cave, and she was now almost seaworthy.

Food, drink and other supplies were ferried in from Portsmouth, and occasionally from the Houmits market on the other side of Seynourg, where the Sea Cow now lay at anchor, waiting for her master.

The palace at Vikings End was now complete, rooms had been cut into the rockface, with stairways leading to an upper level, above which minarets had been shaped, decorated with ornate carvings. All the stone had been smoothed and polished to give the effect of marble. The blocks of stone, hewn from the rock, had been used to extend the lower level onto the beach, its flat roof forming a large balcony from the bedrooms looking onto Moose Pool. Ornate iron grills covered the windows and also formed doorways to the palace's many entrances.

Moose Pool had five small boats pulled up on the beach, built by skilled craftsmen in the form of the viking ship, for the inhabitants of Vikings End to use as pleasure craft. A small hut made of bamboo ferried back from Africa, provided a lakeside bar for the residents, drinks being served day and night by comely dusky maidens.

Each evening, three bucks were selected and let out, watched by armed guards to light the lamps and candles in the hundreds of nooks and crannies all around, and high in the dome of the large cave. Vikings End became a spectacular wonderland of twinkling stars, reflecting from the rock walls and off the surface of Moose Pool.

Lamps were lit in the tunnel and smaller caves, as far as the great iron grill, which was now fixed to the roof and walls a hundred paces in from the entrance leading onto the lagoon and quayside. A locked iron gate across the ledge completed the prison.

Two of the widest sections of the ledge had been utilised. The furthest away from the great cave now had a huge glowing fire, its base as high as a man's waist, set on a mesh of ironwork strung between boulders. Leather bellows were pumped by a stout wooden arm on one side, with a metal tube directed into the base of the embers, to produce a furnace hot enough for the blacksmith to shape iron on a massive anvil. A natural chimney in the rock providing an escape for the smoke.

The other section was even larger, a further half a mile into the tunnel, fifty paces before the inland lake. Here, stonemasons had needed to cut and bore a hole up to the surface, forming a manmade chimney for the cooking fires. Stone ovens and iron hobs were in constant use, three cooks living and working in the area providing food for everyone living in Vikings End. Two caves facing onto the ledge had provided cool natural larders. Stonemasons had cut another area into the rock, forming sleeping and living accommodation for the three busy chefs, who took it in turn to enjoy the leisure facilities on Moose Pool.

Between these two points, iron bars now covered several caves into which the slaves were first unloaded on arrival from Africa.

The sea lagoon provided a natural source of food, wicker pots caught crabs and lobsters which were in abundance. Each day a net was lowered across the water on ebb tides, catching fish retreating into the open sea after feeding from the rocks.

Vikings End was equipped to deal with any emergency, its many smaller caves housing most of the supplies, but Tar had found it necessary to find extra space, and some of their armoury and other equipment were stored further along the coastline, in a couple of smaller well hidden caves.

Tar now had a life similar to that of Turds in Casablanca, with all his needs and desires catered for. He let off a long low rumbling fart as he crossed the causeway to Seynourg and laughed throatily, then continued to rejoin his magnificent life at Vikings End.

He was now a very very rich man.

CHAPTER THIRTEEN

Etheltread

The physician in Dorchester, had given Etheltread a bottle of brandy to keep him quiet, while he reset his leg. It was now strapped neatly, and he could bear some weight on it with the aid of a stick.

His eye was a stickier problem. The only people who dealt with such things were in London, but the physician kept a large box, for just such emergencies. The box contained different coloured pebbles, collected from local beaches, then polished 'til they were shiny. He told Tread, that if he didn't put something in the empty socket, it would close up, and he would never be able to insert anything more in keeping. He was still most surprised when the new Baron of Dorset agreed, selecting grey and black stones. He sorted out an appropriate size, then Tread tried them both, declaring that he was well content when he looked in a glass at the frightening face it reflected.

The weedy little man suggested he might like to wear a patch until he got used to his altered face, but Etheltread declined, pleased with his new appearance.

After a few days, Etheltread had had enough of being made to rest, two more brandy bottles had been emptied, the little physician declaring he had no more.

He'd spent the days and nights in the man's private parlour, using the best chair, with his injured leg resting out straight on another. He had run the little doctor ragged with his constant demands for food and drink.

On the fifth morning after the accident, he stomped around the parlour for an hour, then shouted, "I'm off!"

"You really need more rest Sire," the physician came scurrying in from the surgery.

"I'm off, got business to attend to," Tread declared.

"I'll make up your bill then Sire, but you really must take it easy." The man scribbled some figures, added them up, frowned, then halved the total.

"Two guineas, Sire."

"Far too much," growled Etheltread and slapped a single sovereign on the parlour table, then stomped out through the surgery.

"What about all the brandy?"

"Tasted better," muttered Tread, and was gone.

His first port of call was the first tavern he set eye on, in dire need of a stiff drink, having been without for two days. He stomped up to the bar and stared at the serving wench. The colour drained from the girl's face, as she took a step back, picking up a bell and ringing for the landlord.

"Brandy, very large," ordered Tread in his usual loud voice.

The girl recovered and placed his drink on the bar. The landlord surfaced from a trapdoor in the serving area which led to the cellar.

"Blimey mate," the landlord exclaimed looking from Tread's eye to his extra large drink. "Looks like you're already stoned."

"Anymore remarks like that and I'll double your taxes," Tar growled at the man.

"Blimey Sire, didn't realise it was you, no offence meant," stuttered the landlord.

"None taken, give me another drink. I won't be paying."

"Certainly Sire, right away Sire," replied the landlord after his faux pas.

Tread took four more large brandies, glaring at anyone who dared to stare at him, before he stomped out of the tavern.

His next stop was the livery stable a few buildings along from the tavern, where he hired a horse. He made his way to a tall building in a courtyard, where a brass plate on the wall announced The Offices of Grumblegut Grumblegut and Grumblegut. The door was answered by Grumblegut senior.

"You'd better cross out the middle name on your sign," Tread announced without preamble.

"Good morning Sire. Why is that, pray?" answered Grumbleguts senior, trying to look pleased to see his frightening visitor, whose breath reminded him that he needed a drink.

"Invite me in, open the brandy and I'll tell yer."

Grumblegut senior was addicted to snuff, two rivulets of treacle like substance, escaping from his nostrils, before he arrested them with a stained brown silk handkerchief.

Having listened to Etheltread relate the tragic events, which had already been told by his younger brother, Grumblegut senior didn't seem too distressed, his mind had already calculated the extra profit from the business, which would now be shared by two instead of three.

He excused himself, and left Tread sat in one of the high backed leather chairs at one side of a cheery fire, clutching a triple brandy. The Baron of Dorset had poured himself another, before the stout little chap waddled back into the room, clutching a piece of parchment.

"There is another copy of the will, Sire," trying to smile at his awesome visitor.

"Better read it then," demanded Tread.

Grumblegut senior poured himself a small drink then plonked into the chair opposite.

"The estate comes to you Sire, as the next eldest he beamed. Your father has made provision, one thousand guineas are to be shared annually between all members of the family bearing the name Ethel.

Etheltread sat quietly glaring with his good eye.

"Item number five," announced Grumblegut, taking a deep breath. "One hundred and fifty guineas is to go immediately to my other son Luke."

"Who?" yelled Etheltread leaping from his chair.

"Who," confirmed the old man continuing unruffled, "resides on Seynorgue under the name of Luke Duke."

"I'll kill him," screamed Etheltread.

"The money is to be used to buy himself and his mother a residence befitting the new Duke of Seynorgue," continued GG, waiting for the next blast.

"The hell it will," Etheltreads' face turned from deep red to deep purple, he crashed his goblet of brandy into the fire causing a mighty whoosh.

"What sort of solicitor are you?" he bellowed, "allowing the stupid piggin git to put that in?"

Grumblegut got up and poured his enraged client another drink, then sat down and continued. "The new Duke of Seynorgue will be responsible for all taxes on that piece of land, half of which will be payable to you."

"I should have it all," screamed Tread.

The old solicitor continued in a gentle voice, "His reasoning was sire, that this piece of land and its inhabitants have always proved a problem, and a local person would have more success in running it than your family has. In an effort to reach the Kingdom of Heaven he confessed his sins to your priest, the worst of which seemed to revolve around a woman called Becky and her son Luke. The priest advised him on this course of action, to atone himself to God. Also to pay the priest twenty five guineas a year for his services."

"I'll kill the piggin priest," Etheltread leapt from his chair yet again.

"Let's have a look," Tread grabbed for the parchment containing words which meant nothing to him, then "accidently" dropped it on to the fire.

"Whoops! Better write another one," he chuckled.

The small round solicitor looked aghast.

"You can't do that Sire."

"I just have, now get writing."

Etheltread dictated the new will which omitted any payments to the rest of the family, Luke Duke or the priest.

The solicitor wrote in a slow careful hand, a long hour later it was complete.

"You can't do this Sire," Grumblegut tried again.

"It's done," growled Tread. "Now make another copy, if you want to remain a solicitor to the Baron of Dorset."

With both copies in front of him, Etheltread removed his Father's ring, which he now wore, and placed it into the hot sealing wax at the bottom of each. He then made a cross next to both seals, which, except to a cross expert, would look exactly like his Father's cross.

"Now witness it," he instructed.

The little solicitor wrote under Etheltreads' cross, ILLEGAL on both copies and handed one back to his client.

Etheltread stared at it out of his single eye, unable to read the writing "is this correct?" he demanded.

"Yes Sire," Grumblegut replied truthfully in a strong voice, which belied the tension in his body.

The solicitor returned to his chair by the fire, and sank down shaking, then poured himself a huge brandy after his gruesome guest had stomped out, clutching one of the copies of the new will.

Grumblegut certainly hadn't had the guts to tell this monster there was another copy of the original will. "That will have to sort itself out later," he sighed.

Etheltread rode out of Dorchester heading for Blandford and his brother's Manor where he had never been. He was amazed at the well kept land he crossed, having entered through a large archway, where two stone stags stared down at him. More deer, real ones this time, roamed the gentle meadows either side of the long straight drive which led to a magnificent house.

He dismounted at the block in the yard where several coaches were lined up, a groom hurried across to help him as he swung his straight leg over the horse.

"Go and get your master," Tread glared down at the man, refusing help.

A few moments later Ethelbert appeared.

"Hi brother, hope you're feeling better," he called, staring in disbelief at the gruesome figure before him. Lady Michaela came down a gravel path from the house, gasped, and stood behind her husband.

"Shant be needing your services," stated Etheltread. "Thought I'd come and have a look and decide for meself how much rent I should be collecting from this place."

Immediately on guard, Ethelbert stood in front of the frightening spectacle, which he was about to invite into the house.

"You won't be collecting any rent old chap, I bought this lock stock and barrel off the old man. Grumblegut's have got a copy of the deeds if you don't believe me," the Lord of Blandford stood his ground and stared back at the baleful eye of his brother.

"All I'll be paying you are half the taxes I collect each year."

Etheltread's terrible face looked even more so, as he climbed onto the mounting block and straddled the horse, turning away without another word.

The Baron of Dorset hadn't intended going back into Dorchester, but cut across country to the Grand Manor, now with the bad news he'd just heard, he wanted to check that his brother wasn't lying, and actually did own Blandford Manor.

He rode out of Dorchester even more angry, after Grumbleguts had confirmed that Ethelbert was indeed Lord of Blandford, owned all the buildings and land, with no rent payable.

The poor horse was relieved when his miserable journey back to the Manor was over. Its rider had never been satisfied, geeing him up when he went too slow, and geeing him down when he went too fast.

Etheletread stomped into the great hall. The rubble from the collapsed ceiling had all been cleared away. High above him through a large hole, he could see his father's four poster bed, suspended by stout ropes tied to the roof joists. Two Woodburghers were busy sawing and hammering at the broken beams which had supported his father's bedroom.

Etheltread stomped into the kitchen where Ethelethel and his niece Ethelegs were sat at the kitchen table, preparing vegetables, with a scullery maid and the cook.

The scullery maid looked up, screamed, and ran out of the back door.

"What's up with her, silly cow?" demanded Tread.

The other three looked at the gruesome dirty face in disbelief, before Ethelegs giggled and ventured, "well you do look a bit stony faced uncle."

"Never mind that dear come and sit down take something to drink how's your leg does it still hurt?" Ethelethel gestured to a chair without taking a breath.

"Yes, better and yes," muttered Etheltread.

He was in the midst of relating what had gone on in Dorchester when the two Ethelreds appeared and stood staring at their eldest brother.

"Stop gawping dears come and sit down and listen to what your brother has to say," Ethelethel commanded in one mouthful.

Cook scurried about bringing food and drink, as the family Ethel sat with the servants of the Manor. The scullery maid sidled back in to sit down very close to Ethelegs at the far end of the table.

"Get me the priest," he instructed Ginger II.

An hour later the youngest son returned, accompanied by the family priest, whom he had interrupted writing a sermon at the rear of the family chapel.

The man was ushered into the Great Hall, where the family had now deposited themselves.

Bowing low, he shuffled in. "Bless you Sire and bless your family," his voice coming in its usual lilting chant.

"Don't bother with all that nonsense," growled Etheltread. He proudly unrolled the new will, pointing at the seal and the cross below the writing.

"Read that priest, it's a copy of the will that went up in smoke," he lied.

The holy man glanced nervously at the awesome face before him.

"Well get on with it," demanded Etheltread.

"This is the Last Will and Testament of Ethelfoot Baron of Dorsetshire," the priest read slowly, a small frown creased his brow as he continued. "All my land, property and wealth to pass to my eldest son Etheltread, who will also inherit the title Baron of Dorset on my demise." He stopped, his frown becoming more pronounced.

"Well?" demanded Etheltread.

"It had your father's mark and seal Sire." He crossed himself, "and is witnessed by his solicitor."

"Right, that's it priest, now get out," commanded the new Baron.

The man looked fearfully at his master and the rest of the unhappy family, his mind was in a whirl, knowing the will was wrong, and having read Grumblegut's final word, ILLEGAL.

Should he repeat what was written?

His conscience said yes, but common sense said no. He thankfully but unhappily, made his retreat.

"What about us?" demanded Ginger I.

"Nothin'," sneered Tread.

"We've got to have something dear Papa used to make me an allowance and all your brothers and sisters used to get one too." Ethelethels face for once looked resolute.

"I know," the Baron conceded, "I'll make you each an allowance of twenty guineas a year, which is more than generous."

Four glum faces revealed that they didn't think it was generous at all.

"Ethelbert owns Blandford Manor lock stock and barrel," he went on, "and he doesn't have to pay any piggin rent."

"Oh we knew that," replied the family.

"Why don't you wear a patch over your eye?" Ginger II enquired.

"Why don't you mind your own business?" came back the grouchy reply.

"Well I think it looks very posh, in a frightening sort of way," sniggered Ethelegs. "Your subjects can call you Etheltread the Terrible."

"So do I," agreed the Baron of Dorset, "and they can. Now what have you done with all the stuff which fell through the ceiling?"

Ethelethel fumbled with her dress, fishing a key, which had been suspended on a piece of twine around her neck, from her ample bosom.

"All safe and sound dear the boys all helped to move it before the servants came back on the morning you went to Dorchester its locked in the barn on the other side of the yard." Ethelethel finally drew a long breath.

It wasn't long before the kitchen door was banged open. "Where's the rest of the gold?" the fiercesome figure in the doorway demanded at the top of his voice.

While Tread the terrible went to inspect his inheritance, the family had wandered back to the kitchen where they now sat in silence, each with their own miserable thoughts of how rich they thought they should have been, except for Ethelegs who still seemed quite perky.

"The trunk's nearly empty," he yelled, his face turning various shades of red and purple.

"Its all there dear I've had the key since the boys helped move it," Ethelethel replied gently.

"It piggin ain't, helped themselves is what you mean," Etheltread was almost jumping up and down as he yelled back at his sister. Then his eye fell out.

Ethelegs burst out laughing, then had to hastily duck under the table pulling the scullery maid with her, as her uncle launched cooking utensils at the place where she had sat.

"I'm gonna piggin thrash you," he shouted, rounding the table.

The two girls jumped from their refuge and ran out of the door into the great hall, then outside and disappeared.

"If some of the money's gone dear could someone have got into the barn?" soothed Ethelethel.

"Of course they piggin have," Tread yelled.

"You Gingers, go and find Big Mac, don't tell him what's happened, I want to see all the Burghers in here now, one by one."

It was the evening of the next day before the last servant left the kitchen shaken and scared. The whole time had been taken up by Etheltread roasting Big Mac and grilling the Burghers.

His fears were now confirmed. None of them had the slightest idea about what he was talking about. It was one of the family, and he bet he knew which one. He considered each of them.

Ethelbert had taken him to be patched up in Dorchester, when the gold and other trinkets had been moved.

Ethelethel wouldn't steal a penny.

Ethelegs was too silly and wouldn't have the guts. (Wrong).

Ethelgay was too much of a poof. (Wrong).

Ethelete was dead.

The two Reds were too stupid.

Etheltar had helped, yes Etheltar had helped himself. (Almost right).

He'd have to kill him to get it back he mused, but first he had to catch him. His immediate problem was, that half the gold would have been used to pay the annuity to the crown, which was due just after Christmas. There wasn't enough.

The taxes due to be collected in November from the Lords of the Manors and his own serfs would cover the bill, but still leave his own fortune in tatters.

Etheltread called Big Mac to take a message to Grumblegut, telling him to prepare a hundred notices.

When a messenger returned with a large bundle of parchment in July, Big Mac was once again, with the help of two trusted Burghers, instructed to visit all the Lords of the Manors, then the main towns and larger villages of Dorsetshire to display the proclamations, which stated:

TAX DUE IN NOVEMBER
WILL INCREASE TWOFOLD
By order of
The New Baron of Dorset.

Ethelegs now had to dodge her uncle, his vile temper rising to the surface whenever their paths met.

Megan, the scullery maid only two years younger than her mistress had developed an embarrassing crush, following her around cow eyed, whenever she was not kept busy by the cook.

Six weeks after her uncle's return to the Grand Manor Ethelegs had had enough, not daring to go near him, as this would produce a swipe from the stick he now constantly carried.

She whispered in Ethelethel's ear, then instructed Megan to pack all of her clothes without anyone else knowing. One dark evening the pair of them slipped away in a pony and trap, the valise of clothes resting neatly on top of the pail full of gold coins which she had retrieved from the dairy.

CHAPTER FOURTEEN

Becky the Booful

Becky, Luke's mother had finally come completely out of her shell with the news of Ethelfoot's death.

For the last ten years she had buried the horrors which she had endured deep in her mind. She never told Luke who his father was, not wanting to answer the inevitable questions the boy would pose. Now the fear was lifted, the fear that he still might come and get her was gone.

That joyous day she had been crowned May Queen all those years ago, had turned to terror when Ethelfoot grabbed her from the stage and galloped away from Seynorgue.

She had been locked in the cellar of a large house, with a single hard bed, a rough table and chair. The only light in the damp prison coming through a small barred window, which she could only just see through, when she stood on the chair.

Her food was brought into her by people wearing smocks with a large letter B sewn on them. Her toilet consisted of a bucket which was removed everyday and replaced with a clean one. Water for drinking and washing was also delivered by the B people, who never spoke to her.

One morning, after about a week in the terrible place, the door was swung open by Ethelfoot.

"Right girl, you are now mine," the ugly obese figure advanced into her cell.

Becky cowered into a corner.

"If you do all I tell yer, your life will get a lot piggin better," he growled in a low gravelly voice.

A huge hand reached out to touch her, Becky swung her leg and kicked as hard as she could. The Baron bellowed in pain, doubling over. Becky spat in his ugly face. Staring up at her in anguish, he had retreated backwards from the cellar, still clutching the point where Becky's foot had caught him.

An hour passed, then two large B men entered. Becky was whipped and beaten until she passed out.

Two days went by, in which she was given no food, nobody came to change her buckets and the cellar began to stink.

At last, a gaunt B woman, with hard eyes, unlocked the door, giving her food and fresh water. As she removed the foul bucket she muttered, "Better do what he wants girlie or it'll be the worst for you."

More days passed, once again the Baron visited her cell.

"Come to your senses yet girl?" he shouted at her.

"No, and I never will," she yelled back, the first words she had spoken since her capture. Taking a knife from her plate of uneaten food she thrust the point against her throat. Ethelfoot stepped back, seeing the intent in her eyes.

Once again she was thrashed by the two large men then left with no food and no water.

It was three days before the gaunt woman came to her cell. Becky had resorted to licking the damp walls in an effort to gain moisture. The woman placed a tray with bread and cheese and what appeared to be a jug of wine on the table. The girl was already tipping the jug to her mouth, letting the strange tasting liquid relieve her parched throat, as the woman placed a clean bucket on the floor, and took out her foul slops. She closed and locked the door without a word.

She awoke the next day with her head swirling, her body feeling as if it had taken another beating. Her dress was in tatters, there was blood dried on to her legs, both her arms were covered in bruises. She eased the torn dress away from her body, each of her breasts were bruised with what appeared to be massive bites.

Slowly the awful truth dawned on her, she pulled up the hem of her dress, then stared in disbelief at her lower body covered in blood and bites.

The B woman came into the cell, carrying a bowl of water and a smock.

"Get yourself clean, then put this on," she instructed. She stood over Becky as she washed and dressed.

"Out," she said, pointing at the still open door. Becky was taken up into a large kitchen, then through into another room, where the B woman instructed two gross females, with large blotchy faces, and even larger blotchy arms, "put her to work, and keep an eye on her, if she escapes there'll be hell to pay."

The next miserable months were spent washing filthy laundry in the steamy scullery. No one spoke to her and she received a slap if her work wasn't to the women's liking. The gross pair took it in turns to help cook in the kitchen, but she was never left alone. The only thing she looked forward to was the food, she now had a place at the table in the kitchen, where the servants ate the same food which cook had prepared for the family Ethel.

She now slept in a large dormitory, at the rear of the house, with ten of the Burgher women, as she had discovered they were called, her bed at the back of the room, furthest away from the door.

One afternoon while her two minders were arguing, which they often did, Becky unlatched the door and slipped out unnoticed, then she ran.

Two hours later, she was dragged back to the house, taken down to the cellar and beaten again.

A week of misery with only bread and water ended, when once again the gaunt Burgher woman, who she now knew to be the housekeeper, in charge of all the female servants, escorted her once more to the scullery.

"Do that again and he'll probably kill yer, if he don't I will," she informed her.

Months passed, Becky couldn't understand why her body had started to become so gross, then one day she was taken to the dormitory and locked in, one of the women tended to her without a word.

During a bitterly cold February, although days and months had all blended into one miserable blur, Becky gave birth to a baby boy and was kept locked in for a further three days, until the housekeeper came in, told her to get up and get back to work.

The baby was put in a box in the corner of the scullery, where she was allowed to tend him during meal times.

Ethelfoot never came into the servants area, but his children were regular visitors to the kitchen, pestering cook for titbits. She caught glimpses of him at odd times, through the kitchen window, often she heard his gravelly voice raised at one of the Burghers.

The only person who showed her any kindness was the family's' eldest girl, who often came to the kitchen to see the baby, sometimes bringing clothes cast off from the family's infants.

Her infant grew into a delightful little boy, inheriting his mother's beautiful eyes, which looked enquiringly from his devilish little face, taking in all the comings and goings of the scullery and kitchen. He was allowed to play with two other children, which belonged to male Burghers, when their fathers brought them with them whilst doing work around the outside of the house. Becky tended the child she had named Luke, but could find no love in her heart for him, although her heart missed a beat when on several occasions she saw Ethelfoot in the yard talking to the children.

Becky's miserable existence continued. Years passed, occasionally one of the other servants spoke to her, but never kindly, until one day a golden opportunity offered itself, and she grabbed it with both hands.

Burghers had been building a stone wall to the rear of the house, enclosing the kitchen garden. Twice over the last few months, cattle had broken down the rickety wooden fence, trampling the salad vegetables and tearing down the washing which was hung out to dry.

On the second occasion it was mealtime, everyone rushed to the kitchen window hearing shouts from their Lord and Master. One of the beasts brought a rare smile to her face, a large bedsheet was draped over its head, the terrified animal rushed hither and thither pursued by several Burghers and the Baron. Suddenly it turned, and charged the chasing group, catching Ethelfoot with the side of its body, depositing him in a pile of manure used to nurture the plants.

Now the wall was nearly completed. Luke was playing with Olly and Lucy, the Burghers children, whilst they worked. A rumble and then an almighty crash alarmed the staff working in the kitchen and scullery. Desperate cries for help followed. The two gross sweaty scullery maids rushed out into the kitchen, Becky followed. Cook had already run out of the kitchen door, Becky's two minders chased after her.

A large section of the new wall had collapsed, Becky went outside for the first time since her escape years before. One of the

Burghers was lying next to a great pile of rubble, the other was trapped by his legs yelling at the top of his voice. Only two children were visible, when there should have been three.

"He's under here," the trapped Burgher yelled.

Becky gasped, then to her relief one of the children ran to her.

"The wall fell down Ma," Luke cried. "Olly's underneath it."

The other child was now being cuddled by cook. The two fat scullery maids were screaming. Other Burghers came running, Ethelfoot charged out from the house, demanding what all the noise was about. The Burghers frantically pulled at the large stones which had made up the wall. The current mistress of the house came rushing out with the children and all the interior maids, they stood staring at the mayhem.

Becky gave Luke's small hand a squeeze, went back through the kitchen door, out through the door leading to the great hall then slipped out of the front entrance.

Becky didn't make the same mistake as the last time she tried to escape. She ran for half an hour down the single wide carriage way which she had been carried along all those years ago, then struck off into a large field of cut grass which had been raked into many small stacks, ready to be loaded onto carts and taken in for winter animal feed. Lifting Luke into her arms she raced across the open field, scared that at any minute she would hear a cry from the roadway behind her. Thankfully they made it to the far side undetected. Gratefully Becky lowered the boy down next to one of the stacks, then burrowed into the sweet smelling stalks, dragging the frightened child after her. She made a nest in the centre of the stack, pulling her entranceway closed behind them. Mother and son lay cuddled together, the boy whimpering, Becky's breath coming in small sobs.

It was over an hour before her disappearance was noticed. The Burghers finally uncovering the small dead body, others easing out the man who had both legs crushed. Three sobbing women filed back into the kitchen and sat down shakily at the table, leaving the housekeeper and Burghers tending to the casualties.

"Where's the girl?" cook suddenly exclaimed.

One of the fat scullery maids jumped up and bustled to the scullery door.

"She ain't here missus," the woman turned with a look of fear, the last time her charge had escaped it wasn't only her who felt the sting of the master's whip.

The boy was calm and had fallen asleep on their soft bed. Becky eased herself out to the edge of the mound, poked a small hole and looked out. She breathed a huge sigh of relief, nobody. The carriageway was empty as was the field. With Luke peaceful behind her, she also started to doze. Sounds jerked her instantly awake, all the fear flooding back. Horses were charging along the road, their riders yelling and waving sticks, in the lead was the man included in all of her nightmares, his huge round body astride a great black stallion, he clutched a sword in his great fist. Becky pulled back into their nest pulling her peephole closed and lay quivering next to her sleeping son. She lay for an age, not daring to move a muscle, Luke started to stir. Taking a deep breath the girl inched forward again, slowly pulling aside the grasses, daylight had turned to dusk. No one was in sight. Luke started to whimper again, she began to slide back to him, when a movement at the edge of her vision turned her sense of relief once more into terror. The line of horses were coming back up the road.

The line stopped.

"Do you want us to search the field master?" she heard the Burgher's voice clearly in the night air.

Luke's whimpers were becoming louder, hastily she withdrew and pulled the child to her. They lay together, Becky cuddling the boy to her body quietening his murmurs.

A noise reached her ears, then voices.

"You must be brave, don't make a sound boy, they're bad men who will hurt us," she breathed in the lads ear.

She almost screamed herself, but had the presence of mind to clasp her hand gently across Luke's mouth as a pole was thrust into the mound, then another an inch from their faces. The boy started and tried to struggle, but she held him even firmer.

Quiet, then voices and sounds again.

Then silence again.

They lay together shivering for two more hours before Becky plucked up courage, crawled forward and peered out.

A three quarter moon, low in the sky, cast a ghostly light across the hayfield. The girl stared intently, she could see no horses on the roadway and nobody in the field. Pulling Luke up next to her she made another small hole in the grasses.

"Tell me if you can see anybody," she gently whispered in his ear.

The pair lay motionless, only their eyes moving.

"No Ma I can't see anyone. Should I?" the boy whispered back after several minutes.

Becky waited another hour, then gripping the boy's arms, pulled him gently after her out from their hiding place. She stood motionless, fearing that any moment hands would be clamped on to her.

The only life in the field was Becky and Luke, plus half a dozen rabbits, playing in the loose grass.

They moved from mound to mound, Becky bent low, stopping at each stack looking and listening. They made it to the carriageway, the only fright, when an owl hooted above them, scattering the family of rabbits.

Whispering to Luke to lay at the edge of the field, Becky crawled on to the verge of the track and looked fearfully in both directions.

Nothing.

Beckoning the child, the pair crept along the verge looking ahead and behind. Becky had no idea where she was heading, only that it was away from the fearful place.

Soon woodland bordered onto their side of the roadway, the girl felt safer with an instant hiding place should anyone come along the track. The pair trudged on for several miles, Becky was proud of her small son, who didn't complain. A wooden bridge wide enough for a horse and cart spanned a small stream, the pair clambered down to the water's edge, thankfully drinking and splashing their faces. They then rested for a while, before the girl said "ready to walk some more?"

"I'm hungry Ma." The little chap looked up at her with tears in his eyes.

"We'll find some food soon," Becky comforted, not having the faintest idea where.

On they went, the only sounds coming from wild animals in the thick woodland which now bordered both sides of the track.

Thankfully the night air was still warm, as the pair only had flimsy rags covering their bodies.

The small boy was lagging behind again when the first birds started to call, closely followed by a dawn chorus, welcoming the new day. Becky took Luke's hand and selected a pathway made by game, breaking through the brambles on opposite sides of the track. The lightening sky revealed early blackberries, which they picked cramming the sweet fruit into their mouths. The brambles gave way to beech woods, the ground was carpeted with beech nuts, their small spiky shucks easily opened to reveal the small kernels within.

The girl's mood of despair lifted with food inside her, Luke was engrossed popping each of the shells, but he was desperately tired.

The trees finally came to an end, beyond a grassy meadow was a low hillside covered in ferns, a herd of deer grazing peacefully further up. Through a gap in the growth Becky could see water running down across rocks. She waited for Luke, taking his small hand in hers once again, she led the boy along the meadow, then followed the tumbling stream up into the ferns. The deer stared at them for a while, then continued munching.

They drank from the stream, then carefully parted the vegetation, finally sinking down into the covering fronds.

The sun was high in the sky before the pair awoke. Becky sat up slowly, peering down over the ferns towards the meadow and the wood. The deer had moved down on to the grass, lying peacefully in the warm sunlight.

Nobody's frightened them while we've been asleep, reasoned the girl.

As daylight dimmed Mother and child went down to the wood, Becky carrying a basket made from ferns. They spent an hour collecting beech nuts and blackberries before returning to their soft hillside beds. They ate and slept.

When morning came they feasted again on the nuts and berries they had collected, the deer were further along the slope, they watched while the herd meandered down to the meadow, then lay down where the sun had warmed the ground.

They drank from the stream, then washed and played, certain their distant companions would give due warning of any intruders. Then they rested again safe on the covered hillside.

As the sun sank out of sight the girl asked, "Ready to do some more walking?"

The boy nodded eagerly, bored now with their surroundings.

Once again they filled the fern basket as they walked through the woods, then picked blackberries which they ate whilst they picked their way along the brambly path. It was almost night as they stepped out on to the verge.

"Horses, Ma," Luke tugged at the girl's rags.

They slipped back into the cover and slid beneath the prickles as two Burghers galloped by, in the direction of the Manor.

Two hours later they crept out once more, no one else having come up or down the road. Again they marched, stopping every few paces to listen, and every couple of hours to rest. They had eaten all their nuts, and were now once again desperately thirsty. Either side of the track now, the silver moonlight revealed fields of corn, some of which had been cut.

It was almost dawn. Becky was thinking of somewhere to rest, Luke was getting slower and slower. With harvesting in process, the cornfields were going to be a risky hiding place. Ahead she could see the carriageway crossed a wide cobbled yard, farm buildings were to one side, and further back a large farmhouse.

What did she do? Cross the yard before it got light, or hide in one of the fields. She decided to go on. Putting her finger to her lips warning the boy to be quiet, the pair crept across the cobbles.

That was when their luck changed.

Suddenly two snarling trufflemouzers blocked their path, Becky turned, another collie type dog ran out behind them barking. There was no escape.

A light appeared in one of the hovels windows, then a man at the doorway holding a lantern.

"What's all the noise you hounds?" he yelled, advancing to where Becky and Luke stood. He was large and bewhiskered, wearing a smock.

"Oh, I sees now," he came up to the frightened pair holding the lantern high.

"I've been arf expectin you two, you'd bedder come along with me up to the house."

The man shepherded Becky who was crying, and Luke in front of him, the dogs trailing behind.

"His Lordship said to look on out for a girlie and her son," he said as they came to the door of the farmhouse. The man spat on the ground.

"They're 'ere Mother," he called.

A short plump woman came to the doorway, also holding a lantern.

"You look dun in," she exclaimed. "You bedder come along in."

Becky and Luke followed the little round lady into the hovel.

"You'd best sit down afore you falls down," the man said following the pair, then turned to the dogs who had ventured in behind him, commanding "Out" in a stern voice, but adding "good boys" in a far nicer one.

A low fire was glowing in a huge hearth adding light to the two lanterns, but the little lady busied herself lighting several candles. Becky and Luke sat at a large table, and watched nervously for what was to come next.

The woman turned and faced the pair. "Oh you poor dears, what has that evil man done to ee?"

"His Lordship, the Baron of Dorset, could have done anything," said the man and spat again, this time into the fire.

"Don't do that Father, 'taint nice," the woman admonished.

"Are you going to take us back?" Becky asked slowly.

"Glory no dearie, I wouldn't give a dog to that beast."

Becky let out a sigh, a wan smile creased her face.

"My you are a pretty one," said the woman, "and what a 'ansome little chap."

Luke grinned back at her.

"I spect you're hungry you poor dears, Father stoke up the fire and I'll get some breakfast."

The candles and lanterns had been snuffed out, Becky now sat in front of the fire in a rocking chair, Luke was on the floor in front of her fussing one of the trufflemouzers that had snuck in the back door. For the first time since they had crept out the front door of the Manor she felt at ease.

The four had eaten a huge breakfast of eggs, ham, wild mushrooms and bread, washed down with warm cows milk.

Luke informed the kindly pair, "This is me Ma Becky and my name's Luke."

The whiskered man burst out laughing. Becky described what had happened to her and some of the horrors she had endured.

"Dang if I dunno who you are," shouted the man slapping his thigh. "You're Becky the Booful."

Becky blushed bright red. She learnt that the kindly couple had farmed the land on either side of the carriageway since they were married, thirty years ago.

"Don't you have any children?" she asked at one point.

"Not any more dearie," the lady's face lost its cheery smile, she turned away dabbing at her eyes with her apron. Becky didn't ask again.

She learnt that the couple dreaded Ethelfoot, his family and his Burghers, the woman whose name was Daffy, having to stop her husband spitting each time the Duke's name was mentioned.

The warmth from the fire and Becky's exhaustion soon took effect.

"Come along dearie, bed for you two," the lady ushered them into another room.

"Get those filthy rags off, have a quick rinse there," she pointed to a bowl and jug on a washstand at the side of the room, "then you can snuggle into our bed."

The tired little boy was instantly asleep on the large feather mattress, his Mother next to him covered by cotton sheets and a heavy quilt, luxury the girl had never experienced. There was a gentle knock on the door.

"Come in," said Becky quietly.

"Alright dearie?" asked the little plump lady from the doorway.

"Lovely," replied Becky.

The lady withdrew and was replaced by her husband.

"Sleep well lovely you're safe in 'ere," he said, then before closing the door, added "you can call me Father, and the missus Mother, she'd like that."

It was evening when Becky woke, she looked to the chair by the washstand where she and Luke had discarded their clothes, they were gone. Alarmed, she sat up clutching the bedclothes to her naked body. On the bottom of the bed two dresses were laid neatly with some underclothes, a brush and comb on top. Another small pile of clothes stacked neatly on top of a large trunk in the corner of the room, looked as if they had been left for Luke.

The girl got up, Luke was still fast asleep. There was now a lump of something in the bowl on the washstand, making the water smell sweet, Becky took it from the water, experimentally rubbing it on her body, it was wonderful. She washed off the greasy sweet smelling liquid the lump had produced with clean water then dried herself on a large thick cotton sheet, now hung over the chair. She dressed in the clothes choosing a cream dress, then she noticed a pair of black lace up boots tucked under her side of the bed, they looked as if they might fit. Delighted, she picked one up, a black cotton stocking and a ribbon were tucked inside, she slid the cotton up her leg and tied it with the ribbon above her knee, the boot fitted almost perfectly. Becky was overjoyed, had she found a fairy godmother. With the other stocking and boot securely tied she took the comb and ran it through her shoulder length dark hair, which she had washed in the tumbling stream. Painfully she worked on the knots until she was satisfied, then sat and brushed and brushed and brushed, finally she flicked her head delighted with the effect, her thick locks swinging in a cloud across her face.

Luke was still asleep; quietly she lifted the latch and went into the living room. The plump little lady was sat by the fire knitting.

"My," she exclaimed, staring at the beauty before her. "Father," she called. "Come and see."

The man came in from another room which Becky hadn't seen before, he closed a large sliding door.

"Well well, now we can really see why they called ee Becky the Booful."

A whimper from the bedroom alerted the girl.

"Don't worry dearie, I'll see to the little chap, you can sit and talk to Father."

"Thank you, thank you," the girl laughed, adding, "Mother and Father."

The couple beamed, and Mother scurried into the bedroom lifting her apron to her eyes. The girl and man sat either side of the fire.

"We'd like to keep ee with us," Father said. "But it be too dangerous."

Becky looked sad.

"Don't fret my lovely," the kindly man went on. "We'll get ee somewhere safe. Where was ee 'eading?"

"I don't know Father, just away from that terrible place." She thought for a few minutes, then added, "back to Seynorgue, praps my old hovel is still there." She brightened a little with the thought. "Tis far enough out of the village so's I wont be noticed." Becky went on to tell the farmer how her parents had died and she had looked after herself until that sorry May Day. Their conversation was brought to an end by Mother ushering Luke back into the room. He wore similar clothes to those Becky had seen on the young Ethels, when they came in to raid the kitchen at the Manor. A blue velvet jacket was done up over a white blouse, soft brown leather pantaloons covering his little legs were tucked into a stout pair of boots.

Over supper they continued their conversation discussing what was to become of the two. It was far too dangerous to stay, as Ethels and Burghers constantly used the roadway. The Baron had already been to the farm on the day of their escape. Mother said if they continued on foot they would have to pass through Weymouth, then along the causeways joining Portland Bill and Seynorgue, somebody was bound to spot them.

"Got it," shouted Father slapping his thigh. Then he laughed.

"What?" asked his wife.

The man's whiskered face was creased into many wrinkles as he continued laughing.

"What?" demanded Mother, exasperated.

"I'll take em next week, when I goes to Houmits market, we've got the very place in the cart. I can take em right under those Ethels and Burghers noses," he made as if to spit.

"Stoppit," commanded his wife, now also laughing.

Dusk had now darkened the cheery room. Luke sat once more playing with the trufflemouzer which had snuck past Father's guard again. The old couple got up, Mother lighting several candles dotted round the room, Father one of the lanterns. He beckoned the girl as he slid back the large door, which passed unnoticed in the room, blending with the walls. Lifting the lantern so Mother could pass him to light more candles, which revealed an area with no windows. Along the back wall was a wooden bench scrubbed spotlessly clean, on it a pair of balancing scales and several small sealed oilskin packets. Along one of the side walls several more far larger sealed oilskin sacks. On the floor a bed had been prepared from cushions, blankets and cotton sheets.

"You and the little one can sleep in here tonight, it'll be safer," the little woman bent down and patted the bed.

"What's those?" asked Luke, unable to contain his inquisitiveness.

"They's bales of tobacco Lukey," the little old lady told him. "My brother brings them into Weymouth from Americy," she went on turning to Becky.

"I unloads them from his ship with my cart when I delivers their grain, but we brings them back in the bottom of the cart under the floor," Father added.

Becky looked puzzled.

"All the goods unloaded from abroad in Dorset ports 'as to pay a duty to the Baron," Father pretended to spit. "We built a false floor in the cart, under where we carry the grain, so when we leaves the docks the Duke's man who inspects everything," another imaginary spit, "thinks wees empty."

"Then we puts it into half pound packets and sells it," beamed Daffy.

Becky stared amazed at the dear old couple who looked as if butter wouldn't melt in their mouths, successfully running a massive swindle under the nose of the Baron.

"We couldn't have all these nice things on what the farm earns with the taxes and rent we 'as to pay," Mother confided, fingering the cotton sheets and silk cushions which made up the bed.

It was four more days before Father was due to ride out to the Houmits market to deliver grain to the local baker, also sell some of his duty free baccy. Becky and Luke were treated as the couples own children, which stirred some of the girls long lost feelings from when her own parents were alive. The day before they were due to leave, the pair avoided recapture by the skin of their teeth. Becky was helping Daffy prepare vegetables for dinner, when Luke came rushing in from outside where he had been playing with the dogs.

"Horses," he gasped.

"Who's the boy?" they heard one of the mounted Burghers demanding an answer from Father.

"Boy, what boy?" the old man struggled for time.

"He was playing in the yard when we rode up," the rough voice stated.

"'spect you saw one of the dogs." Father was thinking furiously.

The Burgher was becoming suspicious. "Don't lie to me old man I knows a child when I sees a child," the Burgher started to dismount.

"Oh a child, that was my little niece," shouted the old chap slapping his thigh. "Thought you said it was a boy."

Daffy shoved Becky into the secret room sliding the door shut, then grabbing Luke's hand and whispering in his ear pulled him into the bedroom.

Becky waited, nerves strung taut, her head pressed against the sliding door. A minute passed. Then she heard the hovel's door banged open.

"Where is she then?" demanded a gruff voice.

Unseen by Becky, her son came out of the bedroom followed by the little old lady. Luke was no longer a little boy, now he wore a pretty dress, no shoes and a little bonnet covered his hair.

Becky heard Mother coax her son, "say hello to the gentleman."

Then she heard a voice which was certainly Luke, but an octave higher say, "hello thir ith a nithe day, I'm Luthey."

Becky put her hand to her mouth, suppressing a frightened giggle, as she recognised Luke was immitating one of the Burghers children back at the Manor.

"Was that you outside Lucy?" the gruff voice demanded.

"Yeth, I wath playing with the dogth."

The sound of heavy feet retreating from the room beyond the sliding door, then the gruff voice saying loudly, "you be sure to let us know if you see the pair we're looking for."

Becky started, as the door was drawn back after ten minutes silence.

Father and Mother stood proudly behind Luke. Becky let out a small scream seeing her son in a little girl's attire.

"Hello Mumthy, do you like my dreth?" the boy grinned up at her.

Becky rushed out grabbing the boy to her then burst into tears, all the pent up fear flooding out of her.

"I think you two had better stay in ere 'til you go, they Burghers might come back," laughed Father, spitting in his hand.

All evening the kindly old couple popped in and out of the secret room with more plates of food than they could eat, a pitcher of milk was delivered, followed by more blankets.

"Are you sure you're alright dears?" the little plump woman asked for the umpteenth time as she closed the door, with the pair tucked into their madeup bed.

It was still dark when Father woke them next morning and led them out into one of the barns, shutting the door before he lit a lantern. A horse was already backed into an empty cart. Mother bustled in clutching a large basket, called the girl and her son to her, hugging them both at the same time, then reluctantly let go when Father tugged at her arm indicating to the pair to climb aboard. Fresh hay had been laid on the floor of the cart, there was a stone bottle containing water.

Becky and Luke lay down on the hay then Father fitted boards above them, completely shutting out the light. For a moment Becky panicked then she felt a draft of air beneath her. The cramped space allowed her and the boy to lay on their backs fronts or sides, but not much more. Becky heard Father shovel grain into the cart, the false floor fitted so well that none of the seeds found their way into the secret compartment.

After about an hour the cart jerked. "Are you alright my dears?" Mother called, knocking at the side of their refuge.

"Alright Mother, thank you, thank you," Becky called back.

"Bye Mother," called Luke, and they were off, bumping over the cobbles in the yard.

The girl was relieved when they reached the track and the jolting stopped, the cart trundled along in a gently swaying rhythm.

Becky didn't know how long she had dozed, but pinpricks of light now penetrated their space. They both took a swig at the water bottle. The cart rumbled on, then stopped. She heard a loud voice demanding, "What are you carrying farmer and where yer going?"

She had to suppress a giggle when Father answered, "taking gold bars to the moon."

"Don't mess with me, old man." The other voice was angry.

"Grain to the Houmits market Sir, sorry Sir."

"On yer way then and remember who you're speaking to in future."

Becky could imagine Father spitting over the side of the cart.

After about another half an hour the cart once again bumped over cobbles. There were many noises and smells now, which Becky recognised from years before in the marketplace.

The cart stopped, a voice greeted, "morning Ralf," a name she had only heard Mother use once when she was a little bit cross.

"We'll shovel it straight into my cart," said the voice. "Got anything else?"

Becky heard a muttered reply from Father, then the sounds of shovels plunging into the load, finally scraping the false timber floor just above their heads.

"How much?" asked the voice.

More muttering, then they were off again. Another half an hour's riding, not so smooth now, as the cart bounced along Becky knew it was the track she had given Father directions to follow. The cart stopped.

"Keep quiet," whispered Father through the side of their compartment.

Becky was becoming alarmed, long minutes passed, then suddenly one of the boards above their heads was slid back. The whiskery face the pair had come to love, smiled down at them.

"All's well lovely, your place is still empty, don't look like anyone's ever been there. Out you come then, nobody around."

Father pulled back the remaining boards.

The old hovel was about five minutes walk off the track, Becky, stiff from her ride, but Luke scampering ahead unaffected. It was indeed as the pair's saviour had described, even the book Becky had been trying to read lay open on the bed at the same page.

"Please come and visit us," Becky pleaded as the old man took his leave, having placed the huge basket of food on the dusty table.

"Course I will my lovely, me and Mother wants to see ee both again."

The old chap pulled Luke to him and broke into tears. Becky eventually pulled the boy away and threw her arms around his neck giving him a long loving kiss on his whiskery cheek.

Mother and son walked with Father to his cart, "I've put a little somethin' else for you in the basket," he said, turning the horse back the way it had come.

"Thank you, thank you, I will never be able to repay your kindness," Becky cried after him, between huge sobs as he trundled off down the track.

"Look out for thoth Burgherth," called Luke. They saw the old man shake with laughter, then lean over the side of the cart and spit.

In amongst the basket of food was tucked a small purse containing five gold coins, Becky sat on the bed, pulled the boy to her letting her tears fall uncontrolled.

The old man visited Becky and her son several times over the next couple of years, once bringing his little plump wife with him. Each time a basket of food was left on the now scrubbed table, and each time there was a small purse containing money. Then the visits stopped. Another year went by.

When taxes were due to be collected by Ethels and Burghers, Becky and Luke went into the woods at the rear of the hovel during the days, only returning at night to sleep inside out of the cold air, each morning leaving their home looking as if it was still unoccupied. Occasionally they heard a cart or a horse on the track below the hovel, but no one ever came up the pathway.

Becky and Luke were sat outside the little home, filling a basket with jars of jam and pots of ointment, which she made from berries collected in the wood, the boy was now old enough to take these into market. They were engrossed in their work, the boy chatting as he always did about the wonders of the marketplace he would visit the next day. Suddenly aware, Becky looked up, a man stood on the pathway only yards from where they sat.

"Run," Becky screamed scrambling to her feet.

"Don't be afraid Becky," a kindly voice called, "I'm Daffy's brother."

They both stopped.

"I'm afraid I've brought bad news, Ralf and Daffy are dead."

Becky gasped and sat down again, Luke started to cry.

The man came and sat next to the pair. "When I got back from Americy this time, Ralf came to the ship and told me Daffy was ill. I went back with him to the farm and stayed for a while, then one afternoon Ralf also took to his bed. I found them next morning cuddled together."

Becky slipped onto her side, tears streaming down her face, jerking as great sobs racked her body.

"What's happened to the dogs sir?" Luke stammered between tears.

"Call me Darcy, Luke," said the kindly man, "everyone does. The mouzers died last year, one of Ralfs friends has taken the collie," the man answered in a soft kind voice not unlike his sisters. "Ralf and Daffy are buried in the churchyard down Weymouth, everybody came, church was full."

"Not everybody," Becky sobbed, holding her face in her hands.

"C'mon, I've got somethin' for ee," the man got up and led the pair down the path to where the horse and cart which had brought them home was standing. He lifted down the large trunk Becky had seen in the old couple's bedroom. He lifted the lid and revealed neatly stacked clothes.

"They wanted you to 'ave these," he said, "they belong to their children."

"What happened to them?" asked Luke.

"The girl was about eighteen and the boy ten, when they were run down one evening by a coach carrying the Baron, 'bout six year ago," the kindly man replied. "Twas a accident, but the swine only said they shouldn't 'ave been in the road."

"Oh no," wailed Becky, sinking to her knees her head over the trunk, uncontrollable grief spilling on to the beautifully kept clothes.

Darcy helped carry the trunk up the path into the hovel, he then sat chatting to Mother and son, sharing a bottle of wine he had brought with him, Luke being allowed his first taste.

"I'll come and see ee agin if yer want," he said as he mounted the cart.

"Oh please do," Becky through her arms around their new friend.

That evening Becky and Luke made a wooden cross which they embedded into a mossy hillock in the wood behind the hovel, then scattered woodland flowers all around it.

Now, years on, Becky had become a regular in the Houmits market selling her jams and potions. She'd gone with Luke, the son she now loved with all her heart, the first few times, but he was now far more involved in the trufflemouzer farm. Her pale face once again tanned, adding to her natural beauty. Becky was at last ready to face the world again.

CHAPTER FIFTEEN

The Find

Three young shining white bodies cavorted naked, whooping and laughing in the surf. Around them several trufflemouzers swam and stuck their heads into shallower water catching crabs. More mouzers ferreted along the sandy beach, excited by the smells of sea creatures.

Skinny wartnose Fred decided he wasn't quite so keen on his first taste of sea water, leaving the other two, he waded ashore, then up the beach of the small cove they had discovered.

The three lads had decided to make the most of their two days off from the trufflemouzer farm, and explore another part of Seynorgue. It was possibly the last hot days of the long hot summer, which was fast turning into autumn. Beech leaves already showing red amongst the green as they struck off to the right of Bramleys homestead, clutching two flagons of cider which the wizened old pig man, who now had his own two trufflemouzers, had refused payment for. Pippin his wife, had loaded their bags with cakes and pies, enough for a small army, delighted with her chance of showing off her cooking skills to someone other than her old man.

This was new territory to the three, Luke and Nobby not wishing to repeat their strange, frightening experience, the night they ventured straight on beyond the old pig mans place. After a couple of miles of walking through the beech woods, excited trufflemouzers running in all directions, bringing back presents of rabbits, pigeons and squirrels, the ground rose sharply, beech giving way to pine, in some places thick enough to close out the sky. Thankfully the ground levelled out after the boys had been trudging uphill, after twenty minutes, the trees were less dense, but the surface of the ground was still covered in a thick carpet of pine needles. Fallen pine cones picked up and thrown by the boys provided new excitement for the mouzers, chasing and retrieving, then dropping the missiles at their master's feet tails wagging like mad, barking for more. Wood ants busily attended huge piles of shavings and pine needles, one of which a mouzer inquisitively stuck his nose into, then retreated hastily spending the next few minutes rubbing his snout along the ground, followed by alarmed rubbing of his face with his paws.

"He won't do that again in a hurry," Nobby laughed at the antics of the dog dislodging the angry insects.

More light filtered through the trees, this time from in front of the trio, finally revealing the sea beyond, as the boys descended the gentle slope to a cove.

"This'll do," shouted Luke.

The boys gleefully dumped their bags and shed their clothes, running, yelling and laughing into the water.

Fred rubbed himself off with his discarded clothes, then dressed in the damp garments which the heat of the sun would soon dry. Selecting a spot near the edge of the trees he collected dry wood which was in abundance and started a fire. Seating himself on a boulder he selected six rabbits from the mouzers catch, then deftly skinned them, laying the pelts on another boulder further along the beach. More wood was added to the fire which he circled with large pebbles. Going down to the shore line he proceeded to gut the catch, within a minute he was surrounded by the mouzers, the smell of fresh rabbit enticing them from their new quarries. When he had finished his task, he washed the carcasses in the sea, and returned to the fire followed attentively by the pack, which had consumed most of the guts with relish.

"Sit!" he shouted, a dozen or so wet black furry bottoms obediently plonked themselves in a half circle around the fire opposite him.

He had cut and sharpened sticks on which three of the rabbits were now impaled over the hot embers, propped on the stones at the edge of the fire, when Luke and Nobby dripped up the beach dragging an old fishing boat sail they had found. This was stretched above them, between the pines, and formed a cover, which wasn't really needed. Beneath their tent they stacked pine needles to form soft beds for the night.

The first three rabbits were cooked and replaced by three more, which the boys sat turning on their makeshift spits, as they drank cider and consumed their meal of rabbit, pies and oatcakes, all shared by their small furry friends.

Deciding there was no more to be had, the mouzers wandered off to find a drink for themselves, discovering a small freshwater stream which trickled through boulders out into the sea. With one flagon of cider empty the three boys stretched out on their woodland beds, and were soon asleep.

Luke was awoken by something being dropped on his still naked chest, two hours later. Starting awake he looked down, and was most surprised to see a candle, its bearer sitting looking excitedly into his sleepy face. He stuck out both his arms and poked the two bodies stretched either side of him. "Look," he demanded as the boys stirred.

"Where did that come from?" asked Nobby rubbing his eyes.

The trufflemouzer wagged its tail.

"Him," said Luke, petting the dog which now lay between them.

"Where did he get it?" Fred finally awoke.

"Dunno," said Luke.

"Ask him," said Nobby laughing.

"I will," said Fred, picking the candle from Luke's chest. Fred scrambled out of their camp and waved the candle at the trufflemouzer.

"Find," he commanded.

The mouzer looked up wagging his tail, wandering what his master was talking about.

"Find," demanded Fred again.

The mouzer searched his brain, wasn't Sit or Stay or Here, so he wagged his tail.

"Fetch!" shouted Fred, exasperated, and he pretended to throw the candle along the beach. The mouzer bounded off looking over his shoulder puzzled, then continued to scamper along the sand. The three boys shook the last of their sleep away and gave chase.

Half a mile along, another mouzer came running towards them, also with a candle grasped firmly in its teeth. The first mouzer ran on, then away from the beach to where a small cliff face was set well back from the sea. More mouzers were scratching at stones around a crevice in the rock.

Two more mouzers appeared from the gap, both with candles. The boys could hear barking from further in.

"Can't see a thing," called Nobby over his shoulder, standing in the narrow gap.

"Hang on," said Fred, producing the tinder box which he had used to light the fire, "grab a couple of they candles."

Standing well out of the slight breeze blowing from the sea he eventually got one of the candles alight, then lit another from it, which he passed to Nobby.

The three squeezed through the crack which widened then opened into a cave. Several mouzers were busy scratching at boxes and barrels stacked around the walls. The lid had been worried off one of the boxes, which proved to be the source of the candles. Fred lit one of these from his own and gave it to Luke, then lowered his light to inspect the barrels. Something was chalked on the outside of each.

"Dunno what it says." Fred held the candle closer inspecting the letters.

"I do," said Luke who could read a bit, quietly, "come away from it Fred before we all join the angels, it's gunpowder."

The three boys retreated, somewhat frightened, out of the cave, calling the trufflemouzers after them. Nobby grabbed a handful of candles which they lit back at the camp as daylight turned to dusk.

Nobody had spoken, the boys stoked up the fire, passing round the second flagon of cider, before Fred asked, "Who? What?"

"Dunno mate," replied Luke, but I bet it's all to do with what me and Nobby saw further along the coast."

"Best leave it alone," Nobby was visibly frightened. "Let's pack up and go."

"Don't worry fella," soothed Luke. "Nobody's going to come tonight."

"First thing in the morning then," Nobby demanded.

"First thing in the morning," the other two agreed, trying to keep their own fear in check, about who might want to store gunpowder in such a remote place.

By the time the three lads had made it back to the trufflemouzer farm they were once again in high spirits. Sidney was in the yard, which was unusual for a Sunday, talking to some of the other lads. With their charges safely back in their pens they joined the group chatting to stuttering Sid.

"Sidney's in love," one of the lads turned and whispered, trying to keep his giggles in check.

"Whatcha Sid how's it going?" Luke cheerily greeted the forlorn looking Houmit.

"Nnot ggood Luke, I'm trying tto be friends with Bbessie and she doesn't want to know."

Luke pondered for a moment, then said "you need sorting out mate and we're the boys to do it, c'mon follow me."

The tatty Houmit reluctantly traipsed after the group of lads into one of the whelping sheds.

"First Sidney, you need a bath," stated Luke, the group of lads following agreed, "yes Sidney you need a bath."

"I ddon't have baths," stuttered Sid.

"We know," Luke replied, "how to you expect to win Bessie if you stink?"

At one end of the shed, a large stone former drinking trough was now used to bathe new trufflemouzer offspring and their mothers, a few days after the trauma of birth. Next to it a large cauldron was constantly kept heated over a fire. Two of the boys emptied the boiling water into the trough, two more went outside and fetched cold water from the pump in the yard, pouring their buckets into the trough until the temperature was acceptable.

The warm air in the shed was stirring the various inhabitants in Sidney's hair, straggly beard and clothes.

"I'm itching," he complained, scratching under his arms.

"We'll soon sort that out Sid, get your clothes off," commanded Luke.

By now the family of lice, which infested his head, were all feeling the effects of the steamy atmosphere and Sidney's probing fingers.

"Isn't it always the way?" muttered the mother louse, who had just got her fifty three offspring to sleep. "Just get the kids off and something upsets them and he's never here when I need him, down in that beard playing games with that lowlife again." She was getting really angry now as two grimy didgets pushed past her. Her thirteenth husband, father to the latest brood, had gone out over two hours ago, promising not to be late back, but had become involved with some of his mates, who were taking it in turn to slide down some dried snot encrusted in the lank chin hair.

"I nnever take my cclothes off," moaned Sidney.

"We can see that," guffawed one of the lads.

"Get 'em off or we'll do it for you."

Reluctantly the stuttering Houmit removed his outer garments.

"And your pants," instructed Luke.

"You'll ssee my bbits!" wailed Sidney.

"Nobody's looking forward to seeing your bits Sid, but they're the same as ours, just dirtier."

Nobby creased up into fits of laughter.

At last the skinny white body clambered into the bathtub. Lice jumped in all directions looking for new homes. "Phew," exclaimed mother louse relieved, landing safely on top of a curly headed lad. Shame about the kids she thought for a couple of seconds, still I can soon have some more, she consoled herself, and this is far nicer than the last place, burrowing into the thick locks.

A muslin bag containing animal fat and sweet smelling herbs was used on the reluctant Houmit. Luke excused himself, and went up to the house to have a word with Crufty.

"What about his breath?" One of the lads, who had just got a face full, gasped as Luke returned.

"We'll get to that and his hair." Luke was confident now, and enjoying the challenge.

Sidney stood rubbing himself on one of the sheets used to dry the trufflemouzers. "Ccan I put my clothes bback on?" he shivered.

"No, wrap yourself in one of those," Luke pointed to a pile of dry linen, "then sit down on this chair." Turning to the group he asked, "anybody got any twine?"

The boys looked puzzled. Several lengths of thread were produced from their pockets. Luke selected a piece and made a small running noose in one end.

"What you ggonna do?" Sid was visibly frightened as Luke advanced on him.

"Try and get rid of your bad breath," Luke sternly replied. "I'm taking out your bad teeth."

"No you ppiggin ain't." Sid jumped from the chair.

"If you want a chance with Bessie it's no good you knocking her flat everytime you talk to her," reasoned Luke.

"Alright, it wwon't hurt wwill it?" stammered Sid sitting down again.

"Yes," said Luke, "open you mouth."

He advanced on the Houmit's stinking gaping cavity holding his breath, he slipped the noose over one of the two rotten teeth protruding at odd angles from his bottom jaw.

"Hold his shoulders lads," he instructed, pulling the string and tying it to the latch on the open door. Checking it was secure he gave the door a mighty shove.

Slam went the door, as it swung shut. The thread tightened and ripped one of the decaying molars from Sidney's mouth.

"Ow!" yelled Sid, "Ow! Ow! Ow!"

"You've stopped stuttering Sid," spluttered Nobby, who was still in fits of laughter.

The door was opened again and Crufty appeared bearing a bundle of clothes and a bottle of gin. "What are these terrors doing to you old chap?" his face breaking into a smile. "Here have a swill with this," he handed Sid the gin bottle.

"One more, Sid," instructed Luke, taking the first blackened stump from the noose.

The second tooth proved more resistant and two pieces of twine snapped before it gave up. Sidney spat blood on the floor, took a large swig of gin, swallowed it, then took another mouthful which he sloshed around his gummy mouth.

Fred pushed forward "let's have a sniff Sid," lowering his face in front of the Houmit's mouth. "Phew, taint as bad as it was though," he reported.

"Take a while 'til the holes have healed up," informed Crufty knowledgeably.

"Right, hair cut," said Luke.

A piggy eyed fat boy named Jeremy, who usually took charge when the trufflemouzers were groomed, stepped up. "I'll do it guv." He was rather proud of his hairdressing skills and often gave the kennel lads a trim or a shave.

He'd only been snipping away at Sidney's hair for a few seconds, when he exclaimed "what's this?" He continued cutting and retrieved a furry hat which the hair had grown through.

"Wwondered where tthat had gone," said Sid.

"Got anything in your pockets?" asked Crufty, picking up the Houmit's discarded clothes with distaste.

"Give 'em here," Sidney ferreted about in the bundle producing a few coins, a knife, a piece of string and a bit of cheese.

"You won't be needing these any more then," Crufty took the rags and to Sidney's dismay dumped them on the fire.

"Wwhat am I gonna wwear?" wailed Sid.

"These," laughed Crufty, pointing to the bundle of clothes he had brought from the house. "You're about the same size as me, and you'll look like a new man in new clothes."

The owner of the trufflemouzer farm and his team of lads went outside when Jeremy had declared himself satisfied, leaving Sidney clean shaven, short haired and toothless, still wrapped in the sheet, wishing he had stayed at home. The group waited and waited, finally the shed door opened. Sidney stood proudly, if somewhat embarrassed, wearing a blue blouse, grey three quarter length jacket, black pantaloons and black buckled shoes, all topped off by a new furry black hat. The boys whistled and cheered, and the mouzers in the pens behind them yapped with excitement. Crufty looked admiringly at his old mate.

"No woman could refuse you now," shouted Luke with glee.

"I know," said Sidney haughtily. "I'm off ccourting."

The little gathering watched in amazement as the tatty Houmit of a few hours ago strutted out of the yard.

"Tthanks lads!" he called over his shoulder.

CHAPTER SIXTEEN

Legs 'n Megs

Ethelegs lay in her bed at the Hungry Houmit, listening to the sounds of market day coming through the open window which overlooked the square.

She and Megs, the scullery maid, had arrived the previous day after spending a pleasant month or so in Weymouth, shopping. Both now had fine clothes, they dressed as lady and lady's maid. Having taken one of Bert's buses, which now ran a regular service to Portland Bill and Seynorgue, they had rented a room at the tavern. The pony and trap had been sold to Bert's livery stable. She had arrived unrecognised at the inn, her tomboy clothes worn when partying on Seynorgue only months before, packed into her trunk.

Leaving Ethelegs in bed Megs had gone off to explore, hoping to find the kindly woman she called Auntie, who had looked after her when her mother died during childbirth. Her father, unable to earn a living and look after a baby had left Seynorgue to try and find work. It had been her idea that they revisited her birthplace, putting a few more miles between them, the Ethels and Burghers, who often frequented Weymouth.

It had been a desperate living for Megs' guardian, who barely made enough money to feed herself. What she lacked in assets she made up for with knowledge which was imparted to the girl's sharp mind, teaching her to read and write, and the basics of addition and subtraction. By the age of nine, Megs was clever enough to have worked out that she was too much of a burden to the clever lady.

Picking up scraps on market day was one of the better sources of food for many of the under nourished Houmits. Megs had just found an apple, which was only bruised on one side, and sat down under one of the stalls to eat it, when another urchin child, a little older than herself, shuffled under the stall clutching a carrot.

"I've just met a man who says he's got work," her new acquaintance told her breathlessly. "I've got to meet him at his cart, outside the Hungry Houmit at noon," she went on excitedly. "He says he's looking for girls to go and work in a big house."

Megs rushed home and babbled the good news to her vexed guardian, who tried to explain some of the perils she could face. Undaunted and desperate to prove she could provide, she put her meagre possessions into a piece of sacking, gave the distraught woman a huge hug and was gone, calling over her shoulder, "see you soon Auntie, I'll bring back enough money to make us rich."

The cart was waiting as promised, her new friend and another girl perched in the back when Megs climbed aboard, behind the huge redheaded man wearing a smart smock.

"You're a bit young lassie," he declared.

"I can work as hard as these two," Megs stoutly defended herself.

"Och so be it then we're off."

The man cracked his whip, the horse shook itself and the cart was on its way. Megs chatted merrily with her two other excited young companions, blissfully unaware of the abuse, beatings and drudgery which awaited her at the Grand Manor.

Ethelegs lay deciding whether to get up or stay snuggled in, no contest, she pulled the bedclothes up closer to her chin. Sleep failed to return as she lay wondering what they should do next. The month in Weymouth had been fun, but she had become bored with the endless trips to the shops.

Unseen in the marketplace below, there were already several Burghers who'd accompanied the two gingers for a day out, and were now making a nuisance of themselves amongst the traders. Becky snatched back one of her jars of potion from one of the Burghers, who was trying to secrete it under his smock, but dropped it in her frustration, contents spilling on to the cobbles. The Burgher and his companion laughed raucously, then slid their booted feet over the mixture. "Any good for bunions is it?"

"No it ain't, go away," Becky was no longer afraid even when the two Ethelreds sauntered up. She recognised the pair as the two ginger haired brats who used to raid the kitchen. She stood defiantly, glaring at them.

"Leave her alone!" shouted one of the other traders.

"Yyes lleave her alone," joined in Sid, now a constant companion of Bessie who was doing a roaring trade in furry hats and thick coats, with the onset of winter.

"Gget back to sselling your sstupid hats," mimicked one of the gingers.

The group roared with laughter, which was thankfully brought to a close by another Burgher yelling "hey lads look who's here."

Big Mac had ridden into the square, astride of a large heavy horse that was pushing its way through the market throng towards the Burghers Bar. Big Mac in full Scottish regalia looked neither right nor left intent on reaching his goal, and getting a drink down his neck.

Three Christmas's ago Ethelethel had asked Gay to purchase some tartan cloth which Mac had described to her. His huge frame was now resplendent in tartan kilt, black jacket and long white woolly socks with a dagger shoved in the top of one of them. Another piece of tartan cloth was draped over his shoulder and hung to the back and to the front, a cocked hat topped the attire.

Houmits stared in awe at the majestic figure, fearing the worst, everyone knew who Big Mac was and he was seldom the bringer of glad tidings.

Mac had set off weeks before with two other Burghers, each going their separate ways to post notices, Mac had instructed the pair to meet him in the tavern on the first market day of September, when hopefully their tasks would be complete.

The two other Burghers were already sat at the bar when Mac marched in. "Move laddie," he instructed a Houmit sat on the only other bar stool. The chap who had been drooling over the pretty serving wench turned, then looking alarmed at the massive figure he turned back, took one more gawp at the barmaid, before reluctantly giving up his place.

"Whisky," demanded Mac, slapping down a sovereign.

The girl poured a measure into a small glass, which Mac ignored grabbing the bottle from the startled girl's hand. Half the contents had disappeared down his wide throat before he turned to the two other Burghers, "how did it go laddies?"

"Did what you said," replied one. "Put up the notices and got out quick."

The bigger Burgher burst out laughing, then told them that one of the places he had visited had just lost its village idiot, who apparently had been dared to see how long he could stand on his head in the local duck pond. The villagers were fishing out his body as he arrived.

"Stupid peasants," sneered Burgher number two. "They can have one of the Gingers as a replacement," muttered Mac.

Right on cue in strutted the two Ethelreds, followed by more Burghers.

"What ho Mac!" they both yelled across the bar. "Good fellow, you can buy us a drink, must say you're looking splendid."

Mac, whose back was towards the pair raised his bushy eyebrows, but nodded to the girl to give his masters a drink out of his money, but then hastily picked up the change placed on the counter and secreted it in the sporran at his waist.

There were only a few Houmits in the tavern, but with the arrival of more Burghers they drank up, picked up their furry hats and filed out.

"Put this up." Mac retrieved a rolled parchment from his jacket and handed it to the landlord, who had just joined the wench behind the bar. The landlord who could read a bit, looked aghast when he read that his taxes were to be doubled.

"Do na worry laddie, you'll make enough out of what I spend," Mac boomed finishing his bottle of scotch and ordering another.

"Same again for us Mac old thing," chirped Ginger II.

"Same again for the Masters," ordered Mac, "they're paying."

This provoked an urgent discussion between the two Gingers, which became quite heated before Ginger I came to the bar putting down money. The Burghers looked on, hiding their amusement.

"I expect the lads could do with a top up," Mac declared.

Ginger I if anything looked more vexed than the landlord.

"Thankee Sire," "thankee Sire," "thankee Sire." Each of the Burghers touched their foreheads but turned away clutching their brimming tankards with smirks on their faces.

Outside a cold wind had blown up, scattering the market rubbish. Now it started to rain. A group of visitors came rushing into the tavern, then seeing the bars occupants, hesitated, and retreated, deciding to get wet running across the square to the Hungry Houmit.

The two Gingers were playing darts against a couple of Burghers for money and losing badly, two more Burghers were glaring at each other across the table fists locked, in a bout of arm wrestling. Several Houmits entered, amongst them Luke and Nobby throwing their wet furry hats down next to an empty table. The serving wench scurried across to serve them, glad to be away from the group at the bar.

Mac had now consumed half of his second bottle of whisky, and was becoming melancholy, staring at the rain through the open door. Slinging a massive arm across one of his drinking partners shoulders, he confided "this is no like the weather in Scotland."

"Why's that, boss?" the Burgher asked, pulling away a little, only to be clutched tighter.

"We have real rain in Scotland laddie no like this, and we have mists, och I miss the mist."

Pulling the chap even tighter he rambled on, speech becoming a trifle slurred, "And I miss the heather on the mountains, you've got no mountains in England."

Nobby giggled.

"Watchit," one of the arm wrestlers growled.

Nobby was defiant. "How does his Lordship think we're goin to pay extra taxes?" He glared at the Burgher.

The group of Houmits had been staring at the notice, already aware of its contents, from the rumours which had been spread by mainland visitors to the market that morning.

"That's your problem," sneered the other arm wrestler.

Mac's confidante extracted himself from the huge arm and came to stand by the pair of contesting Burghers, leaving him with the bottle clasped firmly again to his lips.

"And what happens if we can't pay?" another Houmit demanded.

"If you can't pay in November, we'll come back on the first day of January."

"And do what?" Luke stood up.

"Anyone who can't pay will be kicked out," his adversary glared back.

"C'mon boys, we don't need this," Luke retrieved his hat and marched to the door, deciding to settle for the tattier surroundings of the Hungry Houmit.

His mates got up and followed.

"Y'll have to give up those stupid hats if you have to get jobs on the mainland boys," Mac slurred from the bar.

"Better than wearing a skirt!" yelled Nobby, belting past the rest, tearing across the square looking fearfully over his shoulder.

Big Mac slid off his stool, but quickly decided his legs weren't up to chasing the mouthy lad. "Och I'll sort him out later," he said to no one in particular.

The landlord at the Hungry Houmit for once almost had a smile on his generally miserable face. He was pleased with the amount of custom that had been driven in by the rain, but still annoyed, one of the barmaids hadn't turned up, leaving him to serve with only one other girl helping. Trade had been bad recently, with many of his locals deserting his tavern for the plusher surroundings across the square, he was finding it increasingly hard to make a living. He looked around the grimy interior and wondered why.

"Piggin heck Nobby you're pushing it." Luke looked rather proudly at his best friend on reaching the bar where Nobby was waiting to be served.

"Good though weren't it?" Nobby grinned.

The hubbub in the run down bar was all about the hearsay of increased taxes.

"It's true," stated one of Luke's group, "we've seen the notice across the square, 'spect they'll be over here in a minute."

Upstairs, Ethelegs had finally given up trying to get back to sleep, her thoughts keeping her mind buzzing. Now the noise from below made it impossible. She got up washed, then dressed in her old clothes, feeling at once far more comfortable in leather breeches and a loose blouse, than she had in any of the fine dresses she and Megs had purchased. The bedroom door opened and Megs came in a trifle bedraggled. She sat on the unmade bed and started to cry.

"She's dead Mistress," the girl sobbed softly. "Auntie died last year and I never came back to help her."

Ethelegs sat back on the bed putting her arms round the distraught little scullery maid.

"There there little Megs, tis a hard life for these Houmits, p'raps we can make it better," she said, not having a clue as to how.

Little could she have imagined what was to happen that day and in the few months to come.

"Best get out of those wet things, I'll go down and get you a hot drink." Although only a few years older, Megs looked up to Legs almost as a mother.

"Whatcha Legs," greeted several Houmits as she pushed into the smoky steamy room below. A miserable fire was just alight in the filthy hearth.

Ethelegs odd away days on Seynorgue had always been happy ones, she was accepted by the locals as one of them. She had never looked down, as did her siblings, on the fun loving lads and lassies who frequented the market place and the taverns.

"Get behind here and give us a hand?" the moody landlord brightened a little at the prospect of help.

"Right ho guvnor, look out lads I'm coming aboard," Ethelegs squeezed between two waiting Houmits and clambered over the bar.

"What ho Nobby, are you next?" she enquired.

"What ho Legs," replied Nobby grinning, giving her his order.

"Busy innit," Legs laughed as she filled tankards next to her new employer.

"'Bout piggin time," the miserable face looked back.

The drink had lightened the mood in the bar, everyone was now being served efficiently by Legs and the other girl. The landlord stood back, thinking, 'spect they'll be off over the square when it stops raining. Legs took the opportunity in a brief lull to slip back up stairs, with a glass of milk and brandy.

The bar door was thrust open, chatter died then stopped. Nobby slid behind Luke and several of his other mates. Big Mac staggered in, closely followed by Burghers and the two Gingers who, completely misreading the atmosphere called out "what ho peasants!"

Mac advanced on the landlord clutching a rolled up parchment, "Put this on your wall laddie," he instructed.

"And get us some drinks, and be damned quick about it," shouted Ethelred I.

Nobody will ever know who threw the first punch, or the first bottle, tankard or chair. What was certain was that Ethelred I all of a sudden crashed backwards on to a table, scattering drinks and Houmits alike.

The serving wench wet herself as she crouched under the bar, her fingers bleeding from a broken glass. A kicking, biting, scratching, gouging, punching bundle of Houmits and Burghers rolled into the fireplace, several jumping straight out again slapping singed clothing. One of the Burghers produced a knife stabbing at a young female, but was brought up in mid swing as a chair crashed over his head.

Several dogs and trufflemouzers started their own war, having taken random bites at passing legs. Smoke from the fire now added to the already smoky air, clouds of black dust attempting to settle on the heaving mass of bodies.

The landlord grabbed the bucket containing the day's takings, and shouted at the top of his voice, "That's it, I'm off!"

He was starting up the stairs to collect his things as Legs reached the bottom, alarmed by the noise. Mac stood directly in front of her, having singled out Nobby.

"Mac!" she exclaimed.

His massive fist stopped in mid air.

"Missy!" he exclaimed back, then fell over.

"That's him sorted," laughed Nobby, slapping his hands across each other.

Legs knelt by the huge tartan body. "C'mon Mac help me sort this out before they wreck the place," Legs murmured in his ear, using all of her considerable charm.

Slowly the huge frame lifted from the debris-covered floor. He stood and shook himself, resembling the great horse he had ridden a few hours earlier. His shout of "STOP!" drowned all the other yelling, screaming and banging. He was, amazingly, now completely sober.

"Out," he commanded. "Burghers follow me."

A line of bruised and bloodied Burghers filed out of the tavern after the great Scot, followed by bruised and bloodied Houmits. Into the square marched the bemused line, then Burghers started to turn back.

"Enough!" shouted Mac, "or you're sacked."

Resembling a line of forlorn cattle going into the slaughter house, the Burghers followed Mac across the square to their horses and carts, still tethered outside the Burghers Bar. Houmits stood battered and torn in the pouring rain, then slowly drifted off to lick their wounds.

Legs slammed the door of the Hungry Houmit shut and pulled two of the four bolts tight. She stood surveying the broken furniture now covered in soot and ashes, on a floor swimming in ale and broken glass. Five bodies were in various positions amongst the debris, two of which started to stir. The serving wench crawled out from under the counter holding her hand and lent against the back bar still trembling. Megs came down from upstairs, now in dry clothes and stood next to Legs exclaiming "oh my oh my."

A loud knock on the door raised the girls from their stupor, Legs shuffled through the clutter to peer fearfully out of a broken window. She sighed with relief to see Big Mac stood at the top of the steps leading into the bar. Hastily withdrawing the bolts she let him in.

"I've come for me wounded," he smiled.

One of the Gingers sat up. "What ho Mac, jolly good scrap eh?"

The other Ginger was still out cold, as was one of the Burghers.

Mac swung the second Ginger across his great shoulders as easily as a roll of cloth, went out down the steps and deposited the unconscious body, none too gently, in one of the carts the other Burghers had pulled up outside. Ginger I followed him and climbed unsteadily on to his horse which was held by a Burgher.

"There's three more in there laddies, get 'em shifted," instructed Mac.

The other bodies were duly carried or dragged out of the tavern. Two Houmits were propped up on the steps, the other Burgher was slung into the cart next to Ginger II. Mac came back up the steps, not mounting the top two, he was face to face with Legs.

"Thank you Mac, you were the one I always relied on," Legs gasped. "Please don't tell my Uncle that I'm here."

"Och, nothing to do with me missy, I'd sooner see you happy than him."

Legs flung her arms around the broad neck and gave him a long kiss in amongst the red whiskers.

"That's enough of that now lassie," the big man was visibly embarrassed, his face starting to match the colour of his whiskers.

"I'll be back in November," he said pulling away, "but I'm feared that could be an even sadder visit."

With that he was off, mounting his heavy horse leading his troops out of the market square. Legs watched him depart with a tinge of sorrow, Megs came and stood next to her Mistress at the tavern door, relief spreading through her slight frame as she saw the Burghers departing. The two dazed Houmits on the steps were starting to move, rain clearing their thick heads. She helped Legs swing the heavy door shut and then bolted it once more, this time with all four bolts.

"Looks like we've got some work to do Mistress," she said as the pair picked their way back across the bar room floor.

It was mid November before the door of the tavern swung open again to welcome customers. Mac and his Burghers had already returned and collected increased taxes from most of the Houmits. The big Scot came himself and was let into the tavern, taking a drink with Legs but limiting himself, not wishing a repeat of the last performance.

"What will happen to those that can't pay?" she asked with a worried frown.

"Och, his Lordship has told me to show no mercy," Mac's expression showing for once, that he didn't agree with his Master. "He's also bringing soldiers," Mac went on, "he's heard rumours that his brother's ship has been seen by the quay and he's determined to catch him. He thinks that he helped himself from his inheritance at the Manor. We're coming back on the first day of the new year." The pair chatted, Legs happy to hear that Ethelethel was well, asking Mac to let her know that her daughter was in good spirits, and enjoying life away from her wicked Uncle. Once again she bid a fond farewell to her great friend.

The G.B.H. firm (General Builder Houmits) had been employed to repair damage to the walls and windows. The carpenter, whose shed faced on to the square, was employed to make new furniture. Logs were purchased, and stacked in the back yard ready for winter.

The mistress and her maid scrubbed and polished, then scrubbed and polished again, with the help of Abbi the barmaid, who proved to be a willing worker and had knowledge of the workings of the business. The old landlord never came back, so Abbi was given one of the smaller rooms upstairs at the back of the pub. Legs and Megs also moved from the large bedroom, leaving it available for guests.

A man called with a horse and cart. He introduced himself as Evans, then informed the girls that the last landlord still owed him. Megs demanded to see the bill, checking the adding up carefully she eventually said to the man," I don't think we should be liable for all this."

Legs looked at her timid little partner in amazement.

Evans scratched his greying hair. "Well it's what's owed," he eventually stated.

"If we weren't here, you wouldn't get anything," Megs was enjoying her new found power.

Her mistress interjected, "we will pay you half Mr. Evans, I think that's fair, and we'll want to put in a new order, which I will pay you for right away."

Evans brown eyes twinkled, taking in the pretty trio which now stood before him. "Agreed," he said.

Legs involved Abbi in making an order, then doubled it. The old landlord had hardly kept enough stock to keep him going between Evans monthly visits from the mainland. Legs' stash of gold coins had been reduced to half by the time she paid him, having already settled with the carpenter and G.B.H.

The first customers to venture up the steps, and through the now open door of the Hungry Houmit, were amazed at the transformation. Logs blazed in a spotless hearth, a grand mirror above them reflected the shining brass and copper which bedecked the freshly painted walls. New tables and chairs stood on a scrubbed wooden floor. Behind the bar, four large barrels stood waiting, on a shelf above, more bottles than they had ever seen. Tankards of various sizes and shapes hung from the oak beams. By the end of the week the place was packed by Houmits, defecting from the Burghers Bar to their own local.

Christmas was fast approaching. Legs sat with Luke, Nobby and Fred in front of a cheery blaze. Abbi and Megs chatted happily behind the bar. Outside a frost was already forming as evening approached. Ned, Fred's brother, one of the local fishermen, marched in.

"They've taken the lot," he declared.

"What?" said Fred.

"My catch, they've taken the lot and not paid," Ned was close to tears.

"Get him a drink," called Legs.

Ned sank into a chair next to her. "Now what's happened?" she asked.

"Piggin Burghers." He calmed a little taking a sip from the tankard placed in front of him. Ned spluttered, "Been out two days, best catch of cod I've ever had. They came to the quay as I unloaded, and took the lot. Wish we could stop 'em coming on to Seynorgue."

Next morning, Evans revisited the new landlady, leaving an hour later with the biggest order he had ever seen. Legs' stash of money had started to increase again, and she was determined to keep enough stock to last well over the Christmas period, into the new year.

CHAPTER SEVENTEEN

Escape

Fred, Luke and Nobby paid a visit to Ned, putting forward an idea the three had dreamed up on their way home the previous evening.

A week later, a small fishing boat beached in the cove the boys had discovered, at the end of summer.

The four lads had returned to the cave for the second time, and were starting to roll the second barrel of gunpowder out of the darkness, when an almighty fart warned them that they were not alone.

"C'mon out let's have a look at you," a voice demanded.

The boys stopped, frozen in their tracks.

"C'mon out," the voice came again.

"Or we'll come in and get yer," another voice added.

Raucous laughter followed.

Silently the four lads filed out of the cave. A group of rough looking men stood on the beach in front of them. Another boat was drawn up beside Ned's fishing smack.

"We weren't doin' nothin'," stammered Fred.

"What's that barrel doin' in your boat then," demanded to largest of the group who appeared to be the leader.

"We found some stuff in the cave that we wanted to use," Nobby answered, trying to hide the terror in his voice, wondering who the man next to the leader was looking at, one eye appeared to be fixed on him while the other seemed to stare at a seagull further along the beach.

"We weren't doin' nothin' wrong."

"Stealins wrong innit, fought you'd get away wiv it did yer?" demanded another man with only one leg.

"Cut their froats Eth?" the googly eyed man enquired quietly.

The enquiry was taken up by the rest and turned into a suggestion. "Yea, cut their froats," they joined in excitedly, pulling knives and swords from various parts of their clothing.

"Yea, we'll cut their throats," the leader finally agreed.

The boys looked around desperately, ready to run, there was no escape, some of the men had moved round the side and back of them.

"Afore we put you toerags out of your misery," the big man said, "what did you want my powder for?"

Luke's brain had been working furiously.

"We was gonna blow up the causeway," he said trying to show no fear. He had already worked out this was the brother of the Baron of Dorset who Legs had told him soldiers were coming to look for.

"We want to stop the Baron of Dorset coming on to Seynorgue and throwing people out of their homes. He's bringing soldiers, to trap the man who stole his money."

Two of the ruffians had already moved close behind Fred and Ned, a knife and a cutlass ready to end their lives.

The leader held up his hand.

"That lad, is a good idea. How were you going to blow up the causeway?"

"We were gonna put the barrels on top of the thinnest bit," Nobby said woefully, already accepting his fate.

All of a sudden the big man laughed, then he farted loudly causing titters from the rest of his cut throats.

"If you wanted to blow up a bridge Frog," he turned to the man with one leg, "how would you do it?"

"Wouldn't be from the top Eff," laughed the man.

"So when is this Baron of Dorset coming to trap me?" asked the man the others called Eff.

"First day of the New Year," answered Ned, who had so far been too frightened to speak.

"That bit of information, has earned you your lives boys," said Eff. "Back off lads," he commanded. "Get in your boat and go home, we'll do any blowin' up there is to be done."

Each of the four boys let out a huge sigh of relief, realising they had escaped death by the skin of their teeth.

"You don't breathe a word of this meeting to a living soul," Eff instructed as the first barrel of powder was unloaded from the fishing boat. "My men can find you anywhere on Seynorgue, and they'll finish what we started today."

The boys shoved their boat off the sand and waded after her.

"Come down to the causeway at dawn, first day of January we'll show you how the job should be done," Eff called after them, as they scrambled aboard still trembling.

Christmas Eve at the Hungry Houmit was a joyous affair. The large stone pot which had been put on the bar, was emptied out and counted by Megs. Kind Houmits had given what they could spare, for the twenty three families who didn't stand a chance in raising extra money for taxes.

"Its still over two guineas short," after a second count, Megs looked dismayed.

"Well let 'em get chucked out," shouted Ferrety, "I've had to pay my piggin' dues."

"You mmiserable llittle git," stammered Sidney, "ain't you got no sympathy."

"Yea, shutup Ferrety, go and drink over the Burghers Bar, with the rest of the heartless pigs," shouted another Houmit

Legs had gone up to her room while this banter was going on, she now returned and placed three sovereigns on top of the other money.

"That should make everyone's Christmas a happy one," she chortled.

"All except Ferrety's," yelled several of the revellers.

Christmas Day and Boxing Day came and went, a wonderful feeling of togetherness had settled over the inhabitants of Seynorgue.

Luke, Nobby and Fred had been kept busy at the trufflemouzer farm, with two litters of pups arriving early on the 29th December, but they left their charges in the capable hands of the other lads just after midnight, which saw in the New Year.

Together they picked their way down the frosty path leading into the market square. A thin slither of moon gave little light, but was made up for by thousands of stars shining brightly in the cold night air. They crossed the frost whitened cobbles and made their way out on to the roadway leading off Seynorgue.

The darkness limited their vision, and no sound reached them from the causeway beyond. They sat for two hours before Ned joined them.

"P'raps they've forgotten," ventured Nobby.

"P'raps it was all a 'orrible dream," added Fred.

Then in the distance they saw a pinprick of light, then another then another. The line of lights were moving steadily towards them, across the causeway. Through the clear night air they could now hear the sounds of horses' hooves. Still the columns of light advanced, and still there were no other sounds to tell them anyone else was on the causeway.

"Nothins going to 'appen," said Fred woefully.

By now they could see the first of the lights were flaming torches. The sounds of men and horses a lot louder.

Still the column advanced.

BOOM, an almighty explosion rent the frosty air half a mile beyond them, a great white light illuminated the sky. The rocks beneath their feet seemed to tremble.

BOOM, another explosion followed the first, then two more, each time accompanied by the dazzling light followed by the sound of falling rocks.

"Looks like they were there boys," laughed Luke standing and starting to edge out on to the causeway.

No more booms only shouts and curses, frightened horses being steadied by frightened riders.

The sky lightened as they trod warily along the roadway. Beneath the burning torches they could now make out men and horses, their shouts and whinnies becoming louder with every step. Behind them, the voices of Houmits, shaken from their beds, coming to see what the big noise was. Massive pieces of rock littered the surface of the roadway now, which the boys had to climb over. By the time the boys reached the gaping hole and looked down, rolling waves flowed steadily through the wide gap where before they fought to get through the narrow tunnel.

"Look!" shouted Ned, pointing out into the sea on the left hand side.

Three pairs of eyes followed his jutting out finger, in the distance a long boat was moving swiftly away.

Houmits joined the boys, and stood in wonder staring at the gap and the group of Burghers and soldiers beyond.

The large round figure of the Baron of Dorset pushed his way through the men and stared back at them with his one baleful eye. The Baron, obviously furious, was bellowing at Burghers and soldiers alike.

All the Houmits now started to cheer and wave towards the Baron. The man was now beside himself with rage, he hit out at a soldier who inadvertently stood in his way and screamed at his subjects. "Laugh at me would you, my Burghers will soon fill this piggin' hole, then I'll reek a vengeance on you so piggin terrible you'll wish you'd never been piggin' born. I'll burn your piggin' hovels and your piggin' market. I'll kill your piggin' dogs."

Nobby looked nervously to Luke.

Then a strange thing happened.

Seynorgue started to move.

As if it had been tethered to Portland Bill and the mainland by the causeway, Seynorgue now seemed to have a mind of its own, moving further out to sea.

The Baron and his troops stared in amazement at their quarry slipping away.

"We're floating!" a Houmit shouted.

Faces peered over the side of the causeway, no movement could be seen, but they had definitely slipped further away from their tormentors. Houmits rushed back to the edge of the gaping hole and gaped. Half an hour passed. The gap was now twice as wide.

The Baron appeared to have given up and was retreating back towards the mainland, still shouting abuse over his shoulder, interspersed with curses towards his men.

A large tartan clad figure on a heavy horse chuckled silently.

Many Houmits now started scrambling back across the fallen rocks, back towards their homes, but many stayed, as if on guard, unable to believe what had happened.

The wooden letters which had been nailed to the cliff face, telling visitors they were entering Seynorgue had been shaken free by the explosion, and now lay in a jumbled heap.

Houmits ran into the market square, shouting, yelling, cheering. Windows were thrown open by others who had slept through the commotion, to be gleefully informed of what had happened.

When the four lads returned to the causeway at noon, the gap had widened to a mile.

"We're an island," declared Luke.

Further round the coastline a long boat was pulling into a large lagoon, eight tired oarsmen easing their aching backs.

"Fink we all need a rest Eff," said the man at the tiller, staring at his captain with one eye, the other judging the entrance into the tunnel.

CHAPTER EIGHTEEN

Death

Custom had dwindled in both of the taverns since Christmas, and the landlord of the Burghers Bar, had already let it be known that his place was up for sale, if anyone could afford it.

As the square began to lighten on the first market day of the New Year, the usual cheery hubbub of voices was subdued. Astute traders, were well aware that without the influx of people from the mainland, their takings would take a tumble.

Suddenly, cries from two of the traders children, who had been playing on the road leading down to the quay, cut through the other market sounds.

"Horses! Horses!" they yelled at the top of their shrill voices.

"What are you two shouting about?" their father angrily enquired, as he struggled to undo a bolt on the side of his cart, which was refusing to budge.

"There's a big boat Da, and there's horses Da, horses on the quay."

They didn't have to explain anymore, noises from the market died away, as the sound of many hooves now rang out clearly in the morning air. Expectant faces turned to look hopefully, the looks turned to horror as the first rider came into view.

Tread the Terrible astride his great black charger was followed by mounted Burghers and soldiers.

His great booming voice echoed across the square. "I'll spare anyone who can lead me to my brother."

Scared bewildered faces stared back at the Baron.

"You're all going to piggin die, I'm givin' someone the chance to live!" Tread unsheathed his sword.

A lone voice replied, "I'll show ee Sire." Ferrety made his way through the throng of Houmits, to stand beside Etheltread.

"He's hid in the cliffs, tother side of the land," Ferrety pointed, "I've seen his boat."

"And now you're going to see your piggin maker," snarled the great man, deftly leaning over and thrusting the blade through Ferrety's throat.

"That's what's comin' to the rest of yer scum," he yelled, lifting the small limp body for all to see.

He shook the corpse free and kicked his horse, turning in the direction Ferrety had indicated, then rode out of the square followed by his troops.

The long mournful note of the horn was the first sound to warn residents of Vikings End that something was amiss.

This was soon followed by shouts from one of the lookouts above the cave, appearing on the ledge over the beach and Moose Pool. Shots rang out behind him, more shouting and the sounds of metal on metal, rang out clearly as swords were crossed in the tunnels above.

The man on the ledge suddenly tumbled forward, and fell screaming bouncing off the rock wall to lie dead on the beach, blood spurting from the musket wound in his neck.

Soldiers appeared in both of the openings, shots rained down into the tranquillity that was Vikings End.

Unprepared for an attack such as this, the inhabitants ran wildly trying to find cover, but were picked off at will, from the vantage points above.

"Save yourselves!" Tar yelled, running for the entrance tunnel, the bodies of dead and dying all around.

Ropes had now been lowered, soldiers and Burghers descending into the carnage. First on to the beach, Etheltread, followed by the two Gingers gleefully hacking at defenceless men.

The calm blue water of Moose Pool now took on an ominous shade of pink.

Etheltar scrambled along the slippery ledge and made it out to the harbours edge, where the only vessel moored was the old Viking ship.

The Sea Cow was now making different trips, Ringer in command. Picking up slaves and taking them to America where the price was better than England, then returning loaded with cotton and tobacco. She was now two months overdue.

Etheltar yelled at the two men manning the cannons protecting the seaward side.

"Blast the cave boys, it's full of soldiers."

Fresh musket fire was now directed towards him and the cannons from the clifftop.

Tar cut the ropes holding the vessel and jumped aboard. He rushed to the single mast and sliced through the sheets holding the single sail, furled on the crossbar above.

The two cannons were now pointing at the cave entrance, the gunners having swung them completely on the swivels, used previously to give them command of the sea beyond.

Boom! Boom! Two cannon balls chased each other into the tunnel. The first took a deflection from the left side rock wall, angling off to hit the right hand side of the cave, as it sped into the cavern. It flew off that crashing into Tar's palace bringing down part of the front wall. Its speed was slowing now, but still fast enough to ricochet into the left hand side of the cave bringing down rock, before disappearing into Moose Pool.

The second missile, close behind, hit the top of the tunnel, bounced down onto the ledge then flew up again into the main cave, hitting the domed roof, then the back wall before burying itself into the beach.

Two great cracks appeared, then the roof descended on to soldiers, Burghers, Ethels and slavers.

Both gunners now lay dead over their cannons, having been repeatedly hit by musket fire.

The Viking ship was drifting towards the sea entrance, the tide and the now unfurled sail carrying it slowly out, a shaken Tar taking refuge from the gun fire behind the rear cabin.

He lifted his head gingerly, to stare back at his home, as an almighty roar heralded the collapsing roof of the cave. A great cloud of dust exploded from the tunnel entrance.

Tar stared in disbelief, as a whitened figure appeared out of the cloud, then moved quickly along the harbour wall in a fast hobbling gait, one leg stomping out straight in an effort to keep up with the good leg.

His brother clutched a flaming torch of brushwood in one hand, and was using a great sword as a walking stick to speed and steady himself in the other, his gaze fixed on Tar.

He made it to the end of the quay as the ship edged out of the harbour mouth and threw himself aboard, dropping the torch, sword now at the ready.

"I said I was gonna piggin kill yer and now I piggin am."

Tar grabbed a cutlass from a rack of weapons and faced his gruesome adversary.

"Steal my piggin gold would yer?" the single good eye unblinking, fixed on Tar.

The ship had now cleared the entrance and was moving faster, wind starting to fill the sail as it came clear of the land.

The torch Etheltread had dropped was also fanned by the wind, fire had taken hold of some loose rigging.

The brothers circled each other warily.

"Not only me that took the old man's money, cyclops," baited Tar. "The rest of the family helped themselves, you one eyed idiot."

The ghastly white figure let out a screaming yell, lunging forward with his sword, intent on ripping his brother apart.

Smoke was now starting to drift across the decking, flames feeding off the stiffening breeze.

Still the pair circled each other, taking no notice of the heat now being generated, but conscious of retaining their balance on the now pitching deck.

A sudden whoosh of flame distracted Tread's single eye, as the sail caught fire. Seizing his chance Tar lashed at his brother, the cutlass slicing across his good leg. Etheltread screamed, and went down.

"Now who's gonna kill me cyclops?" Tar raised his weapon intent on finishing it, taking a step towards the rolling body before him, with blood spurting from its wound.

His cutlass had started its downward arch towards Tread's neck, when he lost his footing and pitched forwards. Tread still clutched his great sword; he pulled the point upwards, jamming the hilt into the deck between his legs. The force of the downward swing of the cutlass thrust Tar on to the weapon, the point pierced his body at the top of his thigh, the rest of the blade following it through, until it protruded out of his back.

"I'm gonna piggin kill yer," grunted Tread, "piggin told you so."

The old ship, now completely ablaze, finally slipped under the waves, giving up its ghosts old and new to the sea.

CHAPTER NINETEEN

Finders Keepers

All day worried faces had been turned in the direction in which Etheltread had ridden, by nightfall only a few Houmits remained in their homes, the rest having fled into the countryside or taken off in fishing boats. Now their eyes peered fearfully into the gloom with the sound of hooves striking cobbles at the edge of the market.

Only eight riders appeared, leading about twenty unmounted horses, the line made its way slowly across the square and continued on to the pathway leading down to the quay.

Luke was the first to venture out the next morning. He, Nobby and Becky had stayed in the Hungry Houmit with Legs and Megs that night, bravely – or stupidly – deciding not to run.

Soon others joined him, together the frightened group crept down to the quay. It was empty, no fishing boats and no large vessel which had brought the intruders.

Becky let out a huge sigh. "They've gone," she said needlessly.

During the next few days Houmits nervously re-appeared from hiding places on the island. Fishing boats put back into the quay, passengers and crew exhausted and hungry.

A meeting was called. It was decided that volunteers, led by Luke, would go and investigate.

Armed with stout sticks, shovels and pitch forks the group set off in the direction Etheltread had taken, carrying rope and a couple of lanterns for good measure.

The group called at Cruftys on the way, the farm hadn't been harmed. They continued their journey accompanied by excited trufflemouzers.

Bramley and Pippin rushed out at the sound of the dogs, they told the intent group over mugs of cider that the Ethels and Burghers had ridden straight through their valley a few days ago, but only a handful had returned leading many horses.

215

It was already dusk, so the kindly couple invited the group to bed down in their barn for the night.

Luke and Nobby led the band onwards, early next morning, no moans or clangs reached their ears this time as they approached the sloping cliff of rock, they had scaled all that time ago.

Reaching the top and walking gingerly forward across the ridge, they peered down in disbelief at the sea. What was once a harbour, was now a mass of boulders, the wide ridge behind it was now a narrow pathway, below it, a great chasm of rock. There was no way down to the sea or the bottom of the chasm from where they stood.

Trufflemouzers bounded in front of them as they slowly traversed the path to the other side, there was still no way down into the great hole.

"Well, whatever was here, ain't no more," said Nobby, "let's go home."

They shooed the dogs on and started descending the sloping inland rockface. Suddenly in front of them excited barking. The dogs were worrying at the mouth of what appeared to be a small cave. Luke slithered to the entrance. The dogs were rushing in and out, leaping up at Luke. He lowered himself onto all fours and inched into the blackness, his outstretched hand touched something that was not cold rock, he snatched it back in fear.

He knelt, trembling. Almost inaudible above the din the mouzers were making, he heard a voice.

"'Elp."

He reached his hand forward again, and realised he was touching a whiskery face.

"Are you hurt?" Luke whispered.

No reply.

Luke shuffled backwards out of the hole, trufflemouzers all over him, thinking it was a game.

"Light one of those lanterns Nobby, there's somebody in there!" He disentangled himself from his furry friends.

"We can just about get in side by side, can some of you please keep these mouzers off, until we've got this bloke out."

Taking the coil of rope from one of the Houmits, with Nobby by his side pushing the lantern in front, Luke, once again, crawled into the hole. The soft light revealed a man, very pale, laying head towards them. Holding the light has high as he could in the cramped space, Nobby muttered "I can see down to his legs, he don't appear to be trapped."

"Can you hear me?" Luke put his mouth to the man's ear.

No reply.

"Can't do anything in here, let's get him out."

Luke gently eased the man's arms down to his sides, then slipped the rope under one and across the man's chest, then under the other. He pulled the loose end and tied it as tight as he could behind the man's head.

Very slowly the two friends inched back out of the cave, both holding the rope, attempting to drag the injured man with them. It was soon apparent, that their awkward positions did not allow them to exert enough strength to move the body, so they continued backwards only keeping a light hold on the rope until they reached the entrance.

Many hands reached down to help them upright again, then together they slowly pulled the unconscious man out of the black hole in the side of the cliff.

"We've seen him before," muttered Luke, as the man's face came into view.

"Yeah, he was one of those on the beach, when we found the cave with the gun powder," confirmed Nobby.

"An' he mustav been one of them who blew up the causeway," chimed in wartnosed Fred, making the rest of the group aware that he was involved.

Now the Houmits were able to reach under the man's arms and ease him fully out into the open, so that he lay on a smooth piece of rock at the entrance to the cave.

"Here, I've got something," one of the group produced a flask, kneeling by the body he eased the man's lips apart, and tipped a little of the contents into his mouth.

The man's eyelids started to twitch, then they blinked fully open, to reveal different coloured eyes, one looking to the left, the other to the right. "All dead," he forced out two husky words.

Suddenly his whole body shook, his head lifted, the voice now a husky shout yelled the same two words, "All dead!" Then his head dropped back eyes unblinking, staring left and right.

"He's gone," pronounced the Houmit with the flask.

"Guess he's right now then, they are all dead." Fred grinned at the group.

The trufflemouzers, which had been worrying round people's legs during the rescue, now became disinterested, mooching off in various directions to explore and hunt.

"We'd better get a cart and take him down to the village and bury him," said Luke.

The rest looked doubtful.

"Why don't we just shove him back in the hole and block it up?" ventured Fred.

"That," said Nobby, "is the most sensible thing you've said all day."

Excited yapping echoing from within the cave broke into their considerations.

"What now?" the Houmit with the flask asked, then decided he now needed some of its contents, "hope it ain't no more bodies."

"No it ain't, look!" an excited voice from the group yelled.

A mouzer had emerged from the cave, in his mouth a golden crucifix, which appeared to be set with coloured stones, tail wagging like mad he deposited his find at Luke's feet.

He was followed by a second dog, proudly carrying a golden chalice, again beset with coloured stones. A third appeared dragging a small leather pouch. Nobby's eyes wide with excitement bent down to the little furry creature, hands trembling as he pulled the neck of the pouch open, then tipped out a small pile of golden sovereigns.

"These ain't stones," stated the man with the flask, who was now holding the crucifix, "they's jewels."

Now everybody was talking at the tops of their voices.

"We've found treasure."

"Bet there's more."

"Whose is it?"

"Clever mouzers."

"What shall we do?"

"Will we have to give it back?"

"They don't want it, they're all dead."

"Quiet!" yelled Luke above the babble, as yet another Trufflemouzer appeared, gingerly gripping a silver dagger in his mouth, the handle surmounted by a large red ruby.

218

"We are gonna have to go in and see. Who wants to come with me?"

Everybody did.

"Right, me, Nobby and Fred will go in first, then when we come out another three can go in."

Arming themselves with two lanterns and the rope, the three disappeared into the cave. Luke led the way with one lantern, followed by Fred with the rope, then Nobby brought up the rear, clasping the other light.

It was well past where Google had laid before the roof of the cave began to rise. Soon all three were able to stand side by side as the tunnel widened.

Holding the lanterns before them, the light was suddenly reflected by an amazing spectacle.

Piles of precious stones, relieved from the darkness, twinkled in the glow. Artefacts of gold and silver were lit up, some with intricate designs, others embedded with gems. Numerous chests, some closed, some open, revealed thousands upon thousands of gold coins.

"We're rich!" the three lads yelled in unison.

Together they crept in amongst the treasure, voices hushed now as if they were in some holy place.

Beyond the hall it looked as if the roof had given way, as the passage was completely blocked by fallen rock.

They turned back to ponder the treasure trove.

"This lot's gonna take some shifting," said Nobby. "How are we gonna do it?"

"It's gonna take forever to pass this out," added a frowning Fred.

Luke, deep in thought, said slowly, still thinking, "We need something to drag it." He finally said, "I know, grab some of those bigger pieces each boys and let's get back out to the others."

The three re-emerged from the tunnel, each clutching golden swords, Fred was first. "There's oodles of it," he declared to the expectant crowd gathered outside.

Nobby followed, "we're all gonna be ever so rich!" he beamed.

"There's mountains of the stuff," laughed Luke, "we're gonna need some help."

Already his quick brain had formed a plan, he told his two friends what he intended.

"Good idea boss, let's do it," confirmed Nobby.

"Right," Luke stood in the middle of the group. "Next three go in and take a look, bring out whatever you can, then I want you to come with me back to Bramley's."

Half an hour later three happy Houmits re-emerged, each clutching jewel encrusted pieces. Gleefully they told the others in the group the same tales already told by Luke and his friends, of the riches within.

"With me then chaps," said Luke. "Nobby, you know what to do, we will be as quick as we can."

With that the four set off back down the sloping rock, then across the valley heading towards Bramley and Pippin's farm.

The next three Houmits at the cave excitedly took their turn, crawling in to inspect the treasure.

The last three made their way an hour later, with explicit instructions from Nobby, after the others had re-appeared, each clutching artefacts.

Trufflemouzers, who had been hunting and exploring all this new territory, were called back. Already a pile of dead rabbits had been gleefully returned to their masters.

Now the first excited pair were despatched into the cave, responding to the calls from within. Out they came again a few minutes later, tails wagging, each depositing a priceless object at the feet of Nobby and his companions. Another pair were sent in, the problem was stopping the whole pack diving in at once, but soon a steady line of black furry creatures were going into the dark hole, each to be given a treasure by the Houmits within, then gleefully carried or dragged back into the open.

Nobby instructed two of his companions to move the body of Google, to a spot away from the ledge, where it was covered with loose rock. The pair proceeded down the slope to collect firewood. They were amazed on their return, at the size of the pile of trinkets which now formed a glittering heap at the caves entrance.

"Take a rest, if you can call it that boys, these mouzers are going to keep you busy." Nobby and his partner set off to collect more wood.

As dusk approached, and the air temperature started to dip, Nobby called a halt.

The group had all taken turns in the cave, outside of which were now two great piles, one of wood and the other made up of gold and silver artefacts, bags of precious stones and golden coins.

A fire was lit, and soon the merry group of Houmits and mouzers were dining on roast rabbit.

Luke and his three companions sat once again in Bramley's barn, eating oat cakes and drinking cider, as they told the pigman and his little round wife of their amazing find. It was late afternoon and Fred and another of the group went on to relate the wonderful news to the rest of the village, arriving breathless at the Hungry Houmit.

Luke told Bramley of the plan, which had been discussed by the group on their way to the farm.

"No problem boy." The old chap took charge.

After a few hours cutting, hammering and smoothing a wooden sledge was loaded onto the back of Bramleys cart.

It was still dark, dying embers of the fire had been coaxed back into life by one of the group outside of the cave, when a shout from the gravelly valley below brought them all fully awake.

The pack of mousers, instantly alert, tumbled down the rockface at the sound of Luke's voice.

Soon they returned, excited barking heralding the arrival of four panting Houmits, two with coils of rope around their necks, carrying lanterns, two pulling the sledge.

By noon the rest of the treasure was in front of the cave, or already loaded on to the donkey cart, at the bottom of the slope.

The sledge had been pulled into the cave, and the heavy chests loaded on to it, one by one, then pulled out.

More shouts from the valley announced more help arriving. Wartnosed Fred, importantly leading four more horse drawn carts and numerous Houmits.

The whole group arrived back in the village at dusk.

Word had been sent to outlying hovels, every Houmit was there. The biggest party any of them had every known erupted. Carts bunched together in front of the light from the Hungry Houmit, with extra lanterns placed around them, and a huge bonfire in the middle of the square.

They danced and they sang, they whooped and they cheered, they drank and ate free from the fast diminishing stocks of the two taverns.

Bramley, had with the help of many willing hands, loaded a huge barrel of cider on to the last horse and cart as it passed back through his farm.

It was well into next morning, and there were some heavy heads and many bleary eyes when Ethelegs marched into the square and rang the bell which was used for last orders and time in the Hungry Houmit.

"Come on you very rich people, wake up. Today is the start of your new life!" she yelled.

Slowly the Houmits returned to the market square, from wherever they had slept. Not many had made it to their own beds.

Ethelegs seemed the most alert, by now quite used to late nights in the tavern.

"You've got to decide what you're going to do," she prompted the crowd.

Eventually, a voice piped up, "We've gotta put it somewhere safe."

"That's easy," said Legs, "the store room round at the back of the Hungry Houmit is empty."

"Can it be locked and bolted?" enquired a voice.

"Course it can, don't think it would be left open when it's full of booze, with you lot around," laughed Megs, who had now joined her mistress.

"Still need to put a guard on it," piped up another voice, "somebody's gotta be responsible."

"Somebody's gonna have to be a leader," shouted a Houmit stood at the back of the crowd.

All eyes turned towards Luke, who was sat on the tavern steps with Crufty, Nobby and very many mouzers.

"Its ggotta bbe Lluke," Sydney finally managed to stutter.

"Yea Luke!" came back the cry from the rest.

Luke sat where he was.

"Go on boss, it's gotta be you," Nobby whispered in his pal's ear.

"Alright then." The young man with the stunning looks and devilish eyes stood up. "But I will need some help."

"Rreckon your Ma Ma Ma Mar's the best you can gget."

"Yeah Becky, yeah Becky," agreed the rest.

"An' Nobby," demanded Megs.

"Yeah Nobby, good old Nobby," came the agreement.

"Bbramley and an' C Crufty," called Syd.

"Yeah, Bramley and Crufty, good shout SSSyd," they all laughed.

"I want Ethelegs," yelled Luke, "I know she ain't really one of us, but she really is, if you know what I mean."

"Yeah, Legs Legs Legs!"

"That's too many Legs," she blushed at her acceptance by the people.

"Enough," yelled Luke, "we will need some time, and you lot probably need some more sleep. Let's get all the loot into the store room, then we will decide on a couple to stand guard, then another couple and another, so it's protected all the time."

An hour later the treasure was safely stored, two Houmits on guard outside, with the promise from others that they would be relieved.

"All back here at noon tomorrow then," called Luke, as he and his elected band went into the tavern, the rest disappearing to find their homes.

Fred and some of Crufty's staff took the pack of mouzers back to the homestead, for a well earned feed.

By the end of the day the newly elected leaders had put together a plan.

All residents of Seynorgue would immediately receive one hundred golden sovereigns each (this was double what any self respecting Houmit could expect to earn in a lifetime).

Every year this would be added to, with an extra twenty sovereigns each.

Any sons or daughters of these people would each receive fifty sovereigns upon reaching the age of eighteen.

A portion of the loot would be used to replace existing hovels, with stone built houses.

A special place was to be built, where they would meet every three months to discuss how to proceed further, and any of the Houmits could contact them. This building was also to contain a strong area into which the treasure was to be transferred and secured.

The six would also have the authority to spend any extra moneys they thought necessary.

The only problem that they could see was the lack of contact with the mainland, for extra supplies and general trading.

"There's one more thing," said Becky, as the meeting drew to a close. "This treasure belonged to Etheltread's brother, we have only heard the words of a dying man that he and his gang are all dead, and we are assuming that Etheltread himself has joined them. But," she went on, "there may still be somebody out there who wants it all back."

Worried frowns creased the brows of the newly elected members of the senate, until Nobby piped up, "finders keepers, is what I say."

"Finders keepers," they all agreed, but the less their find was talked about the better.

"I know," said Luke finally. "The people must be told that this is not to be talked about to outsiders."

"Yeah," agreed Nobby, "and anyone caught blabbing will have their yearly allowance stopped."

"Seems a bit harsh," murmured Bramley.

"But it's fair, and it will keep us all a lot safer," Luke agreed, smiling at Nobby.

"One more thing though," said Becky, still worried. "We have always been poor Houmits, all of a sudden we are very rich Houmits."

"Shipwreck," chimed in Crufty straight away. "We've salvaged a shipwreck."

"Good thinking boss," grinned Luke. "Now anything else?"

"Yes," said Ethelegs.

Their faces started to drop again.

"Let's all have a drink," chortled Legs.

Immediately their spirits lightened. "Well done Legs," they all agreed.

"By the way Miss Ethelegs," said Luke, suddenly looking stern again.

"What?" The youngest of the Ethel's tribe looked aghast.

"You are an honorary Houmit, and you will be treated the same as the rest of our new islanders," Luke grinned, "meeting closed."

Ethelegs flung her arms around him and gave him an almighty kiss.

Noon the next day, their plans were met with unanimous approval, with everyone agreeing to all the proposals.

For about two months the land known as Seynorgue moved sedately in a southerly direction, the large plate underneath its mass lifted by the warm currents of the Gulf Stream, sometimes turning a little, sometimes not.

Ships' captains rushed to their chart rooms, then back to their spy glasses, staring at the land that shouldn't be there.

Then, on a fine spring morning, a large ship docked at the quay.

Fisherman Ned raised the alarm. "We've got visitors!" he yelled, bursting through the door of the Hungry Houmit, where Legs and Megs, Becky and Luke were gathered.

"Dunno who they are?"

The four rushed to the window, two men were striding purposefully across the square.

"I know one of them," Legs breathed with relief.

"So do I," Becky was laughing as she ran out of the tavern, down the steps and across the cobbles, then threw her arms around the man Legs didn't know.

The other man, eyes twinkling, continued into the Hungry Houmit. "Thought you might be needing an order," he chuckled, as Legs rushed to meet him, planting a most unexpected, but most welcome, kiss on his cheek.

"Looks as though I was right," he grinned, looking at all the empty shelves behind the bar.

"How did you get here?" demanded Luke.

"My old mate, out there in the square with your Ma, brought me. You must be Luke, heard a lot about you."

The man extended his hand in friendship, "I'm Evans," he said.

By now the other pair had caught up, Luke, in an unusual show of affection, greeted the second visitor with a hug.

"Whatcher Darcy," he almost yelled.

"Got yer own big boat I see," Darcy laughed, "it's taken me all night to catch you up."

"This is Ethelegs, my best girl," Luke grabbed the surprised Legs and thrust her forward, then stammered, "that's after me Ma of course."

"Am I?" enquired Ethelegs, starting to blush.

Luke suddenly realised what he had said, he also started to redden.

It all went quiet.

Then Luke regained his composure "Oh yes," he said, "most definitely."

Darcy, Evans and Becky respectfully turned their backs as the young pair embraced.

"I've got a couple of letters for you two," Darcy finally interrupted them. "They were given to me by the harbour master in Weymouth."

He produced two rolled pieces of parchment, marked, BY HAND FROM GRUMBLEGUT AND GRUMBLEGUT SOLICITORS. One was addressed to Ethelegs, Seynorgue, the other, Luke Duke, Seynorgue. Both letters were the same, requesting the pair to attend at the Grand Manor in three day's time.

"Don't worry Becky," he comforted, seeing the look of horror on her face. "I'm assured there is nothing to worry about, in fact it's quite the reverse."

"Don't worry Ma, they can't do nothing to us now." Luke gave Becky a hug, but she still looked apprehensive.

"My Ma's still at the Grand Manor, as far as I know," Legs said. "She won't let anything happen to Luke, if he's with me."

"Will you two go as well?" Becky asked their visitors.

"If it makes you feel any easier, course we will," Evans replied for both.

"Take Nobby as well," Becky said forcefully.

Evans had brought two large bottles of wine, which he produced from the valise he carried.

"A toast I think," he said, uncorking the bottle and pouring it into goblets Ethelegs produced.

"To new friends and a new partnership."

The wine was the best any of them had ever tasted.

"Talking of partnerships, Darcy," said Luke. "How would you like to be our regular supply ship?"

"Love to Luke, but me bread and butter is sailing the high seas and bringing back cargo from Americy. Although I must say a bit of local work would make a nice change for me and me crew."

"We'll pay you," said Luke. "Since you last visited, we've all had a bit of luck."

He went on to tell a tale of a wrecked ship off the coast of Seynorgue. "All the crew were drowned," he said. Becky and Legs, listened to the story with Evans and Darcy. "Me and some of the boys managed to get aboard, before she went down. There was quite a bit of stuff on her," he grinned.

"Well! Well!" said Darcy.

"Good on you," said Evans. Becky and Legs just stared.

Evans and Darcy stayed as guests in the Hungry Houmit for two nights. During their time there a deal was struck with Darcy, who agreed to make a weekly voyage between Seynorgue and the mainland if the Houmits would match his usual profits.

Evans now had two huge orders in his valise, one from the Hungry Houmit, the other from the Burgher's Bar.

Luke, Nobby and Ethelegs sailed with Darcy and Evans back to the mainland, the evening before the day they were requested to be at the Grand Manor.

Grumblegut Senior's journey to the Grand Manor was far happier than his brother's had been, all that time ago. The gout which had plagued him the week before had gone now, just the odd twinge.

He merrily took a pinch of snuff as the Ethel cart he travelled in, bounced through the gates, set in the high stoned wall, which surrounded the Grand Manor.

The door to the building was opened by a large cheery man, whom he had not met before. The man showed him through to the great hall then left him to go and meet another carriage, which was coming up the drive.

Ethelbert came to meet him. "Mr. Grumblegut," he said seriously.

"Watcher cock," old Grumblegut gave him a friendly slap on his arm.

"Are we all here?" enquired the little round man with the beaked nose.

"Nearly," said Bert, "this is my wife Mikki." He then went on to introduce Ethelgay and the vicar. He was about to say, "I think you know Ethelethel," when a shout from outside interrupted him.

"They're here!" came the shout.

Ethelethel shot past him, heading towards the front door, where a smart carriage was disgorging people she didn't know.

Suddenly her face lit up, "Legs!" she screamed, rushing out to meet her daughter.

After many tears and much hugging, Ethelegs was able to introduce her companions. "And this, Ma," she finally said, "is my fella," she proudly pulled her prize forward, for her mother's inspection.

"Pleased to meet you – I've heard so much about you – I knew you when you were a baby," she gasped, all in one breath, hugging Luke.

"And this is going to be your new Da." She pulled Legs from the group.

The man who had tended the door came forward.

"Big Mac!" screeched Ethelegs, "I thought you was dead!"

"Och, not me missy," the big man hugged the quivering girl. "I had no stomach for what your uncle was planning and stayed here, when he sailed to your place with half the Burghers and a troop of soldiers."

"What happened to them?" asked Legs, gasping and sobbing.

"Let's go inside," said her great friend, "we've got a nice fire going, and there's drinks and food for everyone."

"You and Ma?" Ethelegs, was almost jumping up and down as she walked beside Mac into the great hall.

"That's right missy, I hear you've got a bit of a catch yourself."

"Oh Mac, I have, I have – this is Luke."

"I know Luke," said the huge man, giving a huge smile. "I think I know his pal too."

Nobby put his fists up, laughing.

When all the introductions had been made, Legs hugging both of her brothers in turn, Mac related the tale told by the survivors from the raid on Seynorgue.

"So the two eldest brothers drowned together," he concluded. "Your turn now Mr. Grumblegut."

Mr. Grumblegut pulled himself up to his full height, which wasn't very high, and began reading from a large sheet of parchment.

"As next eldest you will inherit the Grand Manor, all its estates and be responsible to the Sovereign for the upkeep of all the land known as Dorsetshire, with the exception of Seynorgue, which is now out of the Sovereign's jurisdiction. You will also inherit the title, Baroness of Dorsetshire." He turned to Ethelethel, who promptly burst into tears.

"Thank goodness," sighed Ethelbert.

"Yes, thank goodness," confirmed Ethelgay. "Not my scene at all ducky," he said to Ethelethel.

"The remaining members of the family Ethel, will share one thousand guineas each year between them," continued Grumblegut.

"That, I believe, is now only Ethelbert, Ethelgay and Ethelegs."

"What about the Gingers?" Legs suddenly realised the twins were missing.

"Went with your uncle, missy," consoled Mac.

"Oh my." Legs burst into tears again.

"A title was also bestowed on you Sir," the little man turned to Luke. "Duke of Seynorgue, of course this has no official reckoning now, as Seynorgue is no longer part of Dorsetshire, but the title was bestowed before your land broke away, so you may use it if you wish. You are also entitled to the one hundred and fifty guineas which was bequest to you in the will of Ethelfoot."

"Hail, Duke Luke Duke!" yelled Nobby.

"Hail, Duke Luke Duke," the rest toasted, lifting their goblets.

Ethelegs looked on proudly.

"The final bequest is twenty five guineas a year which is to be paid to the family vicar."

"Bless you my son," replied the holy man, in his singsong voice.

The merry group stayed overnight at the Grand Manor, which was now a far cry from the dank place Ethelegs had known as a girl. Her mother had already added carpets, curtains and tapestries.

A bright fire was kept going in each of the rooms, warming old stone which had been damp and cold for so long.

Happy household Hammy Burghers bustled about, making sure the guests had all they required.

Before leaving the next morning, Ethelegs secured promises from her mother and future father that they would visit, now that a regular ship was going to service the island. She also invited Ethelbert and his new wife Mikki, whom she liked very much.

Ethelgay, confirmed that he and the Schmoes would play at her forthcoming wedding, and would wait eagerly for the call.

Darcy's ship made the return journey, already loaded with the two huge orders for both the taverns, plus numerous other goods which Becky had listed before its departure from Seynorgue.

It was just over a year since the land known as Seynorgue had broken away.

Every week now, Darcy's ship made a trip to and from the island, transporting goods. He also carried Houmits to the mainland to purchase goods with their new found wealth.

Every few months trufflemouzers were exported, but buyers had to subject to an interrogation from Crufty and his helpers, before they were allowed to purchase one of the pups.

On the 24th February, the residents of Seynorgue felt a bump, then like a huge boat sliding into the shallows, the land came to rest.

On clear days other islands or land could be seen by Houmits from various parts of their island.

Luke, Nobby, Fred and several other Houmits carrying ladders, walked down to the rockface, where the wooden letters had once been attached to tell travellers they were entering Seynorgue. The wooden letters now lay in a jumble.

"We've lost the O," said an astute Houmit.

"We'll make another name from what's left then," said Luke thoughtfully. "Any suggestions?"

THE END
(Or is it?)